Books by Isis Crawford

A CATERED MURDER

A CATERED WEDDING

A CATERED CHRISTMAS

Published by Kensington Publishing Corporation

A Mystery with Recipes

A CATERED CHRISTMAS

ISIS CRAWFORD

KENSINGTON BOOKS
www.kensingtonbooks.com

Longely is an imaginary community, as are all its inhabitants. Any resemblance to people either living or dead is pure coincidence.

KENSINGTON BOOKS are published by

Kensington Publishing Corp.
850 Third Avenue
New York, NY 10022

All Kensington titles, imprints and distributed lines are available at special quantity discounts for bulk purchases for sales promotion, premiums, fund-raising, educational or institutional use.

Special book excerpts or customized printings can also be created to fit specific needs. For details, write or phone the office of the Kensington Special Sales Manager: Kensington Publishing Corp., 850 Third Avenue, New York, NY, 10022. Attn. Special Sales Department. Phone: 1-800-221-2647.

Library of Congress Card Catalogue Number: 2004114316
ISBN 0-7582-0687-9

First Printing: October 2005
10 9 8 7 6 5 4 3 2 1

Printed in the United States of America

For Sarah and Peter Saulson,
for being good friends.

Christmas Eve Menu

Pumpkin bisque
Freshly baked Parker House rolls

Capon with apple and apricot stuffing
Brussels sprouts with chestnuts
Green beans with toasted pine nuts
Potatoes lyonnaise

Buche de noel
Assorted cookies
Coconut and peppermint ice cream with chocolate sauce

Irish coffee

Chapter 1

Libby looked around the TV studio. She just knew she was going to hate being on TV; she was going to hate being on the *Hortense Calabash Show;* she was going to hate being in this stupid contest; but most of all, she was going to hate being away from the store at Christmas time.

"I think I'm going to throw up," she blurted.

Bernie considered the remark for a second. Then she pointed to her pink suede wedges. "Well, don't do it on these. I just got them."

"You're a veritable fountain of compassion," Libby told her sister as she gestured toward one of the TV cameras on the set.

"You'll be fine," Bernie said. "Just think of these as your friends."

"They may be your friends," Libby retorted, "but they're certainly not mine."

"Getting a little snappish, are we?"

Libby began biting her cuticle, realized what she was doing, and stopped herself. "Anyway, I have nothing to wear."

"What's wrong with the tweed skirt and fitted pale blue

blouse we bought down in the city last week?" her sister asked.

Another mistake, Libby reflected. Now she'd have to tell Bernie she'd returned them. She took a deep breath and let it out. "I took them back. They were too tight." She took another deep breath while she watched her sister roll her eyes. "Well, they were," Libby said in what she realized was a defensive tone of voice as she looked at Bernie standing there in her burgundy leather pants and hot pink V-neck sweater. It wasn't Bernie's fault she didn't understand, Libby reminded herself. She'd always been the thin one.

"They made me feel like a sausage."

"No, what you're wearing makes you look like a sausage. I keep telling you, loose clothes make people look fatter, not thinner. And anyway, you're not that fat."

"That fat?" Libby squeaked. "That's a little bit like saying I'm not that ugly."

"I'm not doing this."

"What's this?"

Bernie ignored her and gestured to the black pants and shirt Libby was wearing. "At least don't wear black on camera."

"I'm not going to," Libby said, even though she had been planning to. She felt more comfortable in it. It made her feel invisible. "I'm wearing my brown pants and yellow shirt." When Bernie didn't say anything, she added, "I'm sorry. I just think that spending two hundred dollars on a blouse is a little much."

"Two hundred and ten dollars to be exact," Bernie said absentmindedly as Libby watched her look around the studio. "And it was a Krista Larson for heaven's sake."

"So what?"

"It made you look great, that's what."

Libby watched Bernie walk over to one of the sinks and turn on the faucet. Nothing came out. She walked over to the second sink and tried that faucet. Water poured into the sink, but it didn't go down. It was clogged.

"Good," Libby said.

Maybe they wouldn't have to tape after all. Maybe she and Bernie could go back to the store, and she could finish the batch of Christmas cookies she was in the middle of decorating. After all, they couldn't cook if things in the kitchen didn't work.

She was sighing with relief when Bernie put her hands on her shoulders and said, "Look, let's forget about the clothes. Let's forget about everything. Let's just concentrate on winning."

Libby took a step back. "We're not going to win."

Bernie dropped her hands to her sides. "Why shouldn't we win?" she countered. "We have as good a shot at it as anyone else."

And that interchange, Libby decided, pretty much defined the difference between herself and her sister.

"I think I need a cookie," Libby said.

"Or a stiff drink," Bernie observed.

"A cookie." And Libby started rummaging around in her backpack for one of the chocolate chip ginger cookies she'd made earlier in the day. Given the circumstances, what was another pound or two? She took a bite. The cookie was good, but not good enough. Usually chocolate did it for her, but it didn't seem to be working today. Maybe Bernie was right. Maybe she needed a drink. Something like a Long Island iced tea. Or a large bottle of Pinot Noir. Or a tranq.

Libby took another bite of her cookie anyway as she contemplated what was in store for her and Bernie this evening. It was no big deal. Why should she be nervous? There'd just be thousands of people out there watching her cook. What was the problem with that? Just because she probably wouldn't be able to get any words past her vocal chords because they would be constricted in terror.

And so what if she dropped say . . . a chicken . . . on the floor, or burned it, or it didn't cook all the way through? What then? The great Julia had done things like that all the time on her television show. But, Libby told herself, she wasn't Julia Child. And Julia didn't have the Heavenly Housewife, aka Hortense Calabash, of the *Hortense Calabash Show* critiquing her food.

Not that Julia would have stood for Hortense's nonsense. Julia would have bashed Hortense over the head with a frozen leg of lamb or a Christmas goose if she ever pulled any of her stunts on her. Just the thought of that made Libby smile. But Libby knew she'd never raise a strand of spaghetti to Hortense, let alone a blunt instrument. Ever.

Libby took a third bite of her cookie. As she swallowed, she could almost see the slight flare of Hortense's thin nostrils, the miniscule lifting of one of her eyebrows when she didn't like something. What had she said to Rudolfo, the chef from *Mesmerize*, after she'd tasted the pâté he'd made? Wasn't it something along the lines of, "My, what an interesting group of ingredients you've chosen to use. This tastes rather like a mix between raw eggplant and liver I once sampled in Uzbekistan."

Libby had never seen a man turn white with anger before. He'd spluttered, but no sounds had come out. Needless to say, *Mesmerize* had gone out of business two weeks later. A week after that, Libby had heard through the caterer's grapevine that the pâté had actually been fine. Hortense had just needed a little something to boost her ratings that week. No wonder Rudolfo had sent her a chocolate cake filled with a mixture of ganache and pureed hog intestines as a thank you for being on her show.

Or how about the time there'd been that woman on the show demonstrating one of the recipes from her new cookbook on how to use a pressure cooker, and Hortense had taken a bite of the stew she'd prepared and said, "My this is tasty"—then came the dramatic pause, never a good sign—"if you're partial to the kind of canned stew they sell in the supermarket."

And another career had bit the dust. Libby shuddered as she finished her cookie. What if Hortense said something like that to her about something she and Bernie made? And while it was true that her store, *A Little Taste of Heaven*, had a loyal and devoted clientele, people were fickle. They tended to believe what they heard on TV.

"What do you think she's going to give us?" Libby asked Bernie.

The surprise-ingredient thing was probably the worst part of the whole contest deal as far as Libby was concerned. She spent hours and hours planning out her menus, and here she and Bernie were being asked to cook a whole Christmas dinner with some strange ingredient that Hortense was going to give them in an hour. Then if they won the first round, they'd have to do it again and again.

"A boar's head," Bernie replied. "She's going to give us a boar's head."

"Be serious," Libby said.

"I am. Boar's heads were the most popular item associated with medieval Christmas feasts." Bernie paused for a moment. "Although they didn't have Christmas foods the way we think of them. Well, that's not entirely true. They did have plum pudding and mincemeat pies."

Libby sighed. Her sister was full of more information than you'd ever want to know.

"I wish there was a way we could find out," she mused.

"You and everyone else on the show."

Of which there were seven. Actually, five if you didn't count her and Bernie. Five caterers. Libby rubbed her forehead. She never watched reality shows on TV as a matter of principle and now she was going to be on one!

"Of course, we could always sneak into the cooler and take a look," Bernie said. "I bet they have the ingredients stored in there."

Libby ignored her. It was bad enough they were in the studio.

"This sucks," she said instead. "At least Bree could have given us three or four months notice instead of letting us know at the last minute she'd booked us on here."

"Back to the weight thing are we?" Bernie asked.

"Not at all," Libby retorted, even though she was. If she had had even two months notice, she would have gone to Weight Watchers or Atkins or booked a cruise to Antarctica. Or Siberia.

Libby shut her eyes. She could picture Bree Nottingham, real estate agent extraordinaire, breezing into her store the day she'd made her announcement. Even though it had been cold and gray, she'd been dressed in pink, the color of the moment according to Bernie: pink tweed Chanel suit, pink slingback heels, pink Chanel purse.

"You're so lucky to have this opportunity," Bree had trilled after she'd explained to Libby what she'd done. "I had to fight to get you on the show, but I said, 'Hortense, we have to use some of our local talent. It's only fair.' "

Lucky was not the word Libby would have used.

"Maybe I could come down with typhoid or bubonic plague."

Bernie tucked a strand of hair behind her ear. "It would probably be bad for business."

"Worse than me on television?"

Bernie shook her head. "Get a grip."

"But I'm not a competitive person." Libby moaned.

"You are now," her sister said.

"You sound like Dad."

"I am like Dad."

"I know."

Libby reflected that her dad was extremely excited that

she was going to be on the show. So was her boyfriend, Marvin, for that matter. In fact, that's all her father or Marvin had been talking about for the last three days.

"The whole world will be watching," Marvin had told Libby, a comment that had sent her straight to the freezer for some homemade coconut ice cream.

As Libby looked around the set again, she wondered who the hell had a television studio built onto the back of their house anyway? Hortense Calabash, doyenne of the cooking channel, queen of sauces, and resident of Longely, that's who. Libby couldn't even use the excuse that she and Bernie were too busy in the store this time of year to take the time out to do this.

"Hortense's house is only fifteen minutes away," Libby remembered Bree Nottingham telling her.

Like she was some kind of moron. Of course Libby knew how far away Hortense's mansion was. They lived in the same town for heaven's sake. Not that she ever saw her. They didn't exactly move in the same social set, which was fine with Libby. But then everyone in the world knew where Hortense's house was. Okay. They had known a couple of years ago. According to the latest polls, her popularity was being eclipsed by a show on cooking caveman style. But it was still pretty popular.

"We've been friends since camp," Bree had chirped.

"Good for you," Libby had wanted to say to Bree. That woman had been the bane of her existence since the fourth grade.

"I should kill her," Libby observed. "I'd be doing the universe a favor."

Bernie raised an eyebrow. A well-manicured one, Libby couldn't help noticing. Maybe she should get hers done too. Before tonight. But the thought of having someone put hot wax on her eyebrows and then ripping the hair out made Libby shudder.

"Hortense?" Bernie asked as Libby was contemplating

what the wax thing would feel like on other parts of her anatomy. "What would her legion of crazed fans do? How would they know what to cook or how to serve it?"

Libby frowned. "No," she said. "I meant I want to kill Bree Nottingham for making us do this."

"She didn't make you," Bernie pointed out in her most reasonable—albeit irritating—tone of voice.

"Not in the literal sense, no," Libby conceded. But when the social arbiter of Longely tells you to jump, and you're in the catering business, you ask what hoop she has in mind.

"Well then. There you go," Bernie said. "Anyway," she continued, "this will be good exposure for the store."

"A Little Taste of Heaven doesn't need any more exposure," Libby replied. "We've got more customers than we can handle as it is."

"Not if you hired on more staff," Bernie pointed out.

"We don't have the room."

"We could expand," Bernie replied.

"That would mean moving," Libby said.

"And we're fine where we are," Bernie finished for her.

"Well, we are," Libby retorted as she watched Bernie saunter over to the sink.

She and her sister had had the "moving discussion" at least once a week for the past year. But Libby was holding fast to her convictions. She knew too many other places that had been doing well until they expanded. What Bernie didn't seem to be able to grasp was the amount of planning that the kind of expansion Bernie was talking about would involve.

But then her sister had always been like that. Diving headlong into something seemed to work for her, Libby thought to herself. She didn't know how, but it did. It was like Bernie's shoes. How she could walk, let alone work, in them was something that Libby had never been able to fathom.

As Libby watched her sister pass by the mini Christmas

tree sitting on the end counter, she reflected that it felt strange being on the set. It wasn't as if she was a big fan of Hortense, because she wasn't. In fact, she hated her, hated everything she stood for. But still. She'd watched Hortense's program on TV from time to time with her dad.

She'd seen those cabinets with the red door pulls, the signature gleaming dark red Viking range while sitting in her living room, and here she was on the set looking at them for real. Somehow they seemed smaller in real life than they did on the screen. It made her feel odd in a way she couldn't explain.

"I'm not sure we should be in here," Libby repeated. She knew she'd said it before, but she couldn't help herself. After all, the doors to the studio had been closed, and a sign posted had the words NO ENTRANCE clearly written in big black letters. "We should be in the green room."

"We will be there—eventually," Bernie said. "That's one of the advantages to living nearby. We get to come early."

"But the sign . . ."

Bernie gave her the look. "I didn't see it. Did you?"

"Not after you hid it behind the table."

"I didn't hide anything," Bernie protested. "Is it my fault if the thing slipped?"

"But—" Libby started to protest.

Bernie cut her off before she could say anything else. "I just wanted to take a look around before everyone else comes on the set." She pointed to a door over to the right. "According to Bree, the real cooking is done in the other kitchen. This set is just for the show."

"What are you doing?" Libby demanded as Bernie crossed the room.

"Taking a peek, of course."

"They probably have an alarm," Libby told her.

"Don't be ridiculous." Bernie opened the door and stepped inside.

"Looks like our kitchen," Libby heard Bernie say.

"I shouldn't be doing this," Libby told herself. But she followed Bernie inside anyway. What was it her father always said about in for a penny, in for a pound?

There was a metal table in the center, clusters of pots hanging from the ceiling, steel racks full of assorted pans, and two large ovens that looked as if they'd seen a lot of use.

One of them was on. Libby resisted the urge to peek. That would be going too far. Instead she went over to the table in the middle and picked up one of the glass pinecones that were in a wicker bowl in the center.

"I wonder what these are for?"

Bernie shrugged. "Christmas ornaments?"

"They're pretty." Libby put the pinecone down and looked at the tray of meringue mushrooms on the table. "They're perfect," she said.

"Yours are just as good," Bernie told her.

"Not quite," Libby said as she followed Bernie back out onto the set. Hortense's had more texture to them. Libby was wondering what kind of pastry tube Hortense had used to get that pebbled effect when she realized that Bernie was talking.

"You know," she was saying, "Hortense may be the ultimate bitch, but you have to hand it to her in the interior design department. Although I like what you did better."

Libby smiled. "Me too."

But what Hortense had done wasn't bad at all. She's just gone in a different direction. And it had taken her a lot less time to execute, something Libby reminded herself she should bear in mind for next year. The mini Christmas tree on the end of the counter was decorated with homemade cookies that Hortense had baked, painted with gold leaf, and shellacked on her last show. The bows that were knotted around the garlands of greenery were made out of a cream-colored organza that had been shot through with gold thread.

In addition, Hortense had taken light green glass bowls

and filled them with smooth river stones, into which she'd embedded groups of ivory tapers. She'd put those on the windowsills. A huge poinsettia that Hortense had placed in a reed basket woven in Africa sat on the kitchen table, while a lavender plant sat off to one side of the sink. The effect was both elegant and homey at the same time.

Libby sighed as she looked around. There was no denying that Hortense was a genius at what she did. She excelled at taking simple household objects and giving them a new look. Though drying cattails, spraying them gold, and making them into Christmas wreaths was going a little too far, in her opinion. She was just thinking that the Shredded Wheat wreath wasn't a particularly good idea either when she heard a noise.

"What was that?"

Bernie shook her head. "I didn't hear anything."

"I did. It's coming from behind the door on the left."

"That's Hortense's office." Bernie cocked her head and listened for a moment. "I think you're right. I think someone is in there."

Libby felt a wave of panic. Why did she always let Bernie talk her into these things? "What if it's Hortense?"

"It's not. And even if it is, so what? We're not doing anything wrong."

Somehow Libby didn't think Hortense would agree with her sister's assessment of their situation. "How do you know it's not her?"

"Because she's getting her hair done."

"Are you sure?"

"Of course I'm sure. I know the woman who does it."

"I still think we should leave," Libby said.

"You don't mean that."

"Yes, I do."

After all, Libby reasoned, since they weren't supposed to be here in the first place, why not get out while the going was good.

"Don't you want to find out what's going on?" Bernie said.

"Why assume something is going on?"

Bernie pointed to the door. "Then what's that noise?"

"A mouse?"

"A mouse on steroids."

Libby bit her lip. Why had she ever said anything to Bernie? All Bernie ever did was complicate things.

"After all," Bernie said, "what's the worst that can happen? That we'll be thrown out of here, and isn't that what you want anyway?"

"I hate when you do this," Libby told her.

"Do what?" Bernie demanded.

"Twist my words back at me."

"I'm not twisting anything," Bernie said as she moved toward the door. "Except maybe my ring. I was just repeating what you've been saying the whole day, which is that you don't want to be on the show. Right?"

Libby had to concede that was true.

"So it doesn't matter."

"Yes, it does," Libby said. She knew Bernie's reasoning was faulty; she just didn't know why. "Wait," Libby cried as Bernie grasped the doorknob.

"It'll be fine," Bernie assured her. She pulled.

The door flew open. As Bernie walked in, Libby caught a glimpse of Consuela Batista bending over a file cabinet.

Chapter 2

Bernie stopped short. She didn't know what she'd expected to see, but it certainly wasn't a view of Consuela's ample derriere. Some people, she decided, shouldn't wear pants with large tropical flowers on them.

"What are you doing?" Bernie demanded, not that the answer wasn't fairly self-evident.

As Consuela turned and straightened up, Bernie frowned slightly. She knew she'd seen her before in another context, with a different name, but try as she might, she couldn't remember. The question had been bothering her since she'd first seen the feature about Consuela in *Food* magazine last year. Then she'd forgotten about it until she'd seen her name on the list of contestants.

"Me?" Consuela replied. "Me? How about you?"

"Don't be ridiculous," Bernie said.

"I'm not the one who's ridiculous," Consuela shot back.

Bernie watched Consuela narrow her eyes. *She's good,* she thought appreciatively. Given the circumstances, most people would have looked at least a little guilty or startled, but not Consuela. No, siree. She was practically vibrating with indignation. She looked like a hen about to peck someone to death.

Of course, the way Consuela was wearing her hair might have inspired her behavior, Bernie mused. Over the years, she'd noticed a correlation between bad hairstyles and bad behavior. Bernie was trying to figure out how Consuela had managed to achieve that look—Bernie was guessing paste—and why she'd want to, when Consuela opened her mouth and began shrieking for help.

Again, this was not what Bernie had expected. For a moment, Bernie was rendered speechless as she listened to Consuela's screams. They were, Bernie reflected, impressively loud screams. In fact, they were the kind of screams that nineteenth-century novelists might describe as bloodcurdling, although how blood could actually curdle was something Bernie had yet to figure out. Obviously, blood could boil being a liquid and all. But curdle? No. Bernie didn't think so. As far as she knew, only milk curdled.

"Stop," Bernie shouted; but as she did, she realized that her lungs were no match for Consuela's, who was now shrieking away like some sort of demented banshee, although here again, on reflection, Bernie wasn't sure that banshees shrieked, so this was another infelicitous phrase.

From what she'd read, banshees were supernatural beings in Ireland and Scotland who took the shape of old women and moaned or sung outside of houses where people were going to die. So then where had the expression "shrieking like a banshee" come from? It was probably from a piece of literature. She was trying to figure out which story it could be when the door that led to the other kitchen banged open. Eric Royal, Hortense Calabash's personal assistant, came running in.

Bernie decided he looked like a crane. Now this was a man who needed to update his look. His bowl haircut pointed attention to his large, curved nose, and his clothes, tight bell-bottom jeans, single-button lavender velvet jacket, and white shirt made him look even skinnier than he already was. The whole sixties thing definitely wasn't working for him. But what would? Bernie wasn't sure.

"What is going on?" he demanded.

Consuela stopped her screaming, pointed her finger at Bernie and Libby, and announced, "I caught them snooping around in here. They were looking for the file with the ingredients."

Unfrigginbelievable, Bernie thought. Talk about chutzpah. Talk about unmitigated gall. She was just opening her mouth to say something when out of the corner of her eye she saw Libby moving past her.

"She's lying," Libby yelled as she shook a finger at Consuela. "She was the one looking in the file cabinet."

"Me?" Consuela drew herself up. Bernie was interested to see that Consuela's heels were higher than her's. "You're accusing me?" Consuela asked. "That is ridiculous. I do not need to cheat to win this contest."

"And you're saying I do?" Libby spat.

Consuela shrugged and inspected her nails. Bernie noticed that each one had a silver star in its center.

"Think what you want," she told Libby.

Eric Royal cleared his throat. "Ladies, ladies," he said as he reluctantly moved forward into the fray—a fray it was perfectly obvious to Bernie he didn't want any part of.

Consuela snorted and turned away from him while Libby didn't even look up. *Poor sap*, Bernie thought as she laid a hand on her sister's shoulder, gave it a gentle squeeze, and stepped out in front of her.

"So you're accusing us?" she asked Consuela.

"What did I just say?" Consuela replied.

"Frankly, I'm not sure what to think," Bernie answered. "I'm really quite shocked at this show of perfidy."

"Perfidy?" Consuela repeated uncertainly.

"That's what I said," Bernie told her as she reflected that it appeared as if Mrs. French, her fourth-grade English teacher, had spoken the truth when she'd said, "Children, trust in a large vocabulary. It will always serve you well."

"You're nuts," Consuela retorted, gathering steam again.

As Bernie listened to Consuela rant on about how terrible Bernie was for using a word like that, it occurred to her that the more wrought up Consuela became, the less Spanish her accent sounded and the more New Jersey it became; suddenly she knew where she remembered Consuela from.

"You went to school in Hoboken," Bernie told her, breaking into Consuela's ravings. "Your name used to be Darlene Brown."

Bernie was interested to see that Consuela shut up. Instantly. Bernie could see a flicker of fear passing over her face. And why shouldn't it? After all, Bernie reasoned, Consuela had made her rep as a plucky *Dominica* who'd cooked her way up from the ghetto.

That was her brand, as they liked to say in the advertising business. Bernie wondered what her fans would think if they knew that Consuela was just a middle-class Jersey girl who knew as much about rice and beans as someone from Ohio. No, they wouldn't be too happy, Bernie was willing to wager. Once credibility was lost, it was hard to get it back.

"You're crazy," Consuela told her.

"No. I'm not. You used to go out with Peter Dorset. We met at a party once."

Consuela lifted her chin up. "I've never been to Hoboken."

Bernie laughed. "You are such a liar."

Consuela gasped and put her hand over her heart. "Excuse me?"

As Eric moved forward, Bernie noticed that he had a small stain on the lapel of his lavender jacket. It looked like oil, Bernie thought. Or maybe grease. Eric waved his hands in the air to get Consuela's attention. She ignored him.

"Did I hear you right?" she asked Bernie.

Bernie smiled at her. "Of course, I meant that in the nicest possible way."

She was about to add something else equally insincere when the door opened again and Hortense Calabash, strands of hair wrapped in little pieces of foil, sailed into the room, the arms of her silk kimono flapping behind her. Eric froze. As Bernie watched Hortense approaching, she reflected that she looked a lot older off screen than on, even allowing for her lack of make-up.

"Eric," Hortense demanded. "What is going on here? I can hear the noise in my room for heaven's sake. How can I focus?"

"I'm so sorry," Eric said.

Hortense looked him up and down. A moment elapsed, then she said, "Don't be sorry, Eric. Sorry is a waste of time. Just fix the problem and move on. This is a television show, not a kindergarten." Two red dots of color appeared on Eric's cheeks. He started to say something, but Hortense held up her hand. "I'm not interested in an explanation," she informed him. "I'm really not. Explanations are excuses, and I don't tolerate excuses."

Eric took a step back, looking for all the world, Bernie thought, like a whipped dog.

"Yes, Hortense," he said.

Hortense ignored him and glanced around the room. When she got to Consuela, her eyebrows shot up and her nostrils quivered ever so slightly. She moved toward her. "How good to see you again," she purred as she came to a stop in front of her.

"You too," Consuela muttered.

When Hortense smiled, Bernie reflected that her teeth looked like Chiclets. Whoever had done Hortense's veneers should be sued.

"I hope you're all right," Hortense said.

"Why shouldn't I be?" Consuela asked.

Hortense put her hand over her mouth for a moment and shook her head. It was, Bernie reflected, a gesture designed to show great concern for your fellow man.

"Well, I heard you were having that small problem with your suppliers. I hope you managed to fix it."

Consuela clenched her jaw muscles.

"Everything's fine," she spit out.

"Good. Good. Good," said Hortense. "I'm so relieved." She shook her head and moved over to where Libby was standing. "And Libby," she said, looking her up and down, "our very own star. I'm so glad you and your sister could come."

"Me too," Libby said in what Bernie considered to be a very unconvincing tone.

Hortense reached over and patted Libby's hand.

"Our own little local celebrities." Hortense turned to Eric. "It's true, you know," she told Eric. "What's more, they're crime fighters in the bargain. You didn't know that, did you, Consuela?" Hortense asked.

Consuela shook her head.

"Yes. They're quite famous."

"I wouldn't go that far," Libby demurred.

"You were in the papers," Hortense said. "Bree showed me the article."

Libby flinched, remembering how unhappy Bree had been about the coverage of their first and second ventures.

"It's so reassuring having you here," Hortense continued. She smiled. "That way if anything happens to me, you'll be right on the scene. Don't you find that reassuring, Eric?"

Bernie decided he looked anything but reassured when he said, "Oh yes."

Hortense's lips twitched up into a smile.

"For heaven's sake, I was just joking, Eric. Who would want to harm me?"

"No one, Hortense," Eric replied in what Bernie judged to be a less-than-satisfactory tone.

"Of course not. I just think it's better to be prepared for all eventualities." Hortense patted Libby's hands again. "You know that Bree thinks the world of you, don't you?"

"Yes," Libby said. That was news to her.

"And any friend of hers is a friend of mine, which is why I hope you don't mind my giving you a teeny piece of advice."

Bernie could see her sister's shoulders stiffening as she said, "Not at all."

"Good," Hortense said. "I knew you wouldn't. Bree told me you go for the rumpled look, but I hope you're planning to change into something more flattering than what you're wearing. What you have on makes you look a tad chunky, so I can't imagine what it will do on TV. You do know the camera adds between ten and twenty pounds to your weight?"

"I know," Libby said, her complexion having gone to beet red.

"Wonderful," Hortense said. "Now I suggest you all adjourn to the green room. I have to finish with my hair and get into my Santa Claus outfit. I adore dressing up, and this outfit is so fun. I got it made especially for me by Auberge. Auberge the designer."

"I know who Auberge is," Bernie told her.

Hortense rewarded her with a perfunctory smile. "How clever of you. And by the way, in case any of you are interested, the list of ingredients for tomorrow's dinner is with me." She patted the breast pocket of what Bernie was sure was a one hundred percent silk robe. "And will continue to be, not that it would occur to any of you to try and riffle through my file cabinet to find it. However, I feel one can never be too careful in matters such as these. Isn't that right, Consuela?"

Consuela nodded.

"I'm sorry. I didn't hear you," Hortense told her.

"That's right," Consuela said, looking down at the floor.

Hortense nodded her approval.

"Good. Eric will fill you in on the routine when everyone gets here. We thought it might be good if we did some team-building exercises before the show, right, Eric?"

"Right," Eric repeated.

"Just checking," Hortense said. "Sometimes I think I give you too much to do. I've been wondering lately if I haven't been overburdening you. There's so much involved. Perhaps it would be better if I split this job in two."

"I'm fine," Eric muttered.

Hortense absentmindedly touched one of the foils in her hair. "I'm glad to hear that. I was worried. You seem to be forgetting things, small things it's true, like yesterday when you forgot to put out my eyelash curler; but still, once material starts to unravel, it's hard to stop. Generally, one has to cut the material and resew it."

Was that a threat? Bernie wondered as she noted the expression of fear on Eric's face.

"Or perhaps," Hortense continued, "you need a vacation. You haven't had one in a while."

"I'm fine," Eric insisted.

Hortense looked Eric up and down. Then she finally said, "If you say so."

"I do."

"I work him terribly hard," she confided to Libby. Then she turned back to Eric. "Listen," she said. "Don't forget about the Christmas tree ornaments." At which point she turned and headed toward the door. When she got to it, she stopped and turned around. "Bernie," she said.

"Yes," Bernie replied sweetly, wondering what un-nice thing Hortense was going to say to her.

"I don't mean to appear picky—"

"But that's why you're famous," Bernie interjected. She was gratified to see a slight flush forming on Hortense's cheeks.

"But those shoes," Hortense continued.

"I know. They're Jimmy Choos. Aren't they fabulous?" Bernie gushed. In her opinion, a good offense was always the best defense. Then, for good measure, she flashed Hortense her best smile. "Did I say anything?" she asked Eric, playing the innocence card as Hortense beat a retreat.

"Huh? No. Yes. I mean no. I have to get her tea. She hates being interrupted before a show."

Bernie nodded. "You know that the sinks in the kitchen aren't working properly," Bernie informed him.

"I'll tell Joe." Eric was doing a little dance with his feet. He looked at his watch. "He should be here soon to show everyone around the set and answer any questions that people have."

Now it was Bernie's turn to look at her watch. They had a half hour to go before the meeting. "Maybe we should adjourn to the green room," Bernie said brightly.

"Yes, maybe you should," Eric said. "If you'll excuse me, Hortense is waiting." And he bolted out the door.

"Can you imagine working for her?" Libby asked Bernie as she slipped in beside her.

"That would be my definition of hell," Bernie replied.

"Mine too," Libby replied.

Chapter 3

Libby looked down at her watch. It was only five minutes after four. If someone had asked her, she would have sworn it was six o'clock. At the very least. To distract herself, she studied the buffet set out on a table alongside the far wall of the green room.

She didn't know what she'd been expecting in the way of food but it certainly wasn't this. What you had here was breakfast food and bad breakfast food at that. And then there was the table. It was cliché city.

The bright red tablecloth, the green paper plates, the red plastic knives, forks, and spoons, and the napkins with giggling Santas on them. And then there was the tired-looking poinsettia someone had plunked down in the middle of the table. At least someone should have taken the price tag off. From anyone else, this might have been acceptable but not from Hortense Calabash.

Libby tapped the fingers of her right hand against her chin. What would she would serve in this situation? Something filling but light. Something that could stay at room temperature. Something that would give people energy. Something they could nibble on if they were nervous.

Perhaps bowls filled with different varieties of olives, a

nice cheese platter, and a bowl of Marcona almonds. Then she'd add some good, sliced Italian semolina bread, as well as a basket filled with Cortland and Gala apples and some perfectly ripe pears.

For those who wanted something sweet, she'd put out a platter of assorted, bite-sized cookies and another platter of mini cupcakes. Libby was thinking that she'd decorate the cupcakes with little icing wreaths when Bernie appeared at her side.

"This food is awful," Libby said to her.

Bernie looked down at the table and shrugged her shoulders. "What can I say? It's your standard green room buffet spread. You've got your classic bagels on steroids, your little containers of disgusting-tasting concord grape jelly, other slightly larger containers of cream cheese preserved with enough gum to turn it into a good substitute for paste, bad eight-hundred-calorie muffins, stale donuts, and brown-colored water in place of coffee."

"That's a fairly accurate description," Libby allowed.

"It should be. I've seen enough of them. They probably have the prototype of this in the Smithsonian in an exhibit labeled 'classic bad food of the late twentieth/early twenty-first century,'" Bernie mused. She gestured toward the table. "Have you ever noticed that the farther away you get from something the more faux it becomes—even in food. Take bagels, for instance."

"Must we?" Libby said, knowing a food rant was coming.

Bernie ignored her. "From what I can gather," she said, "bagels originated in southern Germany and migrated to Poland before coming over to this country."

"Did they have to get passports?" Libby asked. "Or did the people on Ellis Island let them in with nothing?"

Bernie shot her a dirty look. "Funny. Did you know the word *bagel* comes from the German word *beugel*, which means *ring* or *bracelet*. Some people have suggested that the bagel's shape, a circle, is symbolic of the continuity of life. Don't you think that's cool?" Bernie asked.

"Fascinating," Libby said dryly.

"Did you also know that bagels are the only bread that is boiled before baking? When they were first made in New York City, they used to be small, dense, and chewy. In fact, if you didn't eat them that day, you could use them as missiles. Of course, their shape made them popular because they were easy to sell.

"Peddlers stacked them on wooden dowels and walked through the streets. But as they got more popular, they morphed into the big pillowlike things we have today. Cranberry-orange bagels? Blueberry bagels? Apple cinnamon?" Bernie shuddered. "Awful. What was wrong with sesame and poppy seed? Or how about cream cheese? You know it was first developed in 1872. By law it has to contain thirty-three percent milk fat and—"

Libby held up her hand.

"What?" Bernie said.

"Enough."

"Aren't you interested?"

"Not at this moment, no."

"Fair enough. But I did distract you," Bernie said.

Libby laughed. "Yes. You did do that." She shook her head and turned and surveyed the other people in the green room. She noticed that none of them were eating anything either. "I just thought that Hortense Calabash would do better," she said, returning to the thought she'd had before Bernie had started talking.

After all, Hortense was the woman who advocated making your own butter, the woman who had intimated on her last month's show that knowing the pedigree of the chicken you were getting your eggs from would be, in Hortense's words, "a highly beneficial thing, because when it comes to food you can never be too picky."

"She's all show," Bernie said.

Libby shook her head. "I don't get it."

"There's nothing to get," her sister replied. "If Hortense doesn't have to impress someone, she doesn't make the effort. In her mind, she's doing us a favor having us here; we're not doing her a favor by being here. The buffet is strictly a pro forma gesture. Everything she does is guaranteed to advance her career."

Libby thought about how the set was decorated versus how the green room was decked out. Her sister was right, she decided.

She'd seen furniture in the Salvation Army that looked better than the couch and chairs in here did. She was thinking about the disparity when a little blond woman with thinning hair muscled her way past her and began rearranging the bagels on the bagel platter.

"Don't mind me," she told Libby. "I just like everything to be neat."

As Libby watched, the woman gathered up all the bagels, sorted them into piles of plain, sesame, and cinnamon raisin, then carefully arranged them by type on the platter.

"There. Don't you think that's better?" she asked Libby.

"Absolutely," Libby agreed. What else could she say?

The woman nodded her head vigorously and began on the muffins.

"By the way, I'm Pearl Wilde," she told Libby and Bernie as she repositioned the muffins so that each one was exactly a quarter inch apart from the others.

"You own Top Table, right?" Bernie said.

Pearl nodded while she contemplated the containers of grape jelly. "We're known for our comfort food."

Expensive comfort food, Libby almost said. Mediocre, expensive comfort food. She'd been in the store once with Bernie. Top Table was located on the corner of Lexington and Seventy-fifth Street and catered to the Park Avenue crowd. The rice pudding had been twelve dollars a serving. Then there'd been the meat loaf for twenty dollars a pound, and the mashed potatoes for fifteen. She'd bought the smallest serving size possible of chocolate pudding and had thrown it in the trash after one taste. The stuff they sold in the vending machines was better.

"I have OCD," Pearl chirped.

"Overly compensating divorcee?" Bernie asked. "Or is it operational communications disorder? I forget."

"She's kidding," Libby said as Pearl drew herself up. "I'm a little obsessive-compulsive myself."

"Most people in this business are," Pearl observed before she went back to rearranging the jelly containers into a perfect pyramid.

Watching her, Libby decided that Pearl should probably be on medication. She might be bad, but Pearl had definitely crossed over the line.

"I just think it's important for presentations to be geometrical, don't you?" Pearl commented as she moved on to the donuts.

"Personally, I try and arrange everything in circles," Bernie was saying as the door opened and a very large man waddled into the room. "It makes more sense feng shui wise."

He looks like a ball, Libby thought, albeit a ball dressed in black. His skin was so pink and shiny it practically glowed. Libby noticed he had tiny feet, or maybe, she reflected, they just looked tiny because of his girth.

Bernie leaned over. "That's Joe Estes, the producer," she whispered in Libby's ear.

"How much do you think he weighs?" Libby whispered back.

"Four hundred pounds. I heard that he got his start producing porn. You know, *Angels and the Devil?*"

"No."

Bernie gave her an incredulous look. "You've never seen it?"

"No." Why did Bernie make her feel totally clueless? "I don't watch that kind of thing." She was about to add something to the effect that she never had when Estes clapped his hands.

"People, let's get this show on the road."

Everyone in the room stopped talking.

"Better. Much better." Estes rubbed his nose with the back of his hand. "Now, the first thing I'd like to do is have you people sit down at the table over there"—he pointed to a oblong table on the other side of the room—"and have everyone introduce themselves, not that you're not familiar with each other. But I always like to observe the formalities."

"This is what they call a meet and greet," Bernie explained to Libby.

Libby didn't say anything. She didn't want to meet anyone; she didn't want to greet anyone; she just wanted to get back to the store so she could finish making her mincemeat pies and start on her butternut squash and apple bisque. As she looked at the people around her, she cursed Bree again. Why was she here? What was the point? There wasn't any as far as she could see, except that Bree wanted her to do this.

Even the twenty-thousand-dollar prize didn't seem like a good enough reason to participate in this. It wasn't as if they were going to be getting the money. They were going to be donating it to their favorite charity. Then Libby felt guilty about that thought. That was a good thing. But still. As far as she was concerned, A Little Taste of Heaven had a lot to lose and very little to gain by participating in the contest.

Estes clapped his hands again. "All right, chickees, gather round," he said.

"Chickees," Libby muttered under her breath to Bernie. "Give me a break."

"That means you three," Estes said as he pointed to Libby, Bernie, and Pearl.

Bernie and Pearl moved forward with Libby trailing.

"Very good," Estes said. "That wasn't so painful was it, dear?" he asked.

It took Libby a few seconds to realize that he was talking to her.

"No," she mumbled. She hated people calling her dear.

"Good, honey." Estes sniffed. "Damn allergies. We're going to do a quick meet and greet, so I want each of you to stand up and say your name clearly and tell everyone a little about yourself."

Libby watched as Bernie rolled her eyes.

Estes pointed to himself. "And I'll start with me. Or is it I? Oh, who gives a damn. As you can see, I have a problem with my weight. It's a glandular thing." Libby heard some titters around the room. "But that aside, I'm forty years old and in perfect health. Hortense and I have been working together for four years with, I think, good results. If you have any problems, any at all, just tell me and I'll do everything I can to resolve them. That's what I'm here for." And then he pointed to the black man sitting down beside the woman with the long red hair.

The man stood up. He had a shaved head and a gold earring and was dressed in a white suit. A black Mr. Clean, Libby couldn't help thinking.

"My name is Jean La Croix," he said. "I'm from Haiti. I run a shop in New York City called La Bon Food. We specialize in authentic Haitian food as well as Creole and Cajun cuisine. My shop has been written up in both in *Food Styles* and in the food section of the *New York Times*. I've catered parties at Trump Towers and the Royal. My gumbo is famous from Maine to California."

Libby suddenly became aware that Bernie had pushed a napkin in front of her. She looked down. On it Bernie had written, "Full of himself, isn't he?"

"Just a tad," Libby wrote back as Jean shot the cuffs on his shirt.

"So," La Croix said to Estes, "where can I put my pans?"

"Your pans?" Estes asked.

"Yes. I assume I am allowed to use my own pans."

Estes looked nonplused. "I . . . I don't think so."

"What do you mean you don't think so?"

Libby watched Estes backtrack. "I'll have to talk to Hortense about that."

"How can you not know?" La Croix flung his arms out. "Not allowing me to use my sauté pan would be like not allowing Da Vinci to use his paintbrush. If I cannot use them, I will have to withdraw."

"How precious," Consuela said. "And by the way, I thought you were from Brooklyn. So is your shop. I heard you got your accent working in the kitchen of Le Mer."

"Like you got yours from New Jersey," La Croix shot back.

"Actually," Pearl Wilde interrupted, "I brought my knives." And she opened up her backpack and laid a boning knife, a paring knife, and a cleaver out on the table. "I always carry them with me," she confided.

"That's very nice, sweetie," Estes said uncertainly.

"I would like to be able to use them as well. I think of them as my little helpers."

Libby noticed that there were beads of sweat on Estes' forehead. "I'm not sure that will be possible," he told her as he extracted a handkerchief out of the breast pocket of his jacket and mopped his brow.

"Well, you said you'd help out any way you could."

Libby could see from Estes' expression that he was deeply regretting those words.

"And I have something else I want to clear the air about," Pearl continued. "I think it might be useful if you moved the glasses to the left of the sink on the set. All things being equal, that seems to me to be a more proper placement."

"Why to the left?" Jean said.

"Because it will balance things out."

"You are crazy," La Croix said.

"Me?" Pearl pointed to herself. "I'm not the one who got myself arrested for—"

Estes hit the table. The glasses on it bounced. "That is enough," he bellowed. "We will iron out these little details later. Right now, I just want everyone to introduce themselves."

"When is the divine goddess gracing us with her ineffable presence?" a man Libby recognized as Reginald Palmer asked.

Libby had been in his store a couple of times. It was two towns over and did things like clotted cream and scones with strawberry jam. Palmer did a fairly pleasant high tea three days a week, but she'd been told that the store's real money came from catering Bar Mitzvahs and weddings.

"Reggie," Estes was saying when the sounds of "Disco Duck" filled the air.

Consuela began snapping her fingers in time to the music while the redheaded woman sitting next to Jean La Croix started rummaging through her bag.

"Sorry about this," she said. Finally she pulled out her cell. "Hello, Ronnie," she said into it. "I'll call you back later. I'm in a meeting. My publisher," she explained as she clicked her cell off and dropped it back in her bag.

Right, Libby thought. Now she knew where she'd seen her before. Her picture was on the cover of a well-reviewed cookbook on how to throw a party for twenty people in a half hour or less. However, two cooking teachers who Libby knew and respected had pronounced it not worth the money it would cost to recycle it.

She brushed back a strand of her red hair and stood up. "I guess I'm next. For those of you who haven't seen my book yet, I'm Brittany Saperstein, and I own Kugle to

All." At which point her cell rang again. She went through her bag till she found it. "Yes, Evelyn, I think you should go with the gold on the walls. Sorry," she said again.

"Could you turn that thing off?" Estes told her as it rang a third time.

"Hello, Judy," Brittany said into the cell. "I'll have to call you back." She dropped the phone back into her bag—a Fendi, Libby noticed. "There's no need to yell," she told Estes.

"I wasn't yelling," Estes told her.

"Well, then raising your voice," Brittany countered.

"It's difficult to conduct a meeting when that thing of yours keeps going off."

"It's not my fault if people need to speak to me," Brittany said.

"Are you going to have it on, on the show?" Estes asked.

"Of course not," Brittany said.

"Then turn it off now," Estes thundered.

"Joe, Joe. It's not good to be losing your temper like that," Reginald Palmer said. "Not good at all. Especially for someone of your size."

"Let's leave my size out of it, shall we?"

"Fine," Reginald said. "I just don't want you to drop dead of a heart attack."

"Thank you for your concern. Now can we get back to the matter at hand? We have a lot to cover before the show."

"Which is why I want to know when we are going to get a chance to speak to Hortense."

"You're not," Estes said.

"What do you mean?" Reginald demanded.

"Exactly what I said. She doesn't want to talk to the contestants before. You'll speak to her on the show. She never speaks to anyone before airtime."

"What utter rot. She talked to me before."

"That was then. Now she likes to meditate and prepare herself."

"You mean have a couple of cocktails," Libby could have sworn she heard Pearl Wilde mutter under her breath.

"But I have something to say to her," Reginald insisted.

"You can tell me and I'll tell her."

"I'm sorry, that's not possible."

"I can get her assistant in here if you'd like. You can speak to him."

"What nonsense. I need to speak to Hortense."

Estes folded his arms across his chest.

"I'm afraid that that's not going to happen," he told Reginald.

Libby was slightly alarmed to see he was beginning to get red in the face.

"But what about my pans?" Jean La Croix demanded.

"What about them?" Estes asked.

"I want to talk to her about those."

"I've already told you I will relay your request."

Jean La Croix slapped the table with the palm of his hand. "That's not good enough."

Suddenly Libby became aware that she was hearing something other than Jean La Croix's voice. She turned to listen. A noise seemed to be coming from the other room, the room next to Hortense's office.

"What's that?" Reginald said.

Estes didn't say anything.

"That's Hortense, isn't it?" Reginald demanded. He began rising from his chair. "She's in the test kitchen, isn't she?"

"I already told you, you can't go in there," Estes said.

"The hell with that," Reginald replied.

Libby watched as he pushed his chair back and strode across the floor. Libby reflected that for a man of his girth,

Estes could move when he wanted to because suddenly he was blocking Reginald's path.

"I meant what I said," he told Reginald.

Reginald opened his mouth to speak but Libby never heard what he had to say, because the blast coming from the second kitchen drowned everything out.

Chapter 4

Even with the door to the room open and the venting fan on, Bernie could still smell the faint odor of gas lingering in the air.

"It's off," Eric Royal said to her. "I already checked."

Bernie nodded absentmindedly. She'd figured as much. Otherwise they wouldn't be in here now. They'd be outside in the fresh air waiting for the emergency crews to come. She was suddenly aware that Libby was standing right next to her and that her complexion was a definite shade of lime green.

Her sister pointed to Hortense's body splayed out on the floor. Bernie studied Hortense for a moment. She was wearing a Santa Claus suit just like she said she would. Silk, Bernie judged, and tailored to within an inch of its life. It was very upscale.

"That could have been me," Libby said.

Bernie turned and looked at her. Libby was wringing her hands.

"How do you figure that?"

"I almost opened the oven," Libby explained. "I wanted to."

"The operative word here is *almost*," Bernie replied while Consuela made the sign of the cross.

"It wasn't your time," she said.

There was no arguing with that, Bernie thought as she turned back to take a good look at Hortense's body.

"How can you do that?" Libby demanded.

"Look at her?"

"Yes."

Bernie shrugged. "Because I can."

Libby was the sensitive one in the family, not her. Although she had to say, Hortense was not a thing of beauty at the moment. But then, of course, no one would look good when they're covered with cookie dough, red and green sprinkles, fruitcake, and shards of what to Bernie appeared to be Christmas ornaments peppering one's chest. She looked at the glass pinecones on the table; then she looked back at Hortense. Definitely Christmas ornaments. The two browns were a match.

It wasn't the explosion that had killed Hortense, Bernie reflected. Or at least not directly. No. The coup de grace had been the piece of glass that was currently sticking out of Hortense's throat. Obviously it had sliced through Hortense's carotid artery. Death had been instantaneous. Or as close to it as you could get.

"I think we'd better call the police," Bernie said, interrupting Eric Royal, Hortense's personal assistant, who was in the middle of flinging his arms about and shrieking, "The blood, oh my God, the blood and around Christmastime too."

"So this would be better if it happened in the summer?" Bernie asked.

Fortunately Eric hadn't heard her, probably because Brittany was screaming so loudly, Bernie reflected. She sounds like a cat in heat, Bernie decided as she watched Jean La Croix lean over to get a closer look at Hortense.

He shook his head. "This, it is very upsetting," he said. "Very upsetting. I must get my equilibrium back."

Brittany stopped screeching and turned to La Croix.

How she'd heard him Bernie didn't know.

"It's always about the great La Croix, isn't it?" Brittany charged.

La Croix straightened the lapels of his jacket. "Art supersedes everything."

Consuela butted in. "Maybe that's true," she told him, "but you're not an artist, you're a cook."

"In my hands, food becomes art," La Croix replied stiffly.

"That's enough," Bernie said as Consuela rolled her eyes.

She was about to say something else when Estes said, "Hortense said she felt something bad was coming. She said she felt as though a tragedy was stalking her. She was psychic, you know."

"No, I didn't," Bernie replied. She'd heard Hortense called many things but psychic wasn't one of them.

"She was. In fact, she was planning on going to a Hindu temple to ask the priests to say prayers so that they would remove the curse she felt had been placed on her and her show."

Eric raised an eyebrow. "I didn't know that."

"It's true," Estes insisted.

"If you say so." Eric turned to Bernie and Libby. "She did say she was glad you were here in case anything happened."

"That proves my point," Estes said.

"She was being sarcastic," Bernie told him.

Estes spread his arms out. "How can you say that, given the circumstances?"

"Fine," Bernie replied. She wasn't in the mood to argue. "Why don't we let the police decide."

"The police," Estes echoed.

"That's what I said," Bernie replied. She watched Estes sneak a glimpse at his watch before gesturing toward the stove. The oven door was now a mass of tangled metal.

Estes sniffed. "Obviously the stove exploded."

"Obviously it did," Bernie agreed. That was undeniable. The question was why had it exploded? Come to think of it, what was Hortense doing in here anyway? "But even if it is an accident, you still have to call the police," she told Estes.

Estes rubbed his nose with the back of his hand. "First of all, I know that," he told her. "I'm not a moron. And second of all, I resent your implication."

"What implication?"

"The implication present in your statement, 'even if it is an accident.' How can it be anything else?"

"Easy," Bernie replied as she squatted down next to Hortense. "Someone could have booby-trapped the oven."

"Perhaps you're saying that to puff yourself up."

"Puff myself up?"

"Make yourself important."

"I know what you mean," Bernie snapped.

"Good," Estes shot back.

This is going nowhere, Bernie thought as she gingerly reached into the breast pocket of Hortense's Santa suit.

"What are you doing?" Libby squawked.

"Seeing if anything is there," Bernie answered.

"Like what?"

"Like the list," Bernie said without turning her head. The pocket was empty.

"The list of ingredients isn't here," she told her sister.

"So what?"

Bernie heard her left knee crack as she got up. She'd better get back to the gym.

"Remember Hortense said the list was in her pocket."

"That was the pocket of her robe. Why assume she was carrying it on her now?"

"Of course she'd have it on her now. We're going on the air soon."

"She might have just been saying that," Libby pointed out.

Bernie was about to answer but before she could, Estes jumped in.

"Let me get this right," he said. "Are you saying Hortense was deliberately killed for the list of ingredients for the cook-off?"

"It's a possibility," Bernie said.

"That's the most ridiculous thing I've ever heard of," Consuela scoffed.

"An insult to our abilities," Jean La Croix huffed.

"And our morals," Pearl added.

"I never saw this list you're talking about," Eric Royal added. "It's in the safe."

Bernie rubbed her knee. "Maybe she took it out."

"I would have known if she had," Eric Royal insisted.

"Well, all I know is that she told me she had it," Bernie retorted. "Right, Consuela?"

"Right," Consuela said sullenly.

"Eric, maybe you should go check."

"I don't know."

Bernie watched Estes give Eric a nod.

"Go ahead," he told him.

Eric was back five minutes later. From the look on his face, Bernie knew he wasn't going to be delivering good news. And he didn't.

"It's not there," Eric told Estes.

"It could be somewhere else," Libby said.

"It could be," Bernie conceded, but she didn't think it would be.

Chapter 5

Suddenly everyone in the room started talking at once. Bernie felt like putting her hands over her ears to block out the noise.

"Quiet!" Estes yelled.

Everyone shut up. *I need a drink*, Bernie thought as she watched the sweat beading up on Estes' forehead. It was hot in the room, but not that hot. Maybe the guy had high blood pressure.

"What do you mean the list isn't there?" Estes asked Eric.

"I checked the safe and Hortense's desk. I couldn't find it," Eric squeaked.

Estes sniffed. "Well go and look again."

"Don't," Bernie said.

Estes stared at her.

"What do you mean don't?" he demanded.

"You're disturbing a possible crime scene. Don't you watch *Law and Order*?"

"Ha. Ha. Ha. For your information, my cousin helps produce that show. Furthermore, just because you were involved in a couple of cases doesn't make you an expert. Far from. You don't know it's a crime scene," Estes told her. "There are lots of explanations for the list not being there."

"You keep saying that," Bernie told him. "I'd like to hear what they are."

Brittany clapped her hands together.

"People, people, we need to focus here. What are we going to do with the list gone?"

"We don't know it's gone," Estes replied.

"But if someone read it . . ." La Croix's voice trailed off.

Everyone was quiet as they all contemplated the implications of that.

"We'll make a new one," Estes said.

"Who will?" Consuela gestured toward Hortense with her chin. "She's dead."

"And that's the point," Bernie said as she grabbed the conversational ball. "We have to call the police."

Estes scowled. "Of course we will. We have to. But let's think about the show."

"I think we should think about Hortense."

"I never said we shouldn't. All I'm saying is that there are big bucks tied up in this show. I'm just trying to protect everyone's investment."

It always comes down to money, Bernie thought as Consuela said, "That's a terrible thing to say."

Estes made a face. "Save your sanctimonious act for someone else."

Bernie could see Consuela bristling. "Sanctimonious act? How dare you?"

"Easy," Estes said, but before he could say anything else, Pearl Wilde tapped him on the wrist. He turned to face her.

"Where do you keep the cleaning supplies?" she asked him.

"Just a minute," Estes told her as he glanced around the room.

He looks relieved that he has something else to talk about, Bernie reflected as Estes' eyes lit on Eric Royal.

"Eric, can you answer Pearl's question?" he asked him.

Eric Royal gestured to the sink. "Under there." Then he laid the back of his hand on his forehead. "I can't believe this," he said. "I told her not to bake those cookies. I told her there wasn't time. But Hortense insisted. She was like that. I told her I'd go check on them. But she said no. She's always having to do everything herself. And now she's dead," Eric Royal concluded.

Unlike Brittany Saperstein's, all that Eric's performance lacked, Bernie thought uncharitably, was some glycerin tears and a swoon onto the floor. But it wasn't fair to compare them, because Brittany wasn't even trying. Bernie watched Brittany looking around the room. Her eyes went everywhere but to Hortense.

"Estes is right. We have to think about the show," Brittany said.

"How can you think about that at a time like this?" Eric demanded.

"Oh, come on. Be honest. Everyone is," Brittany said as the sounds of "Disco Duck" floated out of her handbag.

"Those things should be outlawed," Estes growled.

Interesting, Bernie thought as Brittany opened her bag. Very interesting that Brittany had had the presence of mind in the middle of the pandemonium that the explosion had caused to bring her bag along with her. That spoke of a pretty cool character or preknowledge.

Estes made a grab for Brittany's handbag.

"I'm going to throw that thing out."

"Oh no, you don't," Brittany told Estes as she pulled her bag away.

"Then shut that thing off!" Estes bellowed.

Bernie was alarmed to see a vein under Estes' left eye getting bigger. She hoped he didn't have a heart attack. Two dead people in five minutes would be a little much.

"Just a sec," Brittany said as she fished around inside her pocketbook. Finally she found her cell. "Mommy can't talk right now," she said into it. "Mommy is busy dealing with a dead person. Well, I'm not sure this one will go to heaven. No, Josefina will take you to the party. Bye, bye, sweetums." And she clicked off. She was just about to put it back in her bag when Estes grabbed it out of her hand.

"I'll give it back to you after the show," Estes told Brittany.

"If there is a show," Bernie countered as Brittany grabbed her phone back from Estes.

She clutched it to her chest. "Of course there's going to be a show," Brittany said.

Bernie gestured toward Hortense's prone body. "I think you're forgetting something."

"No, I'm not. Haven't you heard that thing about the show must go on?"

"I'm not sure that saying applies to this situation," Bernie said. She was just about to tell her why when, out of the corner of her eye, Bernie noticed that Pearl was making her way to the sink. She watched Pearl open the cabinet doors.

"Pearl, what are you doing?" she asked her.

Pearl glanced over her shoulder. "Looking for something to clean the walls, of course. And the floor."

"Of course," Bernie said. Wouldn't that be everyone's first thought? "Don't do that. The police won't like it."

Estes lifted his hands in supplication, dropped them to his sides, and looked up at the ceiling. "Why, dear God, does everything happen to me?"

"I think it happened to Hortense," Bernie pointed out.

"Hortense is no longer among us. I am," Estes shot back.

"Precisely my point." Bernie turned her attention back to Pearl. "Pearl," she said in the same voice she imagined she would use on a recalcitrant small child. "I'm afraid you're going to have to leave the walls alone."

Pearl straightened up. Bernie noted that she had a roll of

paper towels in one hand, a bottle of spray cleanser in the other, and a look of steely determination in her eyes.

"I think Top Job would be better, but this will do."

Bernie wanted to say, "Don't do it," but before she could get the words out of her mouth, Pearl walked over and let loose with a spray of cleanser on the wall. "I prefer high-gloss paint for cleaning purposes, but semigloss does just as well, don't you think?" she asked Bernie. "Thank heavens this room wasn't painted with flat latex. For a while, Hortense was thinking of using a flat yellow latex in here, but I managed to talk her out of it."

"Really," Bernie said. She didn't know whether to be fascinated or appalled. "You have to stop," she told Pearl. "You have to stop what you're doing now."

Pearl gave her an exasperated glance.

"But I can't just leave it like this," she protested. "Hortense would be immensely displeased if I did."

"The police will displeased if you don't," Bernie told her.

Jean La Croix waved his hand around the room. "But this is . . . how you say . . . so ugly."

Bernie gestured at the blood-splatter pattern on the wall. "Would it be better if it were attractive? Something you could make into a new wallpaper pattern?"

"That is a horrible thing to say," Jean La Croix huffed.

"You're right," Bernie told him as she refocused her attention on Pearl. "Maybe what you say about Hortense is true," she told her, "but you're going to have to leave things alone anyway."

"I can't," Pearl wailed.

She turned back and directed another shot of cleanser at the wall. Visions of forensic evidence vanishing danced before Bernie's eyes.

"Libby, take the bottle away," Bernie told her sister, who as luck would have it was standing right next to Pearl.

Libby looked at Bernie uncertainly.

"Me?"

"No. The king of Siam."

"There's no need for sarcasm."

Bernie took a deep breath. "Please," she got out through gritted teeth. "Just take the cleanser away from Pearl now."

"I don't know," Libby said as Pearl clutched the bottle to her chest. "Why don't you do it?"

"Because you're closer."

"By five steps."

"Why do things always have to be so complicated with you?" Bernie snapped.

Libby bit her lip. "We shouldn't be arguing."

"No. You're right. We shouldn't be." Bernie thought for a moment. She nodded in Pearl's direction. "Why don't you take Pearl into the green room and make her a nice cup of tea?"

Libby brightened.

"I think that's a splendid idea," Brittany said.

"I think we could all use something," Consuela observed. "Maybe a shot of scotch?"

"Cognac," Jean La Croix said. "What we need is some Cognac."

"How about some cookies?" Libby suggested. "I always find cookies help in times such as these."

Reginald rolled his eyes.

"Really, my dear," he said to Libby. "You've been reading too many British murder mysteries. Next you're going to suggest crumpets."

Bernie watched a flush grown on Libby's cheeks.

"Hey," Bernie told Reginald. "That was entirely unnecessary. Libby was just trying to be helpful."

Reginald put his hands up in a gesture of surrender.

"So sorry. I didn't realize your sister was such a delicate flower."

Bernie took a step toward him. "Don't be nasty."

Reginald appealed to everyone. "What did I say?" he asked.

Bernie caught herself before she answered. Just calm down, she told herself. Calm down and focus on the big picture. The important thing was that they were contaminating the crime scene by being here—if it was a crime scene. After all, Estes could be right, Bernie thought. There was a chance. Albeit a slim one.

Maybe the list was in the bedroom. Maybe the stove exploding was an accident. After all, accidents did happen, stoves did explode because of the way they were installed. Unfortunately, Bernie's gut told her different.

"Who put you in charge anyway?" Estes demanded of Bernie as Libby started leading Pearl out of the room. "I'm the producer. I'm the person around here who's supposed to be giving the orders. Everyone listens to me."

"We're not taping the show yet," Bernie retorted.

"Good point, Joe," Reginald said. He pointed a shaking finger at Bernie. "You're like some Jonah."

"Jonah?" Brittany said.

"If you were in any way literate," Reginald snapped at her, "you would know that I was referring to someone who brings bad luck." He pointed at Bernie. "Wherever you go, bad things happen."

"That's not true," Bernie said, even though she was beginning to believe it might be. After all, she and her sister had been involved in investigating two murders already. "Anyway, no matter what you think of me, you still have to call the police and report this."

"We will. After the show," Estes said.

"Are you nuts?" Bernie demanded.

"We have to go on the air soon."

"Unfortunately, there seems to be a problem." Bernie pointed to Hortense. No one looked down. "What are you going to do for your hostess? Prop her up, attach some strings to her arms and mouth, and have someone move them?"

"That's disgusting," Consuela cried as Brittany Saperstein's cell went off again. "Show some respect for the dead."

"I'm trying to," Bernie said as Brittany answered her call.

"You won't believe what happened," Brittany said into her cell.

"I've had it with that," Estes roared as he made a grab for Brittany's phone.

Brittany feinted, took a step back, and almost tripped over Hortense. "I have to go," she told the person on the other end of the line. "I have a situation here I have to deal with."

"A situation?" Estes growled. "Is that what you'd call this?"

Brittany put her hands on her hips.

"Well, what would you call it?" she demanded.

"A catastrophe," Estes replied.

"Same thing," Brittany said.

"No, it's not," Estes replied. "It's not the same thing at all."

"I have to agree with Estes on this," Bernie said.

"Who cares?" Brittany retorted.

Bernie pointed to herself. "I do."

Consuela gave the gold chain around her neck a tug. "What I want to know," she said, "is what are we going to do about it?"

"Yes," Jean La Croix repeated. "What are we going to do?"

"I'm trying to tell you," Estes said.

"So," La Croix said, "we are waiting."

"We have a problem, and we're going to solve it. As I've been trying to say for the last five minutes, Eric will take her place."

Eric's thumb stopped in midpress of one of the numbers

on his cell phone keypad. His head popped up. "I will?" he croaked.

"You've always told me you wanted to, haven't you?" Estes asked.

Eric lowered the phone to his side. "Well"—Eric began when Estes cut him off.

"In fact, I've overheard you say any number of times that you could do a better job than Hortense."

"I never said that," Eric stammered.

"You most certainly did."

La Croix stepped forward. "So, Eric, are you going to let me use my pans?"

"I don't know," Eric stammered. "It's not my—"

"And I need my knives," Pearl added.

Consuela crossed her arms over her chest.

"If they get to use their things, then I want to use my special salt," she said.

Bernie decided that Eric was acquiring that deer-caught-in-the-headlights look.

Estes stroked his chin. "So, Eric, who are you calling?" Estes asked him.

Eric bit his lip.

"Well?" Estes said. "Are you calling the *New York Post*? The *National Enquirer*? Your grandmother? Your nephew? Who?"

"No," Eric yelped. "I was calling Bree Nottingham."

Bernie watched Estes nod his head. The effect was somewhat like one rubber ball hitting the other. He rubbed his hands together.

"That's the first decent suggestion I've heard in the last ten minutes," he said. "Bree will know what to do."

Libby groaned.

"I think I feel sick."

Bernie took a good look at her sister. In the last ten minutes, the green in her complexion seemed to have mutated from lime to olive.

"Do you want a drink?" Bernie asked her. They had to have alcohol somewhere around here, and heaven only knows she could use one herself.

Libby shook her head.

"A cookie?"

Libby shook her head again.

"You sure?" Libby refusing a cookie? Now things were serious.

"I think I need to lie down."

Bernie was leading her out of the room when Libby turned her head and leaned over. Bernie jumped out of the way, but it was too late. Libby had barfed all over her pink suede wedges.

Chapter 6

Libby rinsed her mouth out with tap water again, then looked at her reflection in the bathroom mirror. She still looked green. Why did she have such a weak stomach? No one else had puked at the crime scene but her. Not one else had made a spectacle of themselves, that was for sure.

She should have gotten some air when she felt herself going queasy, not tried to tough it out. But oh no. Now she was going to owe Bernie for a new pair of shoes. Why couldn't she have thrown up on the floor, for heaven's sake? It would have been cheaper—both financially and emotionally, Libby reflected. She patted her hair in place and went outside.

As she stepped into the hallway, something that Bernie had said to her when she'd been working in L.A. struck her.

"Never underestimate the power of stardust on civilians," Bernie had said. "Proximity to television and movies makes people do nutty things."

Libby had told her she was the one who was nuts, but given what was happening, she was beginning to think her sister had been right. Or maybe it was the power of Bree

Nottingham, real estate agent extraordinaire, who was responsible for the fact that they were going on the air in a little over an hour. Bree. Just the idea that she was waiting for her made Libby cringe. The only good thing was that Bree hadn't seen her throwing up.

"There you are," Bree said as Libby reentered the room. "Are you feeling better?" she asked.

"She's fine," Bernie said. "Aren't you, Libby?"

"Yes," Libby said in as positive a voice as she could manage.

Looking at Bree now, resplendent in her black and white tweed Chanel suit and black Manolo Blahnik stiletto boots, Libby was once again struck by her ability to engineer any situation with the aid of those indispensable aids to modern life—her BlackBerry and her cell phone. It was why she was who she was.

From her experience, Libby would have bet anything that once the police were called, a predictable sequence of events would follow. The police would arrive, the rooms would be taped shut until the forensic team had completed their investigation, people would be interviewed, and the station would be showing a rerun of the *Hortense Calabash Show* this evening.

But that's not what had occurred, no sirree bob, not by a long shot, as her mother had liked to say. Bree had taken one look at Hortense's body, briskly stepped back out of the test kitchen, whipped out her cell, and summoned the Longely chief of police, Lucas Broad, to Hortense's estate.

Libby didn't know what Bree had said to him, because after she'd said something about "my people," Bree had walked away, and Libby hadn't been able to hear the rest of the conversation, although not from want of trying, she had to admit. But whatever Bree had said, she and Bernie agreed it had certainly been effective.

Fifteen minutes later, there was Old Lucy, as her father called him, studying the scene of the "tragic misfortune," as Estes kept insisting on calling it. Then he and Estes and Bree had huddled together for a ten-minute confab, while everyone else milled around the green room. At that point, Libby was all set to have Estes tell everyone the taping was off. Which was more than fine with her.

"No way, Sherlock," Bernie had whispered when Libby had told her. "Bet you ten bucks."

"You're on," Libby had whispered back.

She'd really wanted Bernie to be wrong. All she wanted to do was go home, take a bath, down some aspirin for her headache, and get to work on her soup for the next day. Was that too much to ask? Evidently it was, because two minutes later, Lucy had walked over and announced to everyone that the show was going to go on as planned. The police would work around the shooting schedule.

Bernie had just smiled and stuck out her hand, palm upward.

"Told you," she said.

"The trouble with people today is that they don't have any respect for the dead," Libby had grumped as she slapped two five-dollar bills into Bernie's palm.

"You sound like Mom," Bernie had told her as Bree materialized beside them.

How does she do that? Libby wondered as Bree looked at the money in Bernie's hand, then looked back up at Libby.

"I forgot to pay Bernie for the eggs she picked up this morning," Libby stammered. She didn't know why she was lying to Bree. There was no reason to, but Bree always made her feel crass.

"Actually it was the snails," Bernie added. "Haven't you heard? We're raising our own. Kind of a test run. Did you know that some archaeologists think that snails were the first animal that man domesticated? And that the Mesopotamians ate them as did the Romans and that a French recipe for their use appeared in a 1390 cookbook, although they didn't become popular until the beginning of the sixteenth century."

Bree raised an eyebrow. "Really. How fascinating."

She idly touched her French knot. Libby noted that it was perfect as per usual. Then she wondered if there was anything about Bree that wasn't perfect.

"I need to talk to the two of you for a minute," she informed them.

"Wonderful," Libby muttered under her breath as Bree motioned for her and Bernie to follow her into the hallway.

Knowing Bree, she probably wanted her to cater a sit-down dinner for twenty-five by tomorrow night for under two hundred dollars, Libby thought, as well as arrange for the flowers.

"Now, my dears," Bree said once she, Bernie, and Libby were standing outside the green room, "I have a teeny, tiny little favor to ask of you."

Here we go, Libby thought. Then she realized from the expression on Bree's face that she must have groaned out loud.

Bree had raised her eyebrow again. "Surely you wouldn't begrudge me in this time of need."

"Of course not," Bernie replied for Libby. "She was just groaning because her feet hurt, right, Libby?"

"Right, Bernie."

What else could she say? Not something along the lines of, "You don't ask for tiny favors." They're all either expensive, time-consuming, or both.

Bree looked at Libby's feet and said, "I feel for you, my dear. Bad feet can be such a trial. It's so sad to go shopping and not be able to wear the cute shoes. I would die if that happened to me. But I understand they're doing wonderful things with surgery these days."

"I don't need surgery," Libby said.

She realized she was gritting her teeth so hard her jaw

was aching. She looked down at her feet. She was wearing perfectly respectable black leather ballet flats. Even Bernie had said they weren't bad.

"I never said you did." Bree sighed. "You always have been overly sensitive. I just gave you a fact." Then she changed the subject before Libby could reply. "Poor, poor Hortense. She was going to have her bunions removed. Not that she has to worry about that now."

"Guess not," Bernie said. "Though she might have to worry about a pedicure. I understand people's nails keep growing after they're dead. Maybe that could be a new service for funeral homes. Postmortem pedicures."

"Really," Bree shrilled. "Sometimes I don't know what's the matter with you, Bernie."

This, Libby decided, might be the only subject that she and Bree agreed upon.

"Sorry," Bernie replied, although Libby noted that she didn't look at all contrite.

After a moment of silence, Bree beckoned for Libby and Bernie to come closer.

"Well, the police are telling me"—here Bree lowered her voice even more—"that they suspect a homicide."

"What a surprise," Bernie muttered at the same time that Libby said, "Great."

Why couldn't Hortense's death have been an accident? Libby didn't have time for a crime, not now, not before Christmas and New Year's Eve. This was party season, for heaven's sake. Hortense should have been more considerate.

Bree shot her a dirty look, and Libby shut up, but she couldn't stop running her to-do list in her head. Maybe she was more like Pearl Wilde than she wanted to admit, she decided.

"Did they say why?" Bernie asked.

"They found the gas line disabled and the remains of a disposable flash camera in the oven."

"Disposable camera?" Bernie said. She moved her silver and onyx ring up and down her finger, which Libby knew meant that she was thinking. "Interesting."

Libby said. "I don't understand."

Bree fiddled with the gold buttons on her jacket. "Frankly, my dear, I'm not sure that I do either, but the homicide people are hypothesizing that someone"—Bree lowered her voice again to the point that Libby had to strain to hear her—"booby-trapped the oven. Chief Broad mentioned something about disabling the flash so when the camera went off it sparked and ignited the gas when Hortense opened the oven door. The chief will explain it to you."

"Somehow I doubt that," Bernie said.

She, Libby, and her father were not on the chief of police's favored-persons list. If they were on a list at all, it would be labeled "troublemakers."

"No, he will," Bree said, her tone leaving no doubt that this was not a matter the chief had any say in.

This is going to be interesting, Libby thought as another question popped into her head. "But what about the Christmas tree ornaments? What were they doing in the oven?" For the life of her, she couldn't figure out what Hortense could possibly be using them for.

Bree shrugged. "Chief Broad thinks the murderer put them in there."

"Obviously the murderer is someone who doesn't like Christmas," Bernie noted.

"Or Hortense," Libby felt bound to point out. "But how come the ornaments didn't melt?" she asked.

"Because glass doesn't melt before two thousand degrees," Bernie informed her.

Bree shuddered.

"Poor Hortense. She was my bunk mate in camp," Bree added.

"At least she died doing the thing she loved," Bernie said. "How many of us can say that?"

"True. Very true." Bree dabbed at her eyes. Then she straightened up. "Now, about that favor."

"Yes," Libby said, a sense of foreboding growing in her stomach. She just couldn't cater a dinner. Not now. Not with what they had to do.

Bree looked around again. Then she leaned in. "Well," she confided, "the police think someone here might be responsible, and I'd like you to see if you can find out who it is."

"Us?" Libby squeaked, although in retrospect she realized she shouldn't have been surprised. "You want us to investigate?"

She didn't know whether to be relieved or worried by this turn of events. She was glad she didn't have to cook, but investigating another homicide? Things always turned weird with those. At least with cooking if you followed the recipe, you knew what you were getting, which was more than she could say about investigating a homicide.

"Well, yes," Bree replied. "After all, it's not as if you haven't done this before, because you certainly have. Twice, to be exact."

"Lucy won't like it," Libby said. "He won't like that at all."

"He certainly won't," Bernie chimed in.

Bree flicked a mote of dust off her suit jacket before replying. "Ordinarily you'd be correct in your assessment, but I've persuaded him for the good of the town to set aside his normal way of doing things."

"Doing what?" a voice boomed.

Libby looked up. Chief Lucas Broad had joined them. He was wearing his uniform, but then he always wore his uniform.

Bree smiled sweetly. "Ah, Chief Broad. I was just saying

that you've graciously decided to accept Bernie and Libby's help with our little problem."

"And my father's," Bernie said. "We come as a package."

Libby watched Lucas Broad open his mouth, then close it again. It was no secret that the chief and her father hated each other.

"Isn't that right, Chief?" Bree said.

The chief struggled with the word for a second. Finally he managed to get a yes out. "That is correct," he said.

Libby was interested to note that a look of what seemed like genuine pain was crossing the chief's face as he uttered those words. What does she have on him? Libby wondered as Bree turned to Libby and Bernie and gave them one of her brilliant smiles.

"See," she said, "I told you things would be fine." She waved a hand in their direction. "Now you three arrange things among yourselves. I have some other problems I have to settle." And she walked away.

Libby watched her as she rounded the corner and entered the green room. Then she turned her gaze back to the chief. He was standing there with his arms crossed over his chest, his foot tapping, and a scowl on his face.

"Okay," he said. "Let's get something straight here. I'm doing this for the good of the town. Understand?"

Libby nodded. Somehow she managed to keep from looking at Bernie. If she had, they both would have started laughing.

"That is the only reason this is happening."

"Boy, Bree must have something on you," Bernie observed. "Or your wife."

Why does she have to say things like that? Libby thought as she observed the chief's eyes becoming little slits. Why does she always have to make things worse? Her sister could never seem to grasp the fact that what she said had real consequences, as in who would take care of her father and run the store if Bernie got herself arrested? Libby, that's who.

"That is libel," the chief huffed.

"Sorry," Bernie said. "I was just kidding."

"Libeling a public official is a felony," the chief continued.

"Are you going to arrest me?" Bernie asked.

"She didn't mean it," Libby said, stepping between her sister and the chief of police. "She's upset."

The chief considered Libby's words for a moment. Then he said, "We're all upset by Hortense's untimely demise. She was a well-loved member of the community and will be missed."

Libby caught a look from her sister. If there was anything less true, she couldn't imagine it.

The chief continued on. "Given the nature of everything, I've agreed to conduct things a little differently than I usually would." He coughed into his fist. "We've decided to try to delay publicizing this tragic event. At least as much as we can. Bree has persuaded me that, given the nature of the outrage, it would be better, public-relations-wise, if we had a suspect in custody when we do, which is where you come in."

"Why us?" Bernie asked.

"Obviously," the chief said, "because you're here. Because you know these people."

"We don't know them," Libby objected.

"Of course you do," Lucy said. "You're caterers, aren't you?"

"Yes," Libby said.

"So there you go," the chief said.

Bernie tapped her foot on the floor.

"That's a little like saying that just because I'm Irish, I go to mass every Sunday."

"You mean you don't?" the chief said.

"We're Protestant."

"I don't care. What I care about is that there will be no nonsense from either one of you, understand?"

"What do you mean by nonsense?" Bernie asked.

As Libby watched, the chief's eyes got even smaller.

"I mean the kind of things you and your sister do," he snarled.

"I don't suppose you could be more specific?" Bernie asked, goading him on.

Judging from the expression on Lucy's face, Libby decided this was not a good question.

Lucy raised one of his hands and ticked things off as he spoke.

"No breaking and entering, no misrepresenting yourselves, no illegal entries, no stealing vehicles. In fact, no illegal activities of any kind. Is that good enough for you?"

"Shucks, and I was so looking forward to doing all of that," Bernie said.

Libby noted that Lucy's eyes seemed to be disappearing all together.

"Do we at least get badges?" Bernie asked.

Bernie, just shut up, Libby thought as the chief stuck his face about an inch away from her sister's.

"I'd rather go to hell."

"Well, that's a fairly clear response," Bernie said. "Can we at least see the case file?"

"There is no case file at the present moment, but if there was, the answer would be no," the chief told her.

"Then how are we supposed to work?" Libby demanded.

"The way you always do," the chief said. "By blundering along."

"What if we don't want to do this?" Libby asked him.

He looked at her for a moment before replying. Then he said, "I don't think that's an option."

Bernie put her hands on her hips. "What are you going to do, arrest us?" she demanded.

The chief stroked his chin.

"You know," he said, "it's amazing how many little rules and regulations towns like ours accumulate over the years. Code enforcement, especially in food establishments, is a tricky thing."

"Are you threatening us?" Libby asked.

The chief put his hand over his heart.

"I never threaten," the chief said. "Your father will tell you that. I was merely pointing out the obvious. By the way, the missus would love it if we could have one of your mince pies for Christmas."

Libby forced herself to smile. "No problem," she said.

"And we'd like a double portion of hard sauce."

"Of course," Libby said.

"But skip the rum and brandy."

Interesting, Libby thought. Maybe what she'd heard about Mrs. Lucy going into rehab to dry out was true.

"I guess we can use orange and vanilla flavoring," Libby said.

The chief nodded. Bernie coughed. The chief turned his gaze to her.

"Are you at least going to tell us how Hortense was killed?" Bernie asked.

The chief nodded. "I can do that."

He was almost done explaining when the production assistant came by. "Five minutes to airtime," he said.

"Oh my God," Libby squealed. "I have to put my make-up on."

One thing you could say about Hortense's homicide, she thought as she ran to get her purse, it had certainly taken her mind off of being on television.

Chapter 7

Sean turned his wheelchair away from the television and studied his two daughters. They looked slightly out of breath, and their cheeks were still red from the cold. The weatherman had said it was going down to ten degrees tonight. Looks as if he'd been right, Sean thought as he glanced at his watch. It was early. Libby and Bernie had come right home after the show. He was happy but surprised. Somehow he'd expected they'd be meeting their boyfriends at R.J's.

"You two made your old man proud," he told them. "You really did. But what happened to your hostess, if you don't mind my asking? Why wasn't Hortense on the show?"

Not that he'd admit this to anyone, but he was disappointed. He'd been looking forward to seeing how she was going to make the meringue mushrooms she'd talked about yesterday. He watched Bernie and Libby look at each other.

"Well?" he said after a moment had elapsed. "Did she choke on a piece of fruitcake?"

"Close," Bernie said.

Sean snorted. "I was kidding."

"Well, I wasn't."

Damn, Sean thought. Trouble followed his girls around like lambs followed Little Bo Peep.

"Go on," he told her.

Bernie clasped her hands together and brought them up to her chin. "Someone killed her. At least that's what Lucy is saying."

For a moment Sean was silent. Things rarely shocked him. He'd been a cop too long for that. But he had to say that this did.

"What happened?" he asked.

"There was an explosion," Libby explained.

Bernie put her hands back down. "We all ran in to the test kitchen and found Hortense covered with fruitcake, cookie dough, and blood. Not a good mix; not a good mix at all, colorwise. Hortense would not have been happy."

Libby opened her mouth to say something and closed it again.

Sean noticed his eldest daughter was wringing her hands, something she did when she was extremely perturbed. Libby was the sensitive one in the family. Always had been and, despite his best efforts to toughen her up, always would be.

"Of course," Bernie continued, "no one would be happy in Hortense's situation." She moved her silver and onyx ring up and down her finger. "Anyway, someone rigged the oven so it would explode when Hortense opened it," she explained. "The oven in the test kitchen," Bernie clarified before Sean could ask.

"How strange," Sean mused. "Death by fruitcake. I always knew they were lethal, except for your mother's of course, but I thought it was more of a digestive thing."

"What a horrible thing to say," Libby cried.

Sean sighed. His eldest daughter was tending toward developing a terminal case of sincerity.

He was about to tell her that when Bernie said, "It's not

horrible, Libby. You shouldn't misuse words like that. It dilutes them. The word *horrible* comes from the Latin word *horrere* and means to be terrified. For that matter, *awful* really isn't correct either. How about the word *nauseous*?"

Libby jutted her chin out.

"I couldn't help it, okay?"

Bernie rolled her eyes.

"You could have turned your head away from me."

"Couldn't help what?" Sean asked.

Bernie pointed at her sister. "She threw up on my shoes."

"At least she didn't contaminate the crime scene," Sean observed.

"I wish she had. They were Jimmy Choos."

"Is that some new form of the flu?"

"Very funny, Dad."

"I thought it was."

Libby put her hands on her hips.

"It happened so fast I didn't have the time to do anything else," she explained to him. "And I already apologized about ten times and offered to buy Bernie a new pair of shoes."

"And I already told you, you can't afford to buy me a new pair of those," Bernie retorted.

Sean watched Libby turn to him.

"I don't know how much they cost, because she refuses to tell me."

Sean noted that Bernie was tapping her foot, never a good sign.

"For the record, they were five hundred. On sale. Satisfied?"

Libby looked shocked. Just like his wife would have been, Sean reflected.

"That's obscene," Libby cried. "No one should spend five hundred on a pair of shoes."

"See. I told you, you weren't going to get a new pair for me."

"I didn't say that."

"Well, are you?"

Sean decided it was time to intervene.

"Girls, girls," he said before Bernie could reply. "Have pity on your old man." Their bickering always drove him nuts.

Bernie inspected her nails. "Fine."

Libby drew herself up. "Fine with me too. I'd just like to point out for the sake of accuracy—a trait I know Bernie values—that it was the glass from the Christmas tree ornaments that killed Hortense, not the fruitcake."

Libby always has to have the last word, Sean thought. Just like his wife.

"Don't be so literal," Bernie retorted.

"Like you're not," Libby replied.

Sean glared at both of them. "That is enough," he said, using the tone he'd used on them when they were six and eight.

"Okay by me," Bernie said.

Libby began picking at her cuticle. "Ditto," she said. She turned to Bernie. "And don't tell me the etymology of that word," she snapped at her.

"I wasn't going to," Bernie responded as the doorbell downstairs rang.

Libby excused herself and went to get it.

"She gets like that when she's upset," Sean said.

"I know," Bernie replied.

"So why don't you ease up on her?"

"I guess I should."

"There's no should about it."

A moment later, Sean heard the clomp of footsteps coming up the stairs.

"Clyde," both he and Bernie said together as Clyde stuck his head in the door.

"How ya doin', Cap?" he asked Sean.

Sean nodded. He'd finally given up telling Clyde not to call him that.

"Good," Sean told him. He realized as he said it that he couldn't help but look down at his hands. They weren't shaking. So he hadn't lied. Today *was* a good day.

Clyde handed Sean a package. "Christmas cookies from the wife."

"Thanks," Sean said. Clyde's wife had the reputation of being the worst cook in five towns.

"I suppose you could use them as doorstops," Clyde told him as he moved a stack of magazines off of the armchair, removed his parka, hung it over the back of the chair, and sat down. "Especially the rum balls. Those are lethal."

Sean laughed. "What are you congratulating me on?" he asked.

Clyde looked at Bernie and Libby. "You mean you haven't told him?" he asked them.

Sean noticed that Bernie had suddenly developed an interest in the view outside his room.

"We were getting around to it when you came in," Bernie said.

"Tell me what?" Sean asked.

"You know that Hortense got killed, right?" Clyde asked Sean.

"Right," Sean said.

"Well, you're gonna love the rest of this," Clyde said to him.

"The rest of what?" Sean watched as Clyde rubbed his hands together. "Are you going to tell me or not?"

"Hey, I'm trying to build up the suspense here."

"And I'm going to tell Libby not to feed you anymore if you don't spit it out right now."

Clyde sniffed. "Fine. If that's the way you want to be."

Sean nodded. "It is." He kept forgetting how annoying Clyde could be.

"Okay, Cap, Lucy has asked you guys to help him with the investigation."

"Hortense's?" Sean said. He couldn't believe what he was hearing.

Clyde rubbed his hands together again.

"Well, we're not talking about the queen of England's."

"You're kidding," Sean said.

"Do I look as if I'm kidding?" Clyde asked him.

"No," Sean allowed. He was so stunned he didn't know what else to say.

Chapter 8

The more Sean thought about what Clyde had said, the more flabbergasted he became. He and Lucy had been at loggerheads ever since Sean had been forced out as chief of police of Longely for refusing to back off of a case. And then there had been the two murders his daughters had helped to solve. Both had been high-profile cases. That hadn't endeared him to the chief either.

Clyde grinned. "Amazing world we live in, ain't it, Cap? I was in the station house when Lucy got the call from Bree Nottingham. The chief's expression was very instructive." Sean watched Clyde's smile grow to Cheshire cat proportions. "I haven't seen him this angry since he caught Milo stealing Millicent Fishbinder's panties."

Bernie raised an eyebrow. Sean explained.

"That's because Milo was taking them out of the chief's desk drawer. Said he'd come across them wrapped around a car antenna."

Just the thought made him chuckle.

"Girls, it was a beautiful thing to see." Clyde agreed. Then he turned and looked fixedly at Libby.

When Clyde had walked in, Sean had bet himself that it would take Clyde at least ten minutes to get around to indicating he'd like something to eat. He'd done it in eight. A new personal best.

"I might be guessing here," Sean said to him, "but before you go on, would you be wanting a little refreshment?"

Clyde nodded. "In this cold weather a man has to keep his strength up."

"Pie has known strength-building properties."

Clyde patted his stomach. "So I've been told. Unless it's too much trouble, Libby."

Sean watched Libby smile. She loved when people loved her food, and Clyde was one of her most stalwart admirers.

"No trouble at all," she said.

"I don't suppose you got any more of that pumpkin pie of your's left?" Clyde asked. "The one you make with the fresh-baked pumpkin."

"If you do, I'll take a piece too," said Sean.

Of course everything Libby made was good, but her pumpkin pie was one of his favorites, maybe because she used apple butter in it as well.

Libby beamed. "I'm pretty sure we have a whole pie downstairs," she said.

"Nice girls you got there," Clyde said after Bernie and Libby left the room.

"The best," Sean said.

"You got lucky," Clyde said.

Sean wheeled his chair over to the table across from his bed.

"I sure did."

"Of course," Clyde added, "it helped that they had a good mom."

Sean nodded. He still didn't like talking about Rose. It was too painful.

By mutual consent, he and Clyde made small talk until the girls returned.

Libby came in first, carrying a tray loaded with plates, coffee cups, saucers, spoons and forks, napkins, a whole pumpkin pie, and a bowl of whipped cream, while Bernie followed her in carrying a coffeepot in one hand and a steaming jug of what Sean correctly judged to be hot, spiced apple cider in the other.

"I substituted a half cup crushed pecans for the flour in the crust and added just a hint of cinnamon and sugar," Libby explained to Clyde as she set the tray down on the table. "And this time I baked the pumpkin instead of boiling it. I think baking gives the pumpkin a somewhat drier texture as well as caramelizing the sugar in it, so it has just a hint of caramel. And, anyway, the color is prettier. I also glazed the pecans on top with sugar and just a dusting of black pepper, so you get a nice little contrast going."

"Black pepper?" Sean said doubtfully.

Sometimes Libby tended to go a little too far in his estimation. If you have something that works, why fool around with it?

Libby shook her head in what Sean knew was mock dismay.

"You are such a traditionalist. If you don't want to try it, just take the pecans off." She turned to Clyde. "Do you want whipped cream on your slice?" she asked.

"Of course," Clyde said. "Is there any other way to go?"

"Not in my mind," Sean said.

As far as he was concerned, cholesterol be damned, this was food for one's soul. After all, given his disease, he wasn't going to worry about a heart condition.

"Perfect," Clyde said after he took a bite of pie. "The dash of pepper is inspired. Try it," he said to Sean.

"Yeah, Dad, go ahead," Bernie urged.

Sean sighed and took a bite. The things he did for his daughters. He chewed. "Hey," he said, "this really is excellent."

Libby beamed. "I know."

"So," Sean asked Clyde after he'd taken another bite of pie. "Why is Lucy asking for Bernie's and Libby's help?"

"And yours," Bernie put in.

Sean put down his fork. "Mine?" He'd assumed that Clyde's 'you guys' had referred to his daughters.

"Yeah." Bernie leaned over and patted him on the shoulder. "I told Lucy we come as a package deal. We can't do something like this without you."

Sean scowled. Bernie punched him in the arm.

"Ouch," he said.

Bernie grinned. "Come on. Admit it. You're pleased."

"Okay," Sean said grudgingly. "I'm pleased. Happy?"

"Yes," Bernie said.

He was touched and flattered. Way too much emotion. He took a sip of coffee. It was excellent, but then Libby's always was. She got fresh-roasted beans and ground them herself.

When he'd gotten himself back under control he said, "I don't get it. I don't get it at all." He looked at Clyde, who was spooning another helping of whipped cream onto his plate. "Aside from everything else, why wasn't there an announcement on TV?"

Clyde dipped his fork into his whipped cream and then licked it clean. "Just the right blend of sugar and vanilla," he observed. "It's so simple, yet such a difficult thing to accomplish—at least if my wife is an example."

He cut himself another piece of pie with the edge of his fork. "To answer your question, Cap, there's no announcement on TV because they're not publicizing Hortense's death." Clyde conveyed the pie to his mouth. "At least not yet," he said after he swallowed. "The media hasn't been notified."

Bernie chimed in. "The question is, if someone dies and the newspapers don't report it, has it really happened?"

"How is that possible?" Sean asked. In his considerable

experience, you didn't notify the media, the media descended on you, especially in high-profile cases like this. Someone always talked. Always. "From what you say, it isn't as if this happened in secret."

Clyde dabbed the corners of his mouth with his napkin before putting it back on his lap. "Bree is riding herd on Hortense's PR person. Plus Hortense has no family nearby, or at least no one she's speaking to at the present time."

"Friends?" Sean asked.

Clyde shook his head. "I guess she's not the social type."

"Staff?"

Clyde ate another piece of his pie. "The staff isn't telling anyone on pain of being fired and sued," he said after he dabbed his lips with his napkin again. "Evidently they had to sign a confidentiality agreement before working with her."

"The contestants could talk."

"They could," Clyde agreed. "But then they'd lose their shot at twenty thousand dollars and the chance to do a two-week guest stint as the new host or hostess of the *Hortense Calabash Show*."

Sean raised an eyebrow.

"Suggestive, isn't it?" Clyde said.

"One might say so," Sean said. He put a large spoonful of whipped cream in his coffee and watched as it dissolved. "How long is this going to go on?"

Clyde leaned over, poured himself some of the cider, and took a sip.

"Delicious." He lowered his cup. "They want to stall for as long as they can."

"And how long do you think they can?" Sean asked.

Clyde thought about it for a moment. "Five days at the outside. And that's with a lot of luck."

Sean nodded. That's what he'd been thinking too. "And the rationale for this is?"

Clyde leaned back in his chair and stretched his legs out. "That's interesting too. I overheard Lucy being told that they want everything settled before they announce Hortense's death."

"Because . . ." Sean prompted. Sometimes Clyde was a little slow.

Clyde covered his mouth with his hand and coughed. "They're hoping that if they announce a new format, new host, etc., the news will be less sensational. That way the stock in Hortense's company won't take a nosedive because her shareholders are scared off."

"Makes sense." Sean took a sip of his coffee. "But you think there's more."

Clyde clinked his spoon against his cup.

"Indeed I do."

Sean scratched behind his left ear. "So what's your take on this?" he asked.

Clyde absentmindedly rubbed his right hand with his left thumb before continuing. "My sources—"

"Your sources?" Sean asked.

"Edna Bishop," Clyde clarified.

"Ah," Sean said.

Edna Bishop was Clyde's sister-in-law and worked as a cleaning woman for a service. It always amazed Sean what people said in front of people like that.

"Anyway," Clyde continued, "it seems as if Bree and Jim are hosting a big"—Clyde paused for a moment while he searched for the word—"gathering in the old Randall home for some developers tomorrow."

Bernie snapped her fingers. "I know. A dolt of developers. No? How about a deal of developers? "

"How about you let Clyde continue," Sean said.

Bernie put her hand over her mouth. "Sorry," she said through her fingers.

"Evidently," Clyde went on, "the powers that be are trying to sell the house and the acreage off. They are envisioning"—Clyde gave the word a sarcastic twist—"making a new very upscale housing development, and they don't want any nasty publicity to interfere with it."

"As murder has a way of doing," Sean noted.

"Indeed it does," Clyde agreed. "Even though, technically speaking, Hortense's estate isn't in the township proper. And of course, what they're doing isn't illegal. They're following all the rules and regs."

"I suppose." Sean took a sip of his coffee. "Looking at it that way, I guess you could say they're just managing the media."

"And doing a good job of it I might add," Clyde observed.

Sean felt a pang of envy. Actually, if he was being honest with himself, it was more like a stab. There were plenty of times when he was chief of police that he wished he could have just dug a huge hole and buried the media in it.

Clyde continued. "And here's something else. If you and the girls investigate and don't find anything, then you guys take the fall. So anyway you go, Chief Lucy wins."

"That had occurred to me," Sean said.

Everyone sat and pondered that for a while.

Sean took a last bite of pie. "So what are they doing with Hortense?" he asked as he cleaned up the crumbs with the side of his fork. "Keeping her in the pantry off the kitchen? That would raise a bit of a stink."

Bernie had a sip of her coffee. "I believe they're conveying her to Libby's boyfriend's funeral home."

"It's Marvin's dad's," Libby corrected.

"Libby, Marvin works there," Bernie said.

"But technically speaking Marvin's dad owns it," Sean said, trying to head off trouble. He found it odd, but for some reason what Marvin did still bothered Libby.

Sean gave a little bow in his daughter's direction.

"Sorry," he said.

Libby nodded her head.

Sean sighed. “It’s unbelievable,” he said.

“Well, Lucy isn’t happy about the whole thing,” Clyde conceded.

“I wouldn’t be either,” Sean said. “He just doesn’t have the guts to stand up to Bree.”

“Maybe he’s thinking of what happened to you,” Bernie observed.

Sean put down his fork.

“You don’t know that for sure.”

“Oh, come on,” Bernie said.

Then Libby chimed in with, “Remember, you said—”

“You may be right,” Sean replied, conceding defeat.

Well, Bernie was right, but then again she wasn’t. It wasn’t that simple. This wasn’t the time to explain all the details of what had happened to him to her though. One lesson he had taken away was that it never paid to tangle with the rich and famous.

Not that he regretted his decision. Okay, maybe he regretted it a little. But at least he hadn’t become Bree Nottingham’s errand boy like Lucy. The thought of Lucy’s discomfort at having to ask his girls for help brightened what had otherwise promised to be a rather boring day.

“Okay,” he said changing the subject. “Fortunately, I taped the show. I think it might be instructive if we watched it again and see if anything pops out at any of us.”

“Like what?” asked Bernie.

“Well, that’s what we’re going to find out, isn’t it?” Sean said.

Chapter 9

Sean watched Libby's boyfriend Marvin squirm. He was sitting on the edge of the bridge chair that Libby had brought in for him. Sean was surprised Libby had chosen that particular chair because it wasn't all that stable. Given Marvin, Sean just prayed he didn't slip off and crash to the floor.

"Mr. Simmons . . ."

"Sean."

Marvin let out a nervous snort that made Sean wince. Sean tried to smile, but he had an idea from Libby's expression that it was coming out more like a grimace.

"Sorry," Marvin said.

"There's no need to be," Sean told him.

Sean watched Marvin bob his head up and down. He looked thoroughly miserable. Had he been like that with Rose's father? Sean wondered. He thought back. No. He'd been a little nervous, but nothing like Marvin. He realized Marvin was talking and tried to refocus his attention on what the kid was saying.

"I hope you don't mind that Rob and I dropped in," Marvin said.

"Of course he doesn't mind," Libby answered before Sean could reply.

Probably because she knew what he was thinking, Sean decided. Because he did mind. He minded a lot. Aside from everything else, he didn't like having all these people in his bedroom.

Sean suppressed a surge of irritation as he pressed the STOP button on the VCR. On orders from his daughters, he was working on being polite, but his grip was somewhat tenuous with this form of social interaction. Always had been, actually.

"Not at all," he lied. "We were just watching a rerun of Hortense's cooking show."

Sean further reflected that he should be glad that Marvin was there. He needed to talk to him anyway, and this just saved him from making a phone call. He was about to ask him about the status of Hortense when Marvin leaned forward and adjusted his glasses.

"Chair, chair," Sean cried as Marvin began to tip over. How anyone could be so clumsy and still be alive was beyond him.

"Sorry." Marvin straightened up and pushed his glasses back up his nose with the tip of his finger.

"You don't need to apologize," Sean told him.

Next thing you knew, the kid would be apologizing for breathing.

"Leave him alone," Libby told him.

"I'm not doing anything," Sean protested. "Marvin, am I doing anything?"

"No." Then Marvin pointed in the direction of the television. "You have a VCR?" he asked. "Wow. I didn't think people had those anymore."

"Well I do," Sean snapped.

He tried to like Marvin for Libby's sake, he really did, but the kid had a genius for saying and doing the wrong thing. He just hoped he didn't have to drive with him again. He didn't think his nerves could stand it.

"Dad's technophobic," Libby explained.

"I am not," Sean said.

"You're right," Bernie agreed. "You're not. You're just cheap."

"Hey, don't say that about your dad," Rob told Bernie.

Bernie turned around and punched him in the arm.

Rob rubbed his bicep. "That hurt."

"It was supposed to. Don't go ordering me around. I can say whatever I like."

"Not about your dad, you can't. He's the man, right, Mr. Simmons? I mean Sean."

Sean smiled as he reflected that Bernie's boyfriend Rob, on the other hand, always had the right thing to say.

Marvin bobbed his head up and down. "Yes, he is," he declared earnestly. "Yes, sir."

Looking at Marvin, Sean decided he should really cut him some slack. After all, it wasn't his fault that the kid had a jerk for a father. With a dad like that, anyone would need some help. And the kid did try. He had to give him that.

And he was better than Libby's last boyfriend Orion. Rose would have said Marvin was nice. Whatever that meant. Of course, Rose's father hadn't thought he was nice. Not at all. He'd told Rose, he was a . . . Sean closed his eyes for a few seconds as he searched his memory for the word . . . a hooligan.

"Want some pie?" he asked Marvin. "Looks as if we've got a couple of slices left here."

Marvin nodded. The kid loved to eat, a fact that was obvious from his waistline. Maybe, Sean thought, that was one of the reasons Libby liked him.

"I've got peanut butter, chocolate chip cookies, and apple tarts downstairs if you'd prefer," Libby said.

Sean reflected that one of the nice things about his

daughters running a catering shop was that there were always good things to eat around.

"No, the pumpkin pie is fine," both Rob and Marvin said in unison.

"This is delicious. Did you make this?" Rob asked Bernie after he'd taken a bite.

"She helped," Libby said.

Sean looked down so Rob wouldn't see him smile. Bernie's pie crusts were so tough you couldn't get a fork through them.

"I don't know what she does to get them that way," Rose had said to him after she'd thrown one in the garbage. "I swear I don't. You should take them to the office and use them as weapons."

Such is the power of love, Sean thought as he heard Rob say to Bernie, "You'll have to teach me how to make a pie crust. It's the best I've ever tasted. How do you do it?"

"Well—" Bernie was saying when Libby broke in.

"It's a family secret—"

Bernie finished the sentence. "That's been handed down for generations."

She flashed her older sister a grateful grin, and her sister smiled back.

Those two might bicker a lot, but they didn't hold grudges, Sean reflected. Thank heavens.

"So," he said to Marvin. "Changing the subject. Tell us about Hortense."

"Yes," Bernie said, "enquiring minds want to know."

Sean watched Clyde lean forward.

"Yes, they do," Clyde echoed.

"Well . . ." Marvin stammered, "there's really nothing much to tell."

"As in once you've seen one dead body you've seen them all," Bernie quipped.

Libby bristled. "Bernie, Marvin just said there's nothing to say."

"Libby, he can take care of himself."

"I know," Libby began when Sean held up his hand.

Enough was enough.

Miraculously, his daughters quieted down. He turned his attention to Marvin, who was sitting there looking miserable.

"But Hortense is in your father's place, right?" Sean asked.

Marvin nodded.

"He wouldn't like me talking about it."

Libby leaned over and patted his knee. "He's not going to find out."

Good girl, Sean thought.

"How did she arrive?" he asked.

"The usual way," Marvin muttered.

"You mean in a hearse."

"Well, he didn't mean a Mini Cooper," Bernie said.

Sean glared at her.

"What is wrong with you today?" Rob asked.

"You wouldn't be in a good mood either if you'd just seen someone being killed," Bernie shot back.

Sean watched Rob's eyes widen. "Did you actually see it?"

"No. But we were in the next room. That's close enough for me."

"Me too," Libby said. "Especially when you consider it could have been me."

"But it wasn't," Bernie pointed out.

"But it could have been."

"What do you mean?" Marvin asked.

It took Sean five minutes to get the conversation back on track. "How did the other people react when they heard the explosion?" Sean asked when he had.

He watched while Bernie and Libby considered their answers. They looked at each other.

Finally, Bernie said, "I don't know. We all dropped what we were doing and ran inside."

"Who was first?" Sean asked.

Libby bit the inside of her lip. "It was like we were in a great big knot."

Bernie tapped the heels of her feet on the floor. "I think Estes was first, then La Croix, and Consuela. But I'm not really sure."

Libby looked down at her cup. "I remember Pearl was last because I turned and saw her coming through the door."

Sean nodded encouragingly. "Very good."

"And the rest were sort of in this mass in the middle." Libby raised her eyes. "This is off topic, but shouldn't Hortense be having an autopsy?" Libby asked. "I mean, isn't that a legal requirement?"

"I believe that is scheduled for tomorrow," Marvin said. "Although the cause of death is fairly self-evident."

As he leaned over to get his piece of pie, Sean held his breath. He could see the chair begin to tip. Marvin grabbed the table for support.

"Don't!" he yelled.

But it was too late.

The chair, Marvin, and the table all went crashing to the floor.

Chapter 10

The next twenty minutes, as far as Sean could see, were devoted to his daughters cleaning up the mess Marvin had made and building Marvin's ego back up—in so far as that was possible. If the kid said he was sorry one more time, Sean decided he was going to run him over with his wheelchair. He was sure Clyde would vouch for a justifiable homicide motive if it came down to it.

The hell with Hortense's killer, Sean thought. He had a bigger menace right here in his bedroom. The kid shouldn't be allowed out in public without some kind of warning device on him. That way people could get away from him.

"It's such a shame," Marvin said when they'd finally gotten back on topic. "I used to watch that show almost every day." Then he realized what he'd said and blushed. Again.

"That's okay, Marvin," Libby said. "My dad does . . . did . . . too."

Marvin turned to Sean. "You did?"

Sean looked daggers at Libby whom, he noted, avoided his eyes. "Absolutely," Sean said. And he had, but Libby knew he hated admitting something like that in public.

"Me too," Clyde said. "I especially liked the show

where she taught you how to stuff and roast a chicken." And he sighed wistfully. "I wish my wife had watched it. She says she has no time for stuff like that."

"You could learn how to cook," Libby told him. "I could teach you if you want."

Clyde looked doleful. "Thanks for the offer, but my wife doesn't want me in the kitchen. Says I make too much of a mess."

Rob butted in. "Excuse me," he said, "but are you guys involved in this?"

"You bet your bippie," Sean said.

Bernie wrinkled her nose. "Bippie? What kind of word is *bippie*?"

"It was before your time," Sean told her.

"But what does it mean?" Bernie demanded.

"Does it matter?"

"Yes."

"Why?"

"Because it's going to bother me all night," Bernie complained.

"Let's get on with this," Sean said impatiently.

Getting this group together was a little like trying to herd a flock of ducks. Everyone was waddling off in their own direction. He wheeled his chair around, faced the TV, and pressed PLAY on the VCR. The *Hortense Calabash Show* jumped back into life.

"I look terrible," Libby wailed.

"You look fine," Marvin told her.

"No. I don't. I look fat," Libby cried. "And my hair is terrible."

"No, it isn't," Bernie said.

"That is enough," Sean said in a louder voice than he intended. Sometimes he wished he had sons.

"Sorry," Libby whispered.

Sean grunted. Great. Now he could feel guilty as well as annoyed, a truly great combination. He couldn't help it if he was used to dealing with guys. Guys didn't take things personally—except for Marvin, that is. Better not to go there, Sean thought as he turned and gave the screen his full attention.

Eric Royal was in midspeech, talking about the upcoming contest. He kept on touching the lapel of his jacket. Why would anyone wear something that color? Sean wondered. It was some kind of purple. Something that started with an *L*. Bernie would know. He almost asked her, then thought better of it. He wasn't in the mood to listen to a ten-minute lecture on word origins right now.

He bent forward a little more. Eric Royal looked ill at ease. So did the other people standing on either side of him. Of course, given the circumstances that was to be expected. Except for the Hispanic lady. Consuela. Sean drummed his fingers on the arm of the chair. She looked very relaxed. Interesting. Especially since Bernie and Libby had said they'd caught her rifling through Hortense's files. Very suggestive. Very suggestive indeed.

He turned toward Clyde.

"What do you think?" he asked him.

"I think the Consuela dame looks like she's on a beach somewhere."

"I think so too."

"Why is that bad?" Rob asked.

"Because," Sean explained, "lots of times innocent people are the nervous ones. Probably because they've had less experience with the law."

Clyde interrupted. "Hey, Cap, check out that Reginald person."

Sean followed Clyde's finger. Reginald was standing next to Brittany Saperstein.

"Is that a smile on his face?" Clyde asked.

Sean focused in. It was slight, right around the corners of his mouth, but it was there.

"I think you're right," he told Clyde.

"Reginald was insisting he had to talk to Hortense, but he wouldn't say why," Libby noted.

Sean pressed the STOP button on the VCR. "Anything else?" he asked.

"Well," Bernie said, "Consuela implied that La Croix learned his cooking skills in prison. And," Bernie continued, "Estes said something to Consuela about putting on a sanctimonious act, and I don't think he was referring to our having caught her riffling through Hortense's files, and I'm fairly sure she's misrepresenting her nationality. She's a middle-class Jersey girl, not a Dominicana."

"Why would she lie about that?" Clyde asked.

"Because it plays better," Bernie replied. "As in there are a lot of Jersey girls running around, but not too many Dominicanas who have battled their way up from the slums. After all," Bernie added, "the food business is all about presentation, at least that's what Mom always said, right, Dad?"

"Right," Sean agreed. Out of the corner of his eye he could see Libby was picking at her cuticles, a sign that something was bothering her. "Do you have something to add?" he asked her.

"Well, I don't know if I should say this or not . . ."

"Tell us," Sean urged.

"It's gossip," Libby said.

"Gossip is good," Bernie said.

Libby picked at her nails for another moment.

"Yes," Sean said, "we like gossip." He'd cracked half of his ongoings that way.

"Well, I guess in this case it doesn't matter," Libby conceded.

Sean leaned forward in his chair. Sometimes Libby's voice was so low he had trouble hearing.

"Howie, the guy who runs Veggies Are Us, told me that lots of times when he went over to Hortense's house to deliver her order she was smashed. And that she came on to him. He says she told him that if he didn't do what she wanted, she'd take her business elsewhere, and he told her to go ahead."

"I don't believe it," Bernie said. "She's so high powered, and Howie's such a schlub."

"Stranger things have happened," Sean said. And he should know. He'd seen them all. "Maybe she's done that to other guys as well."

"That's not grounds for killing someone," Rob asked. "Some guys might even see it as grounds for gratitude."

Clyde laughed. "You'd think, but you never know what's gonna set someone off."

"No, you don't," Sean said. "I remember this guy who shot his girlfriend—"

"Ruffino" Clyde said.

"Yeah, Ruffino. Anyway, she was a weaver, and she went to some garage sale and bought this loom and set it up in their bedroom, and he came home, took one look at it, got his Smith & Wesson out of his night table drawer and that, as they say, was that."

"But why?" Libby asked. "That makes no sense."

Sean reached for the remote. "He told me he saw the loom as a sign of disrespect."

He started the tape. Everyone watched in silence. He was about to say something about Pearl Wilde. She seemed to be clutching something in her hand when Marvin cried out, "This is so exciting."

Sean caught Libby's glance and with a great deal of effort on his part managed to refrain from saying what he had been going to.

"Maybe I can drive you around like I did the last time," Marvin continued.

Sean bit his lip. Not if he could help it.

"We'll see," he said.

"That's so nice of you to offer," Libby told Marvin.

Nice for him but not nice for me, Sean thought. Love is

great and everything, but she should have some consideration for her old man.

"So how does this investigation thing work?" Marvin asked.

Sean noticed that his eyes were fixed on the screen.

"How does it work? That's simple. Never the way you want it to," Clyde quipped.

"That's for sure," Sean said. "We're just looking at the suspects right now," he explained to Marvin.

Marvin nodded toward the TV screen with his chin.

"How do you know it's just these people?" Rob asked.

"Because they're the only people that were in the house," Libby replied. "The crew came in later."

Rob took a swallow of his cider.

"But someone could have snuck in and done this."

"That's possible," Sean conceded, "but not probable."

"I don't see why not."

"For openers, it's not a crime of opportunity. People don't disconnect the gas line and come up with a detonating device on the spur of the moment. It's been planned and planned well."

"Maybe we should just look for someone who hates Christmas," Clyde interjected.

Bernie cocked her head. "Why do you say that?"

"Because the murder weapon was a Christmas ornament," Clyde replied.

Sean nodded. The conversation was reminding him that he still had to get the tree decorated. Since Rose's death, he'd pretty much lost what little holiday spirit he had, and the girls were so busy with the store that they didn't have much time to do anything upstairs. He really should get them to get the ornaments out of storage.

"In general," he told Rob, "in an investigation, we start with the most likely suspects and go from there."

Bernie jumped up from her seat.

"What are you doing?" he asked.

Instead of answering him, she sang, “I got the motive.”

Then Libby jumped up, pointed a finger at her younger sister, and belted out, “You got the means and the opportunity.”

What is going on with her? Sean wondered as Bernie spread out her arms and went down to her knees.

“We’ll just go for cop immunity,” she trilled.

“You’re not a vaudeville act,” Sean said. He didn’t think anyone heard him, though, because Clyde, Rob, and Marvin were hooting and hollering.

Bernie hopped up.

“Bravo,” Rob cried.

Bernie and Libby curtsied.

“Thank you, thank you, thank you,” they both said.

“Did you just make that up?” Clyde asked.

Libby and Bernie nodded.

“I’m impressed,” Clyde said. “Very impressed.”

Bernie turned to Sean. “What do you think, Dad?”

“I think you’re in shock,” Sean said.

Either that or both of his daughters were going crazy. His wife had warned him that prolonged exposure to the seamier side of life, as she phrased it, would have an effect on the girls. Evidently she was right.

Rob scraped the last remaining bit of whipped cream out of the bowl with the edge of his spoon.

“So what’s your take on this thing, Sean?”

“Tell us,” Marvin said.

Sean straightened his shoulders. At last, the voice of reason. Marvin did have his uses after all.

“Hortense started baking the fruitcake about an hour before the show, so the oven had to have been rigged then—”

“The Case of the Deadly Fruitcake,” Bernie said. “I like it.”

Is it too hard for you people to stay on topic? Sean wanted to scream. Is that too much to ask? Evidently it was. He felt like tearing his hair out. Unfortunately, he didn't have enough to be able to do that.

Libby sniffed. "I don't see why everyone says such bad things about fruitcake," she said.

"Off topic," Sean said.

"Just a moment," Bernie told him before turning back to Libby. "Modern fruitcakes are a bad concept," Bernie said.

"They don't have to be," Libby retorted.

"But they usually are."

"That's because they use that dreadful candied fruit from the supermarket." Libby bit at her cuticle. "Mine isn't like that."

"No one said they were," Marvin told her. "I can't believe that anything you make would be bad."

Sean watched Libby all but bat her eyelashes at Marvin. Marvin beamed.

"Thank you," Libby said. "That's so sweet."

He was definitely losing control of the situation here, Sean decided. This would never have happened in the old days. He was just about to tell everyone to be quiet when Bernie started speaking again, and he realized he'd lost his chance.

"Did you know," she said, "that fruitcakes used to be considered healthy, nourishing food? They were invented in England. Originally they were called *plum cakes* because back then *plum* was the word they used for dried fruits. And here's something really interesting."

Sean rolled his eyes.

"That is so rude," Bernie told him before continuing on with her lecture. "Dried fruits didn't start arriving in Britain until the thirteenth century."

"You're kidding," said Rob.

Like he really cares, Sean thought.

"No, I'm not," Bernie said. "Dried fruit came from Portugal and the eastern Mediterranean. The British didn't have anything like that in their larders. It makes sense if you think about it."

"How weird," Rob said.

"Isn't it, though," Bernie said. "You always think of stuff like this as having been around forever and it usually isn't. A lot of the foodstuffs we take for granted are the result of increased trade and migration patterns. Like you can trace the movement of the Moors through Spain by the prevalence of chickpeas on the menu. The most obvious example of this in modern times would be macadamia nuts. They come from Australia originally."

"Australia?" Marvin said.

Bernie nodded. "Yes. They're indigenous to that country, but they were introduced to Hawaii, and the crop was so successful there that now Hawaii is responsible for something like ninety percent of the macadamia nuts sold in this country."

Sean sighed. The trouble with his oldest daughter, Sean decided, was that she never knew when to stop. Of course, his wife used to say the same thing about him. In fact, she'd said it quite often.

"Do you think we can get back to the matter at hand?" Sean heard himself saying.

He could tell from the expression on his daughters' faces that his tone wasn't very pleasant, but frankly at this point he didn't really care. At all.

"Calm down, Dad," Bernie said.

"I am calm," he yelled.

"Okay, Dad," Libby said in a tone Sean thought was appropriate to use on a three-year-old. "What do you want us to do?"

Marvin leaned forward. "Yeah," he said. "I'm in."

"We all are," Rob added.

"No, you're not," Sean snapped. "I'm not turning this into some damn circus."

"Dad doesn't mean that," Bernie said.

"Yes, I do," he reiterated.

"We could use some help," Libby said. "I've got a lot of baking and orders to fill for the shop. In case you've forgotten, this is A Little Taste of Heaven's busiest time of the year."

"I haven't forgotten," Sean retorted. He looked at Clyde.

Clyde gave a little shrug. "It wouldn't be bad to have some people you could call on, Cap," he said.

Sean mulled over what Clyde had just said for a moment. Marvin was a walking disaster. There was no disputing that. But what was it Rose used to say about making the best of what you've got?

"All right," he finally said. "But only if you guys follow my directions. And I mean exactly."

"Oh, we will," Marvin said. He raised his hand. "I swear."

God help us all, Sean thought. But given the circumstances, he didn't feel as if he had any other choice.

Anyway, if he didn't agree, Libby would kill him.

Or not speak to him for a week.

Which was worse.

He straightened up in his wheelchair.

Enough whining.

It was time to get the show on the road and figure out who was going to do what.

Chapter 11

Libby poured herself a cup of coffee from the Chemex, turned off the light under the teakettle on the Viking, and went out to the front of the store. She snuggled into her robe as she took a deep breath and inhaled the smells of vanilla and cinnamon and freshly baking bread. She looked out of the windows.

At five o'clock in the morning the street was quiet. The Christmas decorations on the lampposts—this year the town had gone with stars—gave off a vague tinselly glimmer. The only things moving were a few snowflakes gently blowing under the streetlights.

As she watched them floating down, she savored a taste of her own private stash of Blue Mountain Jamaican coffee. Normally she reserved the coffee for special occasions—at a little over thirty dollars a pound, she should—but given last night and what was coming up today, she figured she deserved it.

This was her favorite time of the day, she decided as she took another sip. Even though she liked people, she liked being alone in her kitchen among all of her cookbooks. Browsing through them relaxed her.

She liked being here before Googie and Amber started

working. There was something soothing about getting things ready for the day. She liked listening to the hum of the refrigerator, the way the pipes clanked when she turned on the water. She liked the smell of yeast, the smooth feel of the bread dough under her fingers as she formed it into Parker House rolls, the way the muffin batter poured into the tins, the sweet sharp smell of cardamom and raisins.

As she surveyed the window display cases, she felt a rush of pride. She decided that despite what she'd thought earlier, she'd done a good job decorating the store for Christmas. As good as Hortense. Better, actually. Her mom would have been proud of her.

This year she'd made a gingerbread replica of the street that A Little Taste of Heaven was on. It had taken her weeks to figure out how to do it and to make the patterns. There was the shoe store and the fish purveyor and the drug store, the bookstore and the butcher, as well as A Little Taste of Heaven, of course.

All the stores had windows outlined in white icing and roofs made out of flat red licorice. Their marquees were composed out of pound cake, and she'd written the names of the stores in purple frosting. She'd made lampposts out of sugar cookie dough and frosted them with dark green icing.

But the pièce de résistance, as far as she was concerned, were the two dogs she'd made. They each had chocolate kisses for eyes and white frosting with tan patches on their backs. She'd even made leashes out of spun sugar and put spun sugar collars around their necks. Their owner was wearing a light green shirt and yellow pants and was leaning next to a bench Libby had constructed out of chocolate chip cookies and sugar glue. It had been a work of love.

"Getting ready for the day?"

Libby jumped. She put her hand to her heart.

"Oh my heavens," she said after she'd turned around

and realized who it was. "You scared me. I didn't even hear you."

"Sorry," Bernie said.

"It's okay."

"Thinking about today?" Bernie asked.

"Yes," Libby lied.

Actually she'd been thinking that she should have made a gingerbread car as well and sprinkled some powdered sugar on the roof for snow. Maybe she'd still do that. She looked at Bernie as she took a sip of coffee. Her sister even slept in something sexy. It was demoralizing, Libby thought as she looked down at her long T-shirt and the ratty, terry-cloth robe she'd had since she was twenty-one.

"The coffee's good, isn't it?" she asked.

"The best," Bernie said. "Absolutely the best."

Libby nodded. "How come you're up so early?"

Bernie shrugged. "I couldn't sleep."

"Me neither," Libby confessed.

"I kept on trying to figure out what to get Dad for Christmas."

Libby sighed. She and her sister went through this every year. Her dad was the worst person to shop for bar none.

"And," Bernie continued, "I couldn't keep what happened yesterday out of my mind."

"I'm worried about tonight," Libby found herself blurting out.

Bernie patted her on the back. "You'll do fine."

"But what if we can't think of anything to make?" Libby wailed.

"We will."

"What if what we're making isn't done in time?"

"It will be."

Libby looked at her sister. "Doesn't anything ever worry you?"

"Of course things worry me."

"But you don't seem as if they do."

"I just handle it differently than you do."

"I wish I could be more like you," Libby confessed.

Bernie took another sip of coffee. "You take after Mom, I take after Dad."

Libby sighed again. "I know. And I wish I didn't." She took another sip of coffee and contemplated the gingerbread street. It would be nice if she could spend more time doing window displays. It would probably help boost sales. She caught Bernie looking at her.

"What?" Libby asked.

"I was just thinking about what we're supposed to do this afternoon."

Libby could feel her stomach knot up at Bernie's words. "I've been trying not to." She had so much to do at the store that the prospect of going out and talking to people on top of everything else was not making her a happy camper.

"Why do I have to take Reginald's place?" Libby demanded.

Bernie put her hands on her hips. "Because you asked for it. Because you said it was the closest."

"I meant, why are we doing this at all?"

"You know why," Bernie replied.

Libby leaned against one of the counters. She did know why. She just resented it.

"Anyway," Bernie said, "maybe the people in the new development that Bree is trying to build will shop here."

"I hope so," Libby replied. "I really do."

Perhaps what Bernie was saying was true, but it still didn't help her mood any. Libby clicked her tongue against her teeth.

"You can take Pearl if you want to," Bernie offered.

"That's okay," Libby told her.

Libby shook her head. Reginald's place was nearer, and given the circumstances, she had to be practical. She took another sip of her coffee. "I think Consuela did it."

Bernie shook her head.

"Why?" Libby asked. "She was the only one there ahead of us."

"True," Bernie said. "But anyone could have come and gone without being seen. There really isn't any security to speak of."

"We caught her looking through the files."

"Just because Consuela's a cheat doesn't mean she's a killer."

Libby put her cup down. "Why don't you like her for this?"

"Because this strikes me as a guy kind of crime. Guys like to make things explode. Maybe it's a sex thing."

"So who is your money on?" Libby asked.

"Eric," Bernie said. "He has the best motive. He's taking Hortense's place."

Libby shook her head. "I just don't see him as being able to do this. He's too emotional."

"What's that got to do with anything?"

Libby sniffed. "I just don't see him as having . . . the background to think something like that up. I know I certainly wouldn't. Would you?"

"No. I have to admit that using a camera as a triggering device would never even occur to me." Bernie started moving her ring up and down her finger. "Good point. So what kind of background are we talking about here?"

"Someone with a background in demolition," Libby postulated.

"Or maybe they got the idea from TV or a movie. Or found it on the Internet. It's amazing what's on there."

Libby conceded that that was true. "Hortense was a very annoying lady."

"Extremely. But you don't usually kill someone because they're annoying," Bernie pointed out. "At least not usually."

"But if they're annoying and they're keeping you from getting what you want . . ."

Bernie finished the sentence. "You might feel entitled to do them in."

Libby nodded. "Exactly the word I was looking for. I wonder how much Hortense drank?"

"That should be easy enough to find out," Bernie said. "I think I'll visit Harold's liquor store on my way home this afternoon and see what he has to say."

"Good idea, but remember we have to make three batches of jam cookies this afternoon." Libby drained the last of her coffee from the cup, put the cup in the sink, and washed it. She was drying it when all of a sudden she heard the sentence, "Why doesn't Dad like Marvin?" coming out of her mouth.

"Of course he does," Bernie told her. "He just doesn't like driving with him."

"Well Dad makes Marvin nervous."

"I know. But this time I'm sure Marvin will do better. I'm sure of it." Bernie put her hand up. "Girl Scout's honor."

"You never were a Girl Scout. You got thrown out, remember?"

"I got thrown out of the Brownies."

"Same thing."

"Did anyone every tell you you're incredibly literal minded?" Bernie asked her.

"Look who's talking," Libby shot back.

She walked out front, went over to the display, took a chocolate chip cookie out, and ate it. Desperate times called for desperate measures.

"It'll be fine," Bernie said.

"I'm not so sure. Dad might kill Marvin."

Libby stopped herself from reaching for another cookie.

"No, he won't," Bernie said.

"Or order him out of the car."

"Why do you always think worst-case scenario?" Bernie demanded, but Libby could tell from the expression on Bernie's face that she thought that scenario was a distinct possibility as well.

Libby decided she was going to eat the chocolate chip cookie after all. The hell with television. The hell with her clothes fitting. She needed it. She savored a piece of Lindt chocolate dissolving on her tongue.

"I'm not sure that talking to everyone's staff is the way to go."

"Well, I suggested that we break into everyone's apartments and businesses and rifle through their files, but I was outvoted."

"I can't imagine why," Libby replied.

"I know," Bernie told. "It seemed like a perfectly sensible tactic to me."

"Efficient too," Libby said.

"My point exactly," Bernie said. "However, since I was voted down, talking is the only thing left to do."

Libby sighed. "What do you think would happen if we didn't do this?"

"I think we'd have a very pissed off Bree Nottingham."

"Which would not be a good thing," Libby said.

"No, it wouldn't," Bernie agreed.

"We could probably get by without her," Libby observed.

Bernie tapped her thumbnail against her front teeth. "Well we wouldn't lose our walk-ins, but some of our bigger catering jobs . . ." Bernie's voice trailed off.

"I know."

Libby got her third cookie. Piss off the social arbiter of Longely and there would go half of their business. It was times like this that Libby really missed her mom. What would she have done in this situation?

Libby didn't know, but she was pretty sure Rose would

have found a way to maneuver through it. She always did. Too bad she wasn't around to ask. Oh well. She was about to take a bite of her cookie when she saw Amber parking her car in front of the store. Libby went over and unlocked the front door.

"What are you doing here this early?' she asked Amber once she'd walked inside.

Amber started unwrapping her scarf from around her head. "Brandon told me what happened, so I figured you'd need some extra help baking this morning."

"In his past life he was probably the town crier," Bernie observed.

Libby nodded. Brandon was the bartender at R.J's. Her dad called him "a major informational conduit." Which was another way of saying he had a big mouth.

"I'm guessing that it won't be that long before this hits the newspaper," Bernie said.

Libby bit her cuticle. "I'm guessing you're right," she said as she watched Googie's car pull up in front of the store.

"What is he doing here?" Libby asked. He wasn't supposed to be on till two in the afternoon.

"Oh, I asked him to come," Amber said. "I figured that you could use as many hands as possible. Remember what happened the last time you were involved in an investigation?"

Indeed Libby did. They'd been swamped with people anxious to hear the latest word on what was going on. They'd run out of muffins and scones and cookies by ten o'clock in the morning.

Libby bit her thumb.

"Okay," she said, "let's get to work."

Chapter 12

Ah, Christmastime in New York City. It was pretty, Bernie allowed as she hurried down Lexington Avenue, although *festive* might be an even better word. All the gingko trees wrapped in white lights. Displays in the shop windows. Everything scrubbed and glowing. All those people shoving and pushing in the stores so they could cash out and hurry home.

Yes, holiday time in retail, the time when normally nice people turned into raving lunatics. Maybe she was just feeling a bit grumpy, Bernie reflected, because she'd almost been trampled down by a large woman toting an enormous gilt-wrapped package that was effectively blocking her vision while she, Bernie, was just walking along minding her own business.

And the woman hadn't even apologized! She'd just snarled at her and kept on going. Bernie rubbed her shoulder. It still hurt from the impact. Oh well. Time to concentrate on other things, Bernie thought as she hugged her leather jacket to her chest. Man, it was cold. Why hadn't she worn her boatneck, black cashmere sweater instead of her Krista Larson white cotton blouse? Actually, she knew why. Because the rounded inset collar looked really hot peeping out from under her jacket. Very mixed message. A combo schoolgirl and biker chick. Rob was going to love it when he saw it. Unfortunately, he wasn't going to be seeing it till this evening. By then she was going to have turned into a Popsicle.

The paper had said it was going to be thirty degrees today, which really wasn't very cold, but she'd forgotten to add the wind factor into the equation. Down in the city, the skyscrapers turned the streets into wind tunnels so it always felt ten to fifteen degrees colder than it actually was.

Bernie blew on her fingers as she stopped in front of Pearl's store and peered in the window. Wearing gloves wouldn't have hurt either. Maybe she could pick up a pair from one of the vendors on the street. The shop was crowded with beautiful people and the maids who served them, buying things like corn bread, meat loaf sandwiches on squishy white bread, pot roast and mashed potatoes, or potato and leek soup to consume in their offices or their posh apartments.

Bernie knew that these were things that they would normally never give a second look to. But somehow the fact that they were paying twenty dollars for it made meat loaf chic, thus bearing out her mother's contention that reverse snobbery was a potent merchandising force.

As Bernie raised her eyes, she noticed that off to one side of the window, displayed in a tasteful way but placed so that it was impossible to miss, was the article the *New York Times* had written about Pearl last year. The lead-in read, "Caterer to the social set has her taste buds insured by Lloyd's of London for five million dollars."

Bernie rewound her scarf around her neck. What a gimmick. And why hadn't she thought of it? Didn't most people realize that Lloyd's would insure absolutely anything?

That's what they were famous for. *How could I have forgotten about this?* Bernie asked herself as she reread the article.

Or maybe she hadn't forgotten it so much as repressed it. Just thinking about the article annoyed her. It had annoyed her when it had come out, and it annoyed her now. The thing was nothing more than a big puff piece lauding Pearl's prestigious clientele, her menu, and the excellent quality of her food. It ended by quoting Pearl's slogan, "My Palate Is Your Assurance."

"Assurance of what?" Bernie asked herself.

A passerby looked at her, and she realized she'd been talking out loud, something she did when she got upset. But the truth was Pearl's food was awful. Not mediocre. Not slightly off. No. It was really, really bad. For heaven's sake, Libby had spit out the chocolate pudding she'd bought there, and Libby never refused anything chocolate.

In fact, when Bernie had tasted the pudding she could have sworn it tasted just like one of those packets you get in the supermarket. Which meant to Bernie that despite what people said, yes, you could fool all of the people all of the time.

Bernie hadn't shown Libby the article at the time it had come out because she hadn't wanted to listen to the tirade she knew was going to follow about the uneducated palates of her fellow Americans. Actually, the only thing Bernie had wanted to know when she'd read it was who Pearl's publicist was and could they get him too?

Oh well, Bernie thought as she took a last glance at the piece before she turned and hurried down the street. She wasn't stopping here. There was no point. No one would talk about their employer when they were working in her store. Not if they wanted to keep their job. That was a given.

But she had found someone to speak to. Someone who

was no longer working for Pearl Wilde. He was now employed as a bar back in a place called Sail on Seventy-sixth Street between Second and Third Avenues. It had taken her the better part of the morning to get that information.

Willie, a New York City food guy, notorious gossip, and hypochondriac had been more than usually grumpy, and it had taken the promise of two pumpkin cheesecakes to get Willie to give her what she wanted—to wit, the name of a disaffected worker from Pearl's shop—without telling him why she wanted it.

"I'll tell you the whole story when I can," she'd promised him.

"Which will be when?" Willie had demanded. "Remember, I might not have that long to live."

Since Willie had been saying that since her mother had introduced them over twenty years ago, Bernie had felt no compunction about replying, "Fine, I'll bury the cheesecakes with you."

"Very nice," Willie had said. "Very nice way to talk."

Bernie had laughed.

"Your mother wouldn't have approved," Willie said.

"Yes, she would, you old pretender and you know it. Now tell me what you've heard about Pearl Wilde."

"Does this have anything to do with Hortense's show?"

"Willie," Bernie had said.

"Fine. Fine. I haven't heard anything about Pearl's operation."

"That's not like you," Bernie had told him.

"She's very secretive."

"Most caterers are secretive," Bernie replied, thinking of Libby.

"Well, her cooking crew works at night, and she mostly employs people whose grasp of English is, and I'm being charitable here, minimal."

"So this guy Vasily you were telling me about doesn't speak English."

"No. He does. Just don't ask him anything complex."

Bernie wondered exactly what Willie had meant by that as she glanced at her watch. It was a little after two—Willie had said Vasily could talk to her between two and three. Before that, Sail had the lunch crowd and happy hour started around four.

Bernie walked hurriedly down the street, stopping now and then, despite herself, to glance at a particularly well-decorated window. She especially liked the candy store that had put a chocolate cathedral in the window. A sign next to it stated that it was available by special order. No price was given. But that didn't surprise Bernie. In this zip code if you had to ask, you couldn't afford it.

She didn't know what Vasily could tell her about Pearl, but hopefully it was worth the drive down here, not to mention the money it was costing her to park her car in the garage. She was thinking about how expensive it was to live down here when she arrived at Sail. Bernie tapped her fingernails against her front teeth. She'd been here a couple of times five years ago when she'd been going out with the piccolo player. Then it had been an Irish pub. Not anymore.

The sign was gone. So was the old wood façade. Now it was gray slate. The only way to identify the place was by the neon sailboat in the window. If that's what it was. Bernie squinted her eyes and cocked her head first to one side and then to the other. It kinda looked like a deranged triangle to her. As she stepped inside, she decided that she hated this new tendency of places to hide themselves away. Only the terminally hip need apply, or as Rob would have said, this place was too cool to survive.

Bernie nodded to the bartender and walked over to the back.

"Vasily?" she said to the guy stocking the shelves.

He looked small and muscular and had a large nose and a mop of black hair.

"Da," he said.

"Hey, he's got work to do," the bartender called down. "You want anything, talk to me."

Right, Bernie thought. Just what she needed. Another person to contend with.

Bernie walked back up and flashed the bartender her best smile. He seemed unmoved.

"I'm Vasily's cousin—"

"No, you're not," the bartender said, cutting her off before she could even get the rest of her sentence out. "You want something from him, you have to go through me."

Terrific, Bernie thought as she reached inside her pocketbook for her wallet. This was turning out to be an expensive afternoon.

"What will twenty bucks get me?" she asked.

"Twenty minutes."

"That's ridiculous."

The bartender shrugged.

"But I'll take it." And bill Bree, Bernie said silently as she slid a twenty-dollar bill across the counter with the tips of her fingers.

"Fine," the bartender said as he picked it up and put it in his pants pocket. He leered at her. "Sixteen cases of Sam Adams just came in, and your boy Vasily there has to stack in the cooler, so don't tire him out."

"Sixteen cases is a lot," Bernie noted, ignoring the innuendo.

The bartender smoothed down his hair. "The drinking and eating season is upon us."

"And how."

Bernie had read somewhere that most eating and drinking establishments made anywhere from ten to fifteen percent of their year's income between Thanksgiving and New Year's Day. She knew it was certainly true for A Little Taste of Heaven.

Bernie took a few seconds to check out the decor as she walked over to Vasily. The new owners had gutted the place. The whole thing was chrome, with colored back lights that highlighted the bottles of liquor on the call shelves.

The barstools were arranged in groupings of two and three. What happens if someone wants to sit by themselves? Bernie wondered as she surveyed the back, which was filled with low black leather furniture. Fascist decorating, Bernie thought as she approached Vasily.

Vasily nodded. She nodded back.

"Willie Wiggins said you speak English," she told him. "He said you would help me."

"Ah. My English not so good."

"It seems good enough to me."

"I understand. I no speak."

Bernie took a twenty-dollar bill out of her wallet and held it in front of him. "How's your English now?"

He shrugged.

She took out another twenty. "And now?"

"Now is better," he said, reaching for the money.

Bernie laughed. There was no point in getting angry. "Half now, half later."

"Is good," Vasily said as he pocketed the twenty Bernie had handed him. "I used to ride horses in the big circus," he told her. "But then I do this. I think I go home soon and ride horses again. So what you want to know?"

Bernie told him.

"So why you want to know this?"

"Private reasons," Bernie told him. She watched Vasily think over her answer for a moment.

"She not nice lady," Vasily said after a few more moments had elapsed. "She not nice at all."

"How come?"

Vasily made a rolling motion with his hands. "She was always yellings. Yellings about this. Yellings about that."

"I can imagine," Bernie said, thinking about the way Pearl had rearranged the bagels and the muffins in the green room.

"She not nice. She fires me."

Bernie fought down an image of Pearl circling Vasily with a lighter. "For what?"

"For taking this cheese, but I think she throwing it out, you know?"

Bernie nodded.

"I only take two slices."

"Two slices isn't much."

"That is what I say. She no let us eat."

Bernie shook her head. Now there was a rule that was impossible to enforce. At A Little Taste of Heaven, she and Libby encouraged whoever was working there to eat what they wanted. It was one of the side benefits of working in a job like that.

Vasily put his hand up and made a screwing motion near his head with his finger. "I think this lady a little nutty in the head." Then he pointed to his breast pocket. "We go outside and I smoke, okay?"

"Okay," Bernie said.

Bernie followed Vasily outside.

"You want?" Vasily said, motioning to the pack of cigarettes he'd taken out of his pocket.

"No, thanks," Bernie told him. She'd quit three years ago, and she didn't want to start again. "So what was it like working there?" she asked Vasily after he'd taken his first puff.

"How you mean?"

Bernie shrugged. She didn't know what she was looking for. Actually, to be honest, she couldn't imagine Pearl killing anyone—too messy—but she'd said she'd do this and so she was.

"I mean, was it busy? Were you always working?"

"I don't know about busy. I only work at night."

"At night?" Bernie asked.

"Yes, ten clock to three in the morning. I no like working like that. My system get all confused."

That was kind of strange, Bernie thought. Most catering places started their prep work at four or five in the morning.

Vasily took another puff of his cigarette.

"So what did you do there?"

"I mix things."

"Like what?"

"Like I take a big box and put in bowl and add water and mix and cook on top of the stove. It look a little like snow, but snow tastes better. In my country we don't eat things like this."

Bernie thought about what it could be. "Rice?"

Vasily shook his head. "We make Vodka with it."

"Potatoes?"

Vasily nodded excitedly. "Yes. Yes. This is it."

"Instant mashed potatoes?"

"Exactly," Vasily replied.

My god, Bernie thought. People are paying twelve dollars per pound for instant mashed potatoes.

"Sometimes we play joke," Vasily said.

"What kind of joke?" Bernie asked.

"Sometimes we put in much, much salt. Other times we put in the flavoring that you bake with . . ."

"Vanilla?" Bernie asked.

"Yes, vanilla," Vasily said.

"But didn't Pearl know?" Bernie asked.

Vasily took a last puff of his cigarette and flicked it onto the pavement.

"No. No. This lady cannot taste."

"What do you mean?"

Vasily stuck out his tongue and pointed. "She no have these things." And he pointed to the bumps on his tongue.

"You mean taste buds?"

Vasily nodded.

"Are you sure?" Bernie asked.

Vasily nodded again.

"Person in charge taste all food. Anyway, it all come in boxes. Just add water and mix. This is funny country where people pay people like that to make food for them."

"It certainly is," Bernie agreed.

Well that visit had been worth every penny, she decided as she walked back out onto the street. She called Libby and told her what she'd found out. *I only hope my visit to the liquor store proves as fruitful*, she mused as she stepped off the curb to hail a cab. Of course, Bernie reflected, Hortense could have used any liquor store, but she had a feeling Hortense had stayed close to home, which was why she started her inquiry with Harolds', the store closest to Hortense's house. That didn't pan out. The second place didn't either. But Bernie hit pay dirt at Ye Olde Spirit Shoppe.

According to Fred, the liquor store owner, Hortense drank. She drank a lot.

"How do you know?" Bernie asked.

Fred put his hands together and touched his lips with the tips of his fingers.

"Simple," he said. "You see, " he continued, "whenever Hortense had a party, she'd order cases of Gray Goose. I mean cases. That's an alcoholic's trick. They order five cases for twenty people. Now you know that twenty people aren't going to drink that much. Believe me, she had a lot of parties. And that was a problem because my delivery boys didn't want to go up there. I had to do it myself."

"How come?" Bernie asked.

He leered. "She was always groping them. I would have been happy if some lady had done that to me when I was their age, but kids are different now—and not for the better either."

"I guess that depends on your point of view," Bernie told him.

Chapter 13

Libby put her knife down. She'd been in the middle of chopping up chicken for her curried chicken salad when Bernie called. They'd already sold out of it, and she wanted to get another batch ready before she had to leave.

"Say what?" she said when she heard what Bernie had to say.

"I know," Bernie replied. "It's amazing, isn't it?"

It certainly is, Libby thought. "Maybe this Vasily guy is lying."

"Maybe he is," Bernie agreed. "But I don't think so."

Libby was stymied. How could Pearl do that?

"You can't cook if you have no taste buds," she noted. "That's like a musician who's deaf composing."

"Beethoven did," Bernie reminded her.

Libby cradled the phone between her shoulder and ear and went back to chopping chicken. "That's true." She couldn't help thinking about how horrible life would be without the tastes of coffee and orange and vanilla. "It would be a terrible way to live."

"It would be, wouldn't it?"

"I can't even imagine," Libby replied. And she couldn't.

Libby heard some static and then Bernie's voice came back on.

"From what Vasily said, I'm guessing Pearl is using packaged foods in her place."

Yes! Libby said to herself as she did a little dance. "Remember I said her chocolate pudding tasted like a mix and you said no."

Libby could hear Bernie sigh. "Okay. You were right. I was wrong. Satisfied?"

"I wasn't asking for an apology," Libby said. Always be magnanimous in victory. "Well, I wasn't," she said when Bernie snorted. A thought occurred to her. "That must be why her kitchen crew doesn't speak English and why they work late at night," Libby mused.

"My thinking exactly. That way they can't tell anyone, at least anyone that matters, and no one sees what they're doing."

"Of course," Libby continued, picking up her sister's conversational thread, "lots of places use meat loaf mix and instant mashed potatoes."

"But they don't charge what Pearl charges, and they don't have their taste buds insured by Lloyd's of London," Bernie pointed out.

"True." Libby scraped the chicken off the counter into a bowl with the edge of her knife. "If this were common knowledge—"

Bernie finished her sentence for her. "She wouldn't have a business."

"Exactly," Libby agreed. She paused for a second to inspect the chicken to make sure she'd cut all the pieces into roughly the same size. It was a tiny detail, but in this business tiny details mattered. "I still don't believe it. If that's the case, how was she going to do the contest?"

"Now that," Bernie said, "is an interesting question."

Libby threw some golden raisins into the bowl along with a couple of handfuls of toasted chopped almonds.

"Why is she even on the show? I mean, why would she subject herself to that kind of aggravation?"

"Another even more interesting question."

"How can she possibly win?"

"She can't. Unless the contest is rigged."

Libby looked at her watch as she added the mayo and the curry powder to the chicken salad and stirred the whole thing around. She wiped a dab of mayo off of her finger, covered the bowl with Saran wrap, and stuck it in the frig.

"Have you gone to Reginald's place yet?" Bernie asked her.

"I'm pretty much out the door," Libby lied.

She hung up before Bernie could ask her exactly how much out the door she was. Because the truth was, Libby had no idea what to do about Reginald. She wasn't good like Bernie with stuff like this. She really wasn't chatty. She didn't like to go up to people who she didn't know and start a conversation. Bernie could talk to anyone, but she couldn't.

Libby got some dough out of the fridge and cut it into three portions. At least she could make the crusts for the sweet potato pies while she ditzed out. She knew what Bernie would say, but baking helped her think. Should she go to Reginald's store and talk to him? Should she talk to his vendors? If she did, what should she say to them? "Excuse me. Do you know if Reginald Palmer had a reason to kill Hortense Calabash?" Especially since people weren't supposed to know that Hortense was dead. That certainly didn't help.

What was she looking for anyway? Libby took a handful of chocolate chips from the bowl she kept on the counter, "her stash" Bernie called it, put them in her mouth, and let them dissolve under her tongue. Then she got out the flour and her rolling pin. The rolling pin had been her mother's, and Libby liked its heft and the way it felt in her hands.

She sprinkled the counter with the flour, placed a portion of the dough she'd cut in the center, and gently patted it into a circle. She always did better when she was doing something with her hands.

She contemplated Reginald as she applied steady but firm pressure to the dough with her rolling pin. Who knew something about Reginald that she knew? No one came to mind. She gave the dough two strokes, turned it, and gave it another two strokes. It always pleased her to watch a perfect circle form. She lifted the dough up, plopped it into the pie pan, and began to gently press the dough into it. When she'd formed the edge, she started on the second piece.

As she did, her mind drifted back to the problem at hand. Reginald. What did she know about him anyway, besides the fact that he was a pompous ass? The most prominent thing was that he'd been the chief restaurant reviewer for the *Food Lover's Companion* magazine for five years before he'd quit to open up his shop last year.

Libby remembered her friend Joanna telling her he'd been forced out. She dusted off her hands and picked up the phone to call her. Joanna wasn't in, but her business partner was.

"I think he got the boot because he was taking bribes."

"Are you sure?" Libby asked him.

"I could be wrong," Mike said. "I'm just telling you what I heard."

Intriguing. When she'd seen the store she'd thought a lot of money had gone into it. Maybe that's where he'd gotten it from. It was very chic. All pink and white with high tea served five days a week. A ladies' delight, her mother would have said. As Libby started on the third piece of dough, she came to a decision.

After she finished up with the three pies, she'd just drive over and talk to Reginald directly. There. That was simple.

According to Bernie, she always thought about things too much. Maybe Bernie was right. Maybe she did.

Reginald was manning the counter when Libby walked into his shop. Ladies were sitting at the tables sipping tea and nibbling on what Libby assumed to be watercress sandwiches, a concoction she saw no use for whatsoever. *The place looks like a giant bonbon*, Libby thought as she made her way toward Reginald.

"Ah," he said when he saw her. "The little detective coming to detect, or should I say, one of the Jonah girls is here."

Not a promising beginning, Libby decided. Perhaps she should have had a chat with a couple of the vendors after all.

"Are you ready for tonight's contest?"

Reginald looked at her and lifted an eyebrow. Then he sneered.

"Obviously I'm more prepared than you are. Otherwise you wouldn't be asking."

"I was just trying to be polite," Libby heard herself saying. She could feel her temper rising. The phrase "loathsome little man" popped into her head.

"So was I." Reginald put his hands on the counter and leaned forward. "So what can I do for you? Perhaps a scone with some clotted cream and strawberry preserves?"

Libby took a deep breath and let it out. The time for "the niceties" as her mother called them were long past. "Why did you need to speak to Hortense so badly?" she blurted out. And that made her even madder. This wasn't how she'd intended starting. She just hated that she let herself get so easily rattled.

"I didn't," Reginald said.

"Remember, I was there."

"And your point is?"

"It seemed to me as if you did."

"Well, what can I say? You're wrong. Anything else?"

There it was. The dismissal she knew was coming.

"Ah . . ." Libby found her mind going blank. Finally she came up with, "How long have you known her?"

"Hortense?"

Libby nodded.

"Four or five years."

"How did you meet her?"

Evidently, Libby decided, Reginald must be more comfortable with that line of questioning because he said, "I met her when I was the editor of the *Food Lover's Companion*. We did a piece on her."

This is getting a little better, Libby thought. *Maybe this approach is going to work after all*. Maybe the lesson here was just keep going.

"So who do you think is responsible for Hortense's death?" Libby asked.

Reginald gave her an incredulous look.

"Eric Royal of course."

"Why of course?"

"Think about it," Reginald said. "He was her assistant. Now he's hosting the show. Or what about Consuela?"

"What about her?" Libby asked.

"Well, you're such a great detective, you figure it out. I'll give you a hint," Reginald said after a moment had gone by. "It involves pie crusts."

Libby shook her head. It wasn't ringing a bell.

"Think about it," Reginald said.

"I still don't get it," Libby replied.

Reginald gave her a pitying glance. "All I can say is that I hope you're a better cook than you are a detective, because you're really bad at this. Pathetic, actually." And with that, he turned to wait on a customer.

Libby felt her cheeks as she left Reginald's shop. Even though it was cold out, they were hot. She knew they would be. They were probably bright red. She was so angry she didn't know what to do with herself. She took a deep breath and told herself to calm down. What she needed was a cookie. No. What she needed was a walk. No. What she needed was to go back in there and bash Reginald in the face.

She took another deep breath and tried to focus on the white breath that was coming out of her mouth. Forget about Reginald Palmer, she told herself. She had to get back to work. There were pies waiting to be baked, roasts waiting to be prepared, and Amber and Googie waiting to be supervised.

She was opening the door of her van when she noticed one of Reginald's workers coming out of the side door of Reginald's store. The guy was obviously in a hurry because he practically ran by her. She was turning around when she realized that the kid hadn't closed the shop door all the way.

Just leave, Libby told herself. But she remained rooted to the spot. Reginald saying she hoped she was a better cook than she was a detective had been the last straw. He'd be sorry. She'd show him. Libby looked around. No one was on the street. No one was driving by. She quietly closed her van door and went down the alleyway.

I can't believe I'm doing this, she thought as she pulled the side door to Reginald's store open and stepped inside. She expected to be in one of the storerooms or the back kitchen. Instead she found herself in Reginald's office. Now, what had that kid been doing in here? Libby wondered. Probably something he shouldn't have been judging by the speed with which he'd left. Oh well. Libby certainly wasn't going to say anything that was for sure.

I should leave, Libby thought. Then she considered what Reginald had said to her and decided to stay. *I'll just take a quick look and get out of here*, Libby promised herself as she glanced around the office. The room was fairly bare. There was a calendar tacked up on the wall, three chairs, a file cabinet, and a desk. That was it.

"I'll look through the file cabinet first," she muttered to herself, but when she tried it, it was locked. Okay. On to the next thing. The desk. She walked over.

The desk had a laptop, a jar containing pens and pencils, and a stack of mail on it. Obviously Reginald was a neat freak, Libby thought, picturing her desk at home, which was currently buried under piles of bills, recipes she'd clipped from assorted magazines, and newspapers, coupons, and heaven knows what else.

Libby reached out and picked up the stack of mail. She began to thumb through it. Most of it was bills—she recognized the vendors—but then there was something from the Wexler Wellness Center addressed to Reginald Palmer.

Interesting, Libby thought. The Wexler Center was a rehab center for people with alcohol and drug problems. She was holding the letter up to the light when she heard footsteps. *Damn*, she thought. *If I were Bernie, where would I hide?* Nowhere, she decided. There was no closet, and she sure as hell wasn't going to take a chance crouching under the desk.

"This is why I don't do things like this," Libby said to herself as she stuffed the letter in her pocket and ran out the door. "I don't do things like this because I always get caught."

She was halfway down the alley when she heard Reginald calling to her.

"Hey," he cried. "What are you doing here?"

I must have forgotten to close the door all the way, Libby thought. *I can't believe I could have done that. Just keep walking*, she told herself. *Pretend you don't hear him*. But that obviously wasn't working because a moment later, her arm got grabbed and she was spun around.

"I asked you a question," he said to her.

"I'm sorry. I didn't hear." For some odd reason having the letter in her pocket made her feel braver.

"What were you doing in my office?" he demanded.

Libby summoned up her most outraged expression.

"I wasn't in your office."

"Then why was the door open?"

"One of your guys ran out the door."

"My guys?"

"Yes. He was wearing a black watch cap."

Libby could see a flicker of uncertainty in Reginald's eyes. His grip loosened slightly.

"That doesn't explain why you were in the alleyway."

Libby shrugged. "I thought he had dropped something, and I went to look. But he hadn't." She pointed to Reginald's hand. "Now if you don't mind taking your hand off of me. If you don't, I'm going to call the police," Libby told him.

"That's funny," Reginald said, but Libby noticed he looked more uncertain than he had before.

He gave her a closer look. She kept her face expressionless. A moment later she could felt his grip loosening. She made herself walk to her car, get in, and drive away as if she had all the time in the world. When she was three blocks away, she pulled into a Home Depot parking lot, opened the envelope she'd taken from Reginald's desk, and read the contents. *I did good*, she said to herself as she called Bernie. *I did really, really good.*

Chapter 14

Sean clicked off his cell and rested it in his lap where he could easily reach it again if he needed to.

"Now that's interesting," he reflected out loud.

Marvin turned to look at him. "What's interesting?" he asked.

Sean couldn't help himself. Even though he knew he shouldn't yell, he did. "Don't look at me, look at the road!"

There was a Ford Explorer in front of them that Sean definitely didn't want to have a close encounter with.

"Right."

Sean was relieved to see Marvin refocusing his attention on the vehicles in front of them.

He and Marvin, or was it him and Marvin—he could never get it straight—were now on the FDR Drive heading toward Brooklyn Heights where Jean La Croix's store was located. Sean just hoped they made it in one piece. Between the traffic and Marvin's driving ability, he was not confident about their arrival.

"I'm sorry," Marvin said, turning his head again.

"Look at the road," Sean repeated. He could hear his voice rising and what Libby described as his run-for-cover tone kicking in. "And stop saying you're sorry. Sorry doesn't fix anything. Just keep your eyes facing front. And for God's sake speed up a little. At this rate we'll get to the store in two hours."

He shook his head. He couldn't believe the sacrifices he made for Libby—like consenting to have Marvin as his driver. He just hoped she appreciated them.

"Yes, sir," Marvin said.

Sean noticed Marvin had his shoulders hunched over the wheel. His Aunt Martha used to drive like that—right before they made her give up the car.

"Sean," he automatically corrected.

"Yes, sir, Sean."

He's doing this purposely to make me crazy, Sean thought as he remembered Clyde's words. How could he forget them?

"You can't injure him," Clyde had said. "Remember, Marvin could be the father of your grandchildren someday."

Just the thought made Sean break out in a cold sweat. But what Clyde said was true. He had to get a hold of himself. He snuck a glance at Marvin. The kid looked like a whipped dog. Now on top of everything else, Sean felt guilty.

Yelling at Marvin was like yelling at Rose's Maltese, Sean reflected. All it did was make that thing—he could never think of it as a dog—pee on the floor, a correlation Rose had never failed to point out.

Of course, in the old days he wouldn't have needed anyone to drive him. In the old days he always drove himself. He prided himself on his ability to handle his vehicle in any situation. And now he was stuck being chauffeured around by Marvin no less. Whatever it was he had done in his past life he was paying for it now!

Maybe Marvin was a nice guy—okay, he was a nice guy—but the kid couldn't drive his way out of a paper bag, as his dad used to say. It was as simple as that. How the kid had survived for as long as he had without having someone run him off the road was a mystery. In fact, in the old days, Sean thought he would have been one of the first to do it.

Let's be honest here, Sean admitted to himself. There was something else as well. He also hated the fact that he and Marvin were driving down to Brooklyn in the only vehicle available—Marvin's father's hearse. It creeped him out—Bernie's expression—even though he would rather die than admit that to anyone.

He couldn't help thinking of all the lost souls who were floating around in the back. Maybe a few of them were guys he'd sent upstate. In fact, he was staring straight ahead because he wasn't going to look behind him. Nohow. No way. And this from someone who could look down the barrel of a Glock without a quiver.

And then there was the last thing, probably the biggest thing. Marvin's father didn't even know the hearse was gone.

"He'll never notice," Marvin had said.

"How could he not?" Sean had demanded.

"Because the one he usually uses is in the garage. This one was out back."

"What happens if something comes up?" Sean had asked. Meaning, like what happens if two people croak in different locations.

"Don't worry," Marvin said. "It'll be fine."

"How? What'll your dad do? Use a taxicab?"

Sean rubbed his chin. Marvin had looked at him as if he were demented. The kid had no sense of humor.

"I still think you should have told him," Sean had said to try and make his point clear.

"Then he wouldn't have let me come."

Which might not have been a bad thing. Sean closed his eyes. He could just see them being stopped by the NYPD on a stolen car beef. Wonderful. Wouldn't Chief Lucy just love that? He'd never hear the end of it.

"That was Bernie who called," Sean said after a few minutes had elapsed.

Marvin didn't say anything.

At first Sean judged this a good thing, but after a few moments the silence started getting to him.

"Don't you want to know why she called?"

Marvin still didn't say anything.

"You can talk, you know," Sean told him.

Sean watched the right side of Marvin's mouth work itself into a grimace.

"I know I can. But every time I do, you scream at me," Marvin replied.

"All I'm asking you to do is keep your eyes on the road. That isn't too much to ask, is it?"

"No," Marvin allowed. "But people tend to keep a lookout for hearses."

Sean grunted. This was the first he'd heard of something like that.

"They think it's bad luck to hit one," Marvin continued. "I mean, there might be a body in it or something. I'll show you."

"Don't!" Sean cried.

But it was too late. Marvin was turning the wheel. Sean braced himself for the impact and closed his eyes. He didn't want to watch the collision with the Taurus in the right lane.

"See what I mean?" Marvin said.

Sean opened one eye. They were still in one piece.

"I told you. People really do look out for me."

Sean nodded. That was all he could do. For once he was speechless.

"So what did Bernie have to say?" Marvin asked.

Sean took a deep breath. Then he took another. And another. *Get a grip*, he told himself.

"Anything important?" Marvin asked.

What had Bernie said? Sean asked himself. Jeez. Marvin's maneuver had pushed it clean out of his mind. Something about Reginald? No. It was something about her sister.

"She was just telling me about Libby."

Sean had no intention of sharing the whole story of Libby's adventure with Marvin. He'd probably drive straight into a ditch if he did, but something in Sean's tone must have alerted Marvin, because he said, "Libby! Is she all right?"

"Of course she's all right," Sean said before Marvin could so much as twitch his neck around. It occurred to Sean that the important thing with Marvin was to keep him calm. "Why shouldn't she be all right?"

"I was just asking," Marvin said.

Maybe Bernie's right, Sean thought. *Maybe I am turning into a cranky old man.* But too bad. If he didn't deserve to be cranky, he didn't know who did.

He grunted and launched into his recitation. Marvin tapped his fingers on the wheel of the car while Sean talked.

"So," Marvin said when Sean was through. "What do you think that means?"

Sean smiled for the first time since he'd left the house. Maybe he could teach Marvin how to be a better driver. After all, he'd taught Libby.

"It means that both Pearl and Reginald might have a motive for murder."

"How so?" Marvin asked.

Sean was gratified to note that Marvin's eyes were still on the road. Who knew? Perhaps if he repeated something enough, Marvin might actually be capable of learning it. After all, the strategy had worked with his children.

"Think about it," Sean said. "Pearl having no sense of taste."

"Huh?" he said.

Sean realized he hadn't filled Marvin in on Bernie's latest findings.

"Interesting," Marvin said when he had.

"Very," Sean agreed. "Pearl probably has no sense of smell either because usually those things go together. One of those would be enough to sink her, let alone both. If it got out, it would be the end of Pearl's career."

"Was Hortense blackmailing her?" Marvin asked.

Sean thought about what he knew about her. The words *avaricious*, *unscrupulous*, and *greedy* seemed to apply. "It wouldn't surprise me at all."

"Do you think she was blackmailing anyone else?"

"Reginald comes to mind. According to Libby, he might have a drug problem."

It seemed a fair assumption to make. After all, you don't check yourself into rehab because you want to relax for a couple of days.

Marvin sped up and then slowed down.

"Lots of people do that kind of thing."

"Agreed," Sean said. "But the thing with caterers is you let them into your house. Some people wouldn't feel comfortable doing that with someone who has a drug problem."

"Okay. But even if what you say is true," Marvin said. "It doesn't follow that Hortense was blackmailing him."

"But we don't know that she wasn't," Sean replied.

"She could have been blackmailing other people as well."

"She could be blackmailing the whole bloody lot of them for all we know," Sean retorted. He slouched down in his seat. And maybe she was. He hoped not because the point of this exercise was to eliminate suspects, not widen the suspect pool.

Marvin digested that for a few moments. Then he said, "How are you going to find out?"

"I'm going to do what I always do. I'm going to ask questions."

Of course, Sean reflected, he wasn't sure what kind of questions he was going to ask. But that would come later. Right now he was going to concentrate all his energy on his upcoming interview with Jean La Croix, aka John "Boomer" LaMonte, a graduate of the Attica State cooking school.

Sean realized he was smiling. Good ole Clyde. He'd sure come up with some good information this time. He was glad he still had him in his corner. Too bad he wasn't driving with him anymore. They used to have fun going around. And speaking of driving . . .

"Slow down!" he yelled at Marvin, who had just sped up as the Lexus in front of them was slowing down.

"Sorry," Marvin said.

"It's okay."

Marvin looked surprised.

"Really," Sean said.

Remain positive, Sean told himself. Positive energy was the ticket with Marvin. As Marvin turned onto the exit that would take them onto the Brooklyn Bridge, Sean looked at a tugboat chugging down the East River. It made him remember how much he liked the water. Maybe he and Libby and Bernie could take a drive over to the beach this summer. Make a day trip out of it. Then his mind started drifting back to the problem at hand. Yes, he was definitely looking forward to talking to La Croix—that is, if Marvin didn't kill them both before they got to Brooklyn. Although, Sean supposed that if you were going to croak, a hearse was as good a place as any to do it.

And, of course, if they did make it into Brooklyn, they'd have to find La Croix's place, which in Brooklyn was always a challenge.

Chapter 15

Sean took a deep breath and let it out. He'd been doing a lot of deep breathing this past hour or so, enough so he was beginning to feel as if he was in a scuba diving class. Or a Lamaze class. He couldn't decide which.

It had taken Marvin almost three-quarters of an hour to locate La Croix's shop. Before that, they'd driven around Brooklyn, discovering a slew of places that Sean would have preferred not to be in. Anytime he saw a fence with the words ARMED RESPONSE painted on it, it was a good indication to him that he was in the wrong part of town.

This had happened because in addition to everything else, it seemed as if Marvin's map-reading skills were not exactly up to snuff, and when Sean had taken over the map-reading duties, it turned out that Marvin had a certain amount of problems taking directions. If he told Marvin to go right, he went left. If he told him to go left, he went right. And if Marvin got the direction right, he overshot the turn, which meant they had to go around the block, which in certain parts of Brooklyn meant they ended up in who knew where because people had stolen the street signs.

I'm not going to complain to Libby though, Sean

thought. No, siree. He wasn't going to mention Marvin's driving. The last time he'd done that, he'd had to listen to a twenty-minute speech peppered with words like *understanding* and *compassion*, *self-control*, and acronyms like ADD or AHAD or CST or whatever new condition the doctors were pushing pills for these days. If you asked him, those were just code words for not paying attention, but no one was asking him.

Sean opened the door and began getting out of the hearse, a process, he bitterly reflected, that took him far longer than it should.

"Are you sure you don't want me to come in with you?" Marvin asked.

"I'm positive," Sean said. "I need you to stay here and mind the car."

Which was true. The block La Croix's shop was on was extremely narrow, and there was no place to put the hearse. Marvin was now double parked in front of La Croix's store. Sean hoped La Croix was looking. He hoped he was superstitious. Maybe seeing the vehicle would shake him up a little. And anyway, he wanted Marvin close at hand if he needed him. Although he didn't think it would come to that.

Marvin pointed to the cars he was blocking.

"What if someone needs to pull out? What do I do then?"

"What do you think you should do?" Sean wanted to snap. But he didn't.

Instead he said, "Then you have to just keep circling around the block."

Then he pulled himself out of the car, straightened up, and slowly headed toward the back where Marvin had, over his objections, stowed his wheelchair.

At first he hadn't been going to use the dratted thing—he really didn't need it; well, sometimes he did—but then he decided that he should. First off, people in wheelchairs weren't considered a danger; in fact, they weren't considered anything at all, which in this case was good because he wanted to catch La Croix off guard.

Secondly, used the right way, a wheelchair, especially a motorized one, could inflict a substantial amount of damage to a man's feet and ankles. Not that he expected things to get to that point, but it never hurt to expect the worst. That way you were never disappointed.

"I can do that," he snapped at Marvin, who was lifting the wheelchair out of the hearse and onto the sidewalk by the time he got around to the back. "I'm not a complete cripple yet."

Marvin put on his whipped-dog expression, which annoyed Sean even more. He distracted himself by studying La Croix's shop. It looked good. He had to give the man that. Very tasteful with the front painted in various shades of golds and the fresh blue spruce boughs intertwined with white lights strung around the store's entrance. The window decorations were good too.

Actually they were clever. Someone had made cardboard cutouts of various chickens and ducks, had dressed them up as elves and Santas, and had them dancing around a table piled high with presents. It was nice, but, Sean noted with pride, the display in A Little Taste of Heaven looked better.

"Here we go," he said to Marvin as he plunked himself down in the wheelchair and headed for the door.

"Luck," Marvin said.

Sean didn't answer. He was too busy focusing on what was about to happen. Anyway, he didn't believe in luck. Never had. Luck was something you made for yourself.

A lady who was going into the store just ahead of him opened the door and held it for him. Even though it pained him to do it, he nodded his thanks to her and went inside.

The store was crowded. People were three deep in front of the counter. They were acting as if La Croix was giving away gold.

A Little Taste of Heaven was busy, but it wasn't as busy as this—unless, of course, you counted the time Laird Wrenn had died and everyone wanted the straight scoop from Libby and Bernie.

Not that Sean minded the crowd. Far from it. In fact, as far as he was concerned, the more people in here the better. And best of all, the man calling himself Jean La Croix was waiting on customers. Sean decided it couldn't be better if he had ordered it this way.

Sean moved forward a little. Everyone in the crowd parted to let him through. This, Sean decided, was one of the only benefits of being—what was the expression—vertically challenged? Or was it some other hornswoggle term? He could never keep track of all the PC-speak.

"It's showtime," Sean muttered to himself. He straightened his back, leaned forward in the chair, and yelled out, "Hey, Boomer. John Boomer. I can't believe you're out, man."

La Croix's head snapped up. For a second his jaw dropped. Then he caught himself, and his face worked itself into a mask.

Gotcha, John, Sean thought with satisfaction. *I gotcha good*. He'd send over one of Libby's apple pies to Clyde when he got home.

"I'd heard you were in the slammer for another five years," Sean continued. "Guess Sparky got it wrong."

Sean watched as La Croix's eyes worked the crowd and finally landed on him.

"I don't know what you're talking about," La Croix said.

His voice was flat. But then, Sean reflected, ex-cons always knew how to control themselves.

"Sure ya do," Sean went on. "Don't you remember I

was right next to you on Block B? I was two cells down. Assault with a deadly weapon. You were in on a burglary beef."

Sean was amused to see that everyone was moving away from his chair, not so much as to give offense, but enough so that they weren't right next to him. As if he were contagious.

"Who the hell are you?" La Croix demanded.

Sean leaned forward a little more. "I'm Wooky. Don't you remember me, man?" Then before La Croix could reply, Sean gestured to his wheelchair and said, "I'm down on my luck, and I figured that since I graduated from the same cooking school you did, good old Château Attica,"—Sean made sure to pronounce *Attica* clearly— "maybe you could hook me up with something." He looked around appreciatively. "This is one sweet setup you got here. It must have cost you beaucoup bucks."

La Croix pointed to the door. "Get out of my place," he ordered.

Sean put both his hands up in the air. "Hey, man, I woulda done what you do—you know, served an internship with that old lady, but she bit the dust, so you're my next in line."

"Out," La Croix repeated.

Sean laughed. "What's the matter? You gonna forget about your old buddy? After everything I done for you?"

"He's no buddy of mine," La Croix told everyone. "I never saw this man in my life. He is a, how you say, a lunatic."

Sean did outraged. It was something Clyde told him that he did well.

"Hey, I ain't no nutcase. My PO said you done worked for that Hortense dame. In fact, he's the one who suggested I look you up. He says she likes guys like us." Sean made his voice go low and breathy. "You know, guys with tool belts."

I guess my suspicions were right, Sean told himself as he watched La Croix fly around the counter and come racing toward him.

"Don't hurt me, man," Sean whined as La Croix stood towering over him.

"I'm not going to hurt you," La Croix said. "But I want you out of here. I want you out of here now. Otherwise I'm calling the cops."

Sean noted that although La Croix's tone of voice was calm, a vein was twitching under his right eye.

"You don't got to be like that," Sean said, and he turned and began motoring out. "I was just asking you to help out an old buddy is all."

La Croix followed him. Sean was interested to see that the hearse wasn't there. But then why would Marvin be where he needed him? The kid had probably gone off to get a latte or something.

When the store door closed behind him, La Croix leaned down and grabbed Sean by his shoulders and squeezed. Sean could feel the strength in the man's fingers.

"I don't know what you think you're doing," La Croix hissed, "but if you do this crap again, I'll rip your vocal cords out."

"How about if you just make my stove explode like Hortense's?" Sean asked.

"What's that supposed to mean?"

"Guess."

"You're accusing me of murder now?"

Sean shrugged, even though La Croix's fingers were boring into his shoulders.

"You know what they say about if the shoe fits."

La Croix cut him off. "Listen, crip," he snarled, "I don't know who you are, and I don't care. You can mouth off all you want as long as you don't do it in front of my store."

"So you didn't work for Hortense Calabash?"

"What did I just tell you?"

"Well, actually, I lied in there," Sean confessed. "I'm not an ex-con, even though you are. What I am is a journalist, and I'm writing an article about you; you know, something like 'From Attica to Brooklyn Heights—A Caterer's Journey'—and I just want to get my facts straight."

Now La Croix was so close to him Sean could feel the man's breath on his face.

"You do that and you'll regret it."

"That would be interfering with freedom of the press. And by the way, take your hands off my shoulders."

La Croix leered. "You know, if I press a little harder, I can make it so you can't use your arm anymore. That way you'll be minus two legs and an arm. In fact, let me demonstrate."

"What about your customers? They might not like that."

"They won't know."

"Well, before you do that, let me show you what a wheelchair can do."

And Sean ran his chair over La Croix's feet. He could feel La Croix let go of his shoulder. As Sean did it again, out of the corner of his eye he could see Marvin pulling up to the curb.

"By the way, Boomer," he said as he headed toward the hearse, "you should work on that French accent of yours. It tends to vanish under stress."

La Croix started hobbling toward him.

"I think you broke my little toe," he cried.

Sean tsk-tsked as he watched Marvin getting out of the hearse. He was now by the curb.

"What's happening?" Marvin said.

"I'll tell you later," Sean said as he got out of his chair. "Let's get out of here."

Marvin didn't move. He seemed transfixed.

"Now," Sean said.

"I'm going back and getting my knife," La Croix growled.

Marvin sprang into action. In fact, Sean reflected, he'd never seen him move so fast. Marvin grabbed the wheelchair, threw it in the back, ran back, and helped Sean into his seat.

"Relax," Sean told him as Marvin was frantically trying to get the car key in the ignition. "The guy isn't going to do anything."

"How do you know?"

Sean buckled his seat belt. "Years of experience."

"Really?" Marvin pointed.

Sean followed his finger. La Croix was coming out of the shop door waving a cleaver over his head.

"I guess I pissed him off," Sean observed.

"I guess you did," Marvin said as he finally got the key in the ignition and turned it.

"Maybe we should leave," Sean suggested as La Croix stalked toward their vehicle. "I wouldn't want him to mark up your dad's vehicle."

"Oh, heavens no," Marvin replied.

The next thing Sean knew, they had peeled out, leaving a dazed UPS man in their wake. Sean turned and waved at La Croix. He knew it was childish, but at this stage of life he saw no reason to resist an available pleasure.

"Well, I think we've established one thing," Sean said as Marvin made a wrong turn and went onto Seventh Avenue. "Actually we've established two things. We've established that Jean La Croix is a man with a secret to hide and that he is someone who is capable of doing something like booby-trapping the oven." Sean looked at Marvin. "What? You don't agree?"

"No, I agree," Marvin said quickly. "It just doesn't seem like a lot to go on."

"Oh, it's enough," Sean told him. "Believe me, people

have been convicted on less evidence than that." Sean rubbed his hands together. "Turn left. We have to go left," Sean cried as Marvin took a right.

Sean sighed. They were never going to get back to Longely. They were going to be lost in Brooklyn forever.

Chapter 16

Libby looked down at her dad. He was sitting in his wheelchair alternately taking bites from one of her lemon bars and sipping from his cup of tea. Maybe she shouldn't say anything to him. Maybe she should just let it go. . . . Her mom would have, but she wasn't her mom.

But maybe her mom's approach was right. *Why does everything have to be such a big deal with me?* Libby wondered as she caught sight of her nails. God. She was peeling them, and she hadn't even realized it. Now they looked a mess. She could just hear everyone out in TVland saying, "What does that woman do to her hands?"

Libby was wondering if it was too late to do anything about them when she realized her father was speaking to her.

"I like the shirt you're wearing."

Of course he liked it. It was one of Bernie's. Not that she was going to say that.

"Thanks," Libby told him. "I just got off the phone with Marvin."

"Really?"

"Really."

She watched her dad take another bite of the lemon bar—it was one of the store's best-sellers. She was convinced it was the zest and fresh lemon juice that did it. Then he brushed some of the powdered sugar off the corners of his mouth, after which he stirred his tea and took another sip.

"How's he doing?"

"The same as he was doing an hour ago."

Sean shrugged. "Just asking. Did his father notice the hearse was gone?"

"No, thank heavens." Given what Marvin's father was like, that was something Libby didn't even want to consider.

"Hmm." Libby watched as her dad absentmindedly rested his palms on the wheels of his chair. "Not a very observant sort of fellow, is he? It's kind of like not noticing a limo is gone from your garage."

"Dad, forget the limo." Libby tried to moderate her voice. "He told me what you did."

"What I did?"

"With La Croix."

Sean folded his hands in his lap and looked up at her again. Libby noticed that he was getting some noticeable lines around his eyes.

"I didn't do anything to La Croix. He tried to do something to me."

"You could have gotten stabbed," Libby said.

"I think the correct word would be *chopped*, and I didn't."

"But you could have."

She watched as her dad took another sip of tea and put down the cup. She noticed that his hand was trembling less than it had a year ago.

"Nice," he said. "Nothing like a spot of tea during the Yuletide season. Is this the new Earl Gray?"

Libby almost burst out laughing. "You can cut the brogue out. You were born in this country. And don't try and change the subject on me. I hate when you do that."

Her dad gave her a look of total innocence.

"Me?"

"I don't see anyone else in the room."

Her dad looked around. "There's the ficus tree your mom used to speak to. Doesn't that count?"

"I'm not kidding." Libby tried to not let herself be distracted. Her father was really good at that. "You provoked this man. You could have gotten badly hurt."

Her dad brushed a speck of sugar off his sweater. "I appreciate your concern," he said. "But the way I see it, what I did wasn't any worse than what you did at Reginald Palmer's place. In fact, it was better. At least I had someone with me," he observed. "What would have happened if Reginald had caught you in his office? Best-case scenario, he would have had you arrested. That's at best. As for the worst, I don't want to think about that. Remember, we're dealing with a murder suspect here."

"Bernie told you," Libby cried when her father paused to take a breath. She couldn't believe she'd done that.

"I told him what?" Bernie asked.

Libby whirled around. Bernie and Rob were standing in the doorway. Why hadn't she heard either one of them coming up? she wondered. Maybe she was going deaf. She should really get her hearing checked. But that, she reflected, like everything else, would have to wait till after the holidays.

"What did I tell him?" Bernie asked again.

"You told him about my going into Reginald's office."

"You make it sound as if that's a bad thing," Bernie replied. "You didn't tell me not to."

Had she? Libby tried to remember. My God. Maybe Bernie was right. Maybe she hadn't.

"Actually," Bernie said to her, "I think what you did took a lot of guts."

Libby watched her dad move some specks of powdered sugar to the side of the plate. "Stupidity is more like it."

Libby could feel herself bristling. "How come when Bernie does something like that it's okay and when I do it, it isn't?"

"Yeah, Dad," Bernie chimed in.

Libby shot her sister a grateful glance, and Bernie winked back.

Her father was beginning to reply when Bernie interrupted him. "I mean, if Libby hadn't gone into the office, we wouldn't have known that Reginald has a drug problem."

Libby watched her dad frown.

"I suppose," he allowed. Then he turned toward her. "But, Libby, it's bad enough worrying about her." He pointed to her sister. "You're supposed to be the sensible one in the family."

"Well maybe I don't want to be that anymore," Libby snapped. "Maybe I'm tired of being sensible. Maybe I want to go off to Antarctica or hike through Death Valley or wear four-inch stilettos." She faced Bernie. "And you don't have to roll your eyes."

"You will never wear stilettos."

"How do you know what I'll wear?"

"You are so PMSing."

Libby was opening her mouth to answer when her dad's voice rang out like a shot. "Girls."

She shut up. So did Bernie.

"That's better," her dad said to both of them. "A lot better." Then he said to Rob, "Whatever you do, son, don't have daughters."

Rob laughed, which made Bernie laugh, which made Libby laugh.

All right, Libby admitted to herself, maybe she was a little stressed out. Maybe her to-do list was getting to her after all. Maybe she was stretched a little thin right now. What she really needed to be doing was be downstairs making more Yule logs and Christmas cookies. Both were going so fast she couldn't keep them in stock.

And she didn't even want to think about Mrs. DeLitte's pre-Christmas literary affair. Why she had agreed to make cookies in the shape of chimney sweeps was beyond her. She obviously hadn't been thinking clearly at the time.

The shape hadn't been the problem. She knew someone who had made the mold for them. And she'd already baked them. The cookies, gingersnaps with hints of cardamom, had come out wonderfully well. But now she had to ice the darned things with lemon-flavored icing.

She'd done a couple already, and outlining the broom straws had taken way longer than she had anticipated. In fact, she should be down there now doing that. So should Bernie for that matter. She was just about to tell Bernie that when Bernie held up a string of Christmas lights in the shape of chili peppers.

"You like?" Bernie said.

"I like," Libby replied. And she did.

Bernie smiled.

"I thought they were fun in a tacky retro kind of way. They reminded me of the fifties and the whole pink flamingo thing."

Libby shook her head. Why her sister couldn't say anything in a straightforward manner was beyond her.

"I found them in the Dollar Store."

"The Dollar Store?" Libby couldn't believe it. "You went to the Dollar Store? Good grief. "

Rob grinned. "That's my influence. I'm bringing her down in life."

Bernie grinned back at him. "Anyway," she continued, "I thought Rob and I would put them up in the store window, and if we have enough, we'll put a few strings up here."

Libby watched Bernie look around.

"What do you think, Dad?"

"I think it would be good."

"How about this?" And Bernie whipped out a container of snow-in-the-can.

"Absolutely not," both she and her dad said in unison.

"Why not?" Bernie asked. "I think it would be funny."

"Well, I don't," Sean said. "Your mother would roll over in her grave. Besides, that stuff is impossible to get off."

"Fine."

Sean took the can from Bernie and put it down on the floor next to his magazines. Maybe he'd give it to Clyde. His wife liked things like that. He straightened himself up. "Now that we've got that settled, I think it would be good if we could go through what we've accomplished today."

Libby sighed.

"It'll only take a moment," her father was saying when Libby heard the downstairs door open.

A few minutes later a "Hello? Anyone home?" came trilling up the stairs.

Libby looked at her sister and father. They looked at her.

"Bree Nottingham," they all said in unison.

Her dad groaned. Libby was about to say something when Bree, resplendent in her mink coat, appeared at the doorway of her father's bedroom.

"I hope you don't mind," she chirped. "But I was passing by and decided to stop and see what progress my detectives are making."

The phrase "my detectives" made Libby want to strangle Bree, and from the look on Bernie's face, Libby could tell she felt the same way.

While Libby was contemplating the pleasures of life

without Bree, the object of her contemplation smiled at her and said, "I wonder if I could trouble you for a cup of tea."

Libby watched as she lightly touched the hollow of her throat with one perfectly groomed nail, which of course made Libby think about the state hers were in.

"Of course," Libby said.

"And a biscuit or two," Bree added. "I haven't had a chance to eat anything at all today."

"Who wears fur these days anyway?" Bernie muttered in Libby's ears as they trudged down the stairs.

"Maybe PETA will get her," Libby replied as she and her sister entered the kitchen.

"I'd pay to see that," Bernie said, taking one of the small two-cup teapots off the shelf.

"I'm sure lots of people would," Libby agreed as she took some cookies out of their container and practically slammed them on the plate.

The last thing that she had time to do today was listen to Bree Nottingham. When she and Bernie returned upstairs, Bree was sitting with her father on one side and Rob on the other. If she had a hair out of place, Libby couldn't see it.

Today she was resplendent in a black turtleneck sweater, a fawn-colored suede wraparound skirt, and high suede boots. Perfect as usual, Libby thought as she studied the boots. Her calves were probably too heavy to be able to wear something like that, she concluded gloomily.

"How nice," Bree told Libby as she took the teapot from Libby's hands. "You didn't have to go to all this trouble. A cup of Lipton's would have done."

It was all Libby could do to stop herself from rolling her eyes.

"Is this China tea by any chance?" Bree asked.

"Why, yes it is," Bernie said before Libby could tell her it was from India.

"Good," Bree said. "I always feel Indian tea is too heavy."

Libby concentrated on the tree outside of her father's bedroom window because she was afraid she'd start laughing if she looked at Bernie's smirk.

"So how is my band of merry little detectives coming along?" Bree asked as she poured herself a cup of tea and took a sip. "Wonderful," she exclaimed. "So restoring in this Christmas rush."

Libby couldn't decide whether she wanted to throw up or burst out laughing.

"We've made some progress," her father informed Bree. And he told her what they'd found out so far.

Bree nodded. "That's marvelous. I know Hortense would be pleased."

"How is Hortense, by the way?" Libby heard Bernie say. "Funeral plans coming along?"

Bree gave Bernie a forbidding stare. "I assume she's doing as well as can be expected given the circumstances, and yes, the arrangements are coming along quite nicely."

Sean coughed. Everyone turned back to him.

"I was wondering if there was anything you could add about Hortense?" Sean asked her.

Bree put her cup and saucer down and took a nibble of her lemon thin. "Such as?"

"I don't know. From what the girls tell me, you were her friend."

Bree nodded. "Childhood friend."

"I just wondered if you had any information that could help us locate her killer."

Bree stroked her mink coat thoughtfully. "Hortense had a lot of enemies."

"Makes sense to me," Libby interjected before she could stop herself.

Bree shot her a dirty look.

"Well, it's true. Even you said she was"—Libby searched for the word Bree had used—"problematic."

Bree rearranged the folds of her coat. "No. That's wrong."

Libby was about to tell her it wasn't when her dad intervened.

"I'm sure Libby misremembered," he told Bree while he shot Libby a warning look. "Isn't that right, Libby?"

"I suppose," she said grudgingly.

She knew what her father was doing, but it irked her all the same. Even if he was right and even if it was in her best interest to not get into an argument with Bree. She had too much to do, and once Bree got started she never shut up. She just went on and on and on.

Bree nodded her head in what Libby supposed was a magnanimous gesture. She was always gracious in victory.

"What I said," Bree continued, emphasizing the word *said*, "was that a lot of people had problems with her. Most people don't like powerful women. I myself can attest to that. They feel threatened by them."

"Can you be more specific?" Sean said. "We are on a tight schedule here. I'm sure it won't be long before the media catches wind of this. Frankly, I'm surprised they haven't already."

Bree inspected her fingernails. "Well, there is always Consuela," she said. "She and Hortense absolutely loathed each other."

"Why is that?" her dad asked before either Bernie or Libby could.

Bree told them.

Chapter 17

Bernie looked at Hortense's house as she and Libby drove up the long driveway and hung a left into the parking lot that Hortense had used for her studio. The house was huge. Or maybe *gigantic* would be a better word. Or possibly *enormous*. Bernie couldn't decide which word would be better.

It was also landscaped within an inch of its life, but the landscaping was made to look as if it had just happened, which Bernie knew from her days in L.A. was the most expensive kind of landscaping there was—and the most difficult to accomplish. It was kind of like make-up, Bernie reflected. The best kind was the kind that made you look good but didn't call attention to itself.

Bree had told her that Hortense had spent ten thousand dollars decorating her house with wreaths and evergreens for the holiday season. Ten thou was a lot, she and Bree had agreed. Bree hadn't been sure about the big red bows on the windows, but Bernie thought they were a nice touch. Whatever else you could say about Hortense, she had a good eye for detail.

"The place is big enough to house a small village," was the way Bree had described Hortense's house to her.

It was true, Bernie decided. It was big enough to house a small village, maybe even two. *If I had that kind of money,* Bernie reflected, *I'd rather spend it on clothes and travel.* But since she never would have it, it wasn't going to be an issue. But still, it would be nice to live in a place with more than one bathroom. She loved her house. She just hated sharing the bathroom with her dad. He couldn't seem to understand her need for three kinds of shampoos and four kinds of conditioners.

Oh well. There are worse things in life, she thought as she watched Libby concentrate on maneuvering the van into the space between the Ford Explorer and Consuela's BMW. The lot was almost full, which meant Libby was going to have a fit because she always liked to be one of the first to get there instead of one of the last.

Well, actually, she'd already had her fit. And, of course, Libby had blamed their tardiness on her. But it wasn't her fault that her mascara had rolled off the sink and landed behind the towels on the floor and hence was invisible, or that her pink gloves had ended up in the pocket of her brown leather jacket, which was the last place she would have expected them to be.

That was the trouble with being near someplace, geographically speaking, Bernie decided. It was like going to your neighbor's party. You always thought you had plenty of time, so you futzed around and got there late, while the person who had to come from an hour away was always on time. But at least Libby had calmed down. Especially once Bernie had pointed out that screaming at the top of her lungs didn't do good things for her powers of speech, which she was going to need once they were on the air.

"Not bad," Bernie said, nodding in the direction of Consuela's car.

The vanity plates on the black BMW read CNSUELA.

"She must be doing pretty well," Libby observed as she pulled into the space and killed the engine. She patted the van's dashboard. "We love you anyway," she crooned to it. "We love you even if you are old and beat up."

Bernie took off her hat and ran her fingers through her hair. "I bet she leased it."

"Could be," Libby said.

Normally her sister would have been very interested in the status of Consuela's car, but Bernie could tell from the expression on her face that she was preoccupied with something else.

"You're still thinking about what Bree told us, aren't you?" Bernie asked.

Libby turned toward her. She was frowning.

"At least now I know what Reginald meant," Libby said. "I just can't believe she'd do something like that. It's terrible."

Bernie laughed. "You sound as if you've just found out Hortense was a serial killer."

"This is worse."

Bernie sighed. Her sister was such an unbelievable dork sometimes.

"Okay," Libby relented. "Maybe that was an overstatement. But still. Using prepackaged pie crusts!"

Bernie put her hands over her heart. "Oh, the horror of it all."

"I'm serious."

"I know you are. That's what's so scary."

Libby made a face at her. "No. Really. You have to admit that's pretty bad. Especially coming from the original 'do-it-from-scratch' person, the person who suggested that everyone make their own homemade butter because it's so much better."

Bernie reached over and brushed a speck of dirt off of Libby's cheek. Sometimes she forgot how naïve Libby could be. She'd believed in Santa until she was ten years old and the tooth fairy until she was twelve.

"No. I don't suppose you would, would you?" she told her.

"What's that suppose to mean?" Libby demanded.

"Nothing," Bernie said.

"Then why did you say it?"

Bernie pulled down the mirror on the passenger side so she could apply her lip gloss. The holidays certainly didn't bring out the best in her sister, that was for sure. Neither did public appearances, for that matter. Combine them both and you got someone who was impossible to deal with. She turned to look at Libby again. She was picking at her nails.

"You'll do fine," she told her. "You did fine last time we were on the air," she said.

Libby reached in her backpack and took out a cookie. "When I looked at myself I wanted to hide under the bed. I never realized my stomach and butt were that big."

"They're not, but if you feel so strongly, then don't eat those," Bernie told her, pointing to the chocolate chip cookie Libby had just taken a bite of.

"You shop, I eat."

"It's not the same."

"It certainly is. Anyway, chocolate has health benefits. I'm surprised you don't know that."

Bernie sighed. When Libby got like this she wanted to whack her across the face and tell her, "Get a grip. Listen to what you're saying!" But since she was never going to do that, she decided to change the subject to something more neutral, like Consuela and Hortense.

"I can see why Hortense got so mad at Consuela," Bernie said. "Telling *Great Food* that Hortense used prepared pie crusts was definitely not a good thing to do."

Libby wiped the crumbs off her lap.

"I know. I wonder why Consuela did it."

"I'm guessing to get back at Hortense for something she said. Or because she was jealous." Bernie pulled the mirror down and studied her make-up. "This is what the literary among us would call a paroxysm in a pie plate, a scandal in a Sachertorte."

"Or a mountain in a meringue."

"That works," Bernie said as she took her finger and wiped a dap of lip gloss off the corner of her mouth.

Libby grinned.

"The magazine didn't print the accusation though."

Bernie put the mirror back up.

"No, Libby, they didn't."

"I wonder why?"

"Let me think. Maybe because Hortense would have threatened to sue them for libel. I mean, given the lawyers that woman probably had on retainer, writing that would be like baiting the bull. It wasn't worth it. Even if the magazine printed it as a blind item. Anyway, food magazines don't have gossip columns, although the way chefs are becoming TV personalities, maybe they should. Actually, it wouldn't surprise me if they did in the near future."

"And of course Hortense found out."

Bernie shrugged. "Magazines routinely check their sources, a fact Consuela must have known. And even if she didn't, she must have known word would have gotten back to Hortense, the food community being the small world it is."

And it was. Not for the first time, Bernie reflected how everyone in it seemed to live in everyone else's pocket.

Libby turned to her. "Consuela must have been so mad about something that she didn't care what happened."

"Agreed," Bernie said. She'd had a few of those days herself, especially when she'd found Joe in bed with that . . . that . . . no, don't go there, Bernie told herself. Try to look at it in a positive light.

"Here's my question," Libby said. "If Hortense hated her so much, why did she invite Consuela on the show? It makes no sense to me."

Bernie thought about that for a moment. "Because she wanted to humiliate her? Because she was a sadist?"

"Possibly," Libby agreed. "But then why did Consuela agree to come? I mean, I wouldn't do something with someone who I knew hated me. I'd be afraid she'd do me a bad turn."

"Maybe she was afraid not to," Bernie observed.

"But why? That means that Hortense had some kind of hold on her."

"And we're going to try and find out what it was." Bernie handed Libby her lip gloss. "Here. Try this."

Libby took a deep breath. "I guess it's showtime."

"I guess it is."

Bernie patted Libby on the arm. "We're gonna kill 'em," she said.

Libby raised an eyebrow. "I think under the circumstances that's not a good phrase."

"I think you're right," Bernie conceded.

Libby grinned. "But I know what you mean."

Chapter 18

Bernie stopped in the doorway of the green room and peered in. Yup. Everyone was there except them. She and Libby took a step inside. Two seconds later, Estes came waddling over to them. Why do people do that to themselves? Bernie wondered as she looked at what Estes was wearing.

The red and green sweater with reindeer embroidered on it was not a good choice sartorially speaking, Bernie decided. That sweater wouldn't look good on anyone, but couple it with Estes' green and red plaid pants, not to mention his girth, and you had a walking clothing disaster of monumental proportions. Obvious the man wasn't married or his wife hated him, Bernie decided. Otherwise she'd never let him walk out the door like that.

Bernie was trying to see if Estes was wearing a wedding ring as he pointed to the clock on the wall.

"Where the hell were you?" he demanded. "We have ten minutes to airtime. You were supposed to have been here fifteen minutes ago. Why are you late?"

"They're late because they've been too busy trying to find out which one of us killed Hortense to pay attention to the time," Reginald called out. He pointed to Libby. "Ask that one."

Estes' face grew flushed. He turned to Libby.

"What have you done?" he demanded.

"I didn't do anything," she replied.

A statement, Bernie reflected, that wasn't exactly true. But Bernie was happy to see that Libby was getting a little better at holding her own. Her chin was up and she had her hands on her hips.

"I'll thank you not to make things worse than they already are," Estes told her.

Bernie laughed. "And how is that possible?"

"I just don't want to see the *Hortense Calabash Show* get tagged as a bad luck show. Then I'll never get people to come on it."

"Bad luck show?" Libby asked.

"Yes." Estes rubbed his nose. "A bad luck show. Like *Poltergeist*."

"That was a movie."

"Fine. Then the *Brick House Saloon*. Five people on the set were seriously injured."

"Because they were careless," Bernie said.

"That's not what the tabloids said," Estes pointed out.

Consuela interrupted. "Do you really think this show is cursed?"

Give me strength, Bernie thought. "No. I don't think this show is cursed," Bernie told her. "I think we have someone on the show who didn't like Hortense a whole hell of a lot, and the police think that too."

"The police?" Pearl squeaked as she popped up from behind the chair Reginald had been sitting in, dust rag in hand.

The woman looks terrified, Bernie reflected. She wondered what she had to be terrified about. And what she had been dusting? The rungs of the chair?

Brittany sniffed. "I can't believe you think we're all suspects," she huffed.

"The police do," Bernie shot back.

"Ridiculous," Brittany said.

That woman is wearing way too much Prada, Bernie thought as she watched Brittany drift toward the door.

"Then who do you think ah . . . assisted Hortense toward the other side?" Bernie asked her. "Or do you think this was an accident too?"

"I don't know." Brittany combed back her hair with her fingers. "Maybe a vagrant who wandered in did it? Maybe one of the camera crew did?"

"Why should it be one of them?" Bernie asked her.

"Why shouldn't it?" Brittany countered.

"Because this murder wasn't random," Bernie told her.

"Murder is such a harsh word," Reginald observed.

"Then what would you call what happened to Hortense?" Bernie asked him.

"A mishap. Just like Estes said."

Brittany pursed her lips. "In the end it doesn't really matter," she said after a moment of reflection.

"Doesn't matter?" Libby said. "Someone being killed doesn't matter?"

Brittany gave her a pitying look. "My dear girl, I meant that in the cosmic sense. We're all just grains of sand on the cosmic beach of life."

My god, Bernie thought. Could we get anymore trite?

But apparently Brittany could, because the next words out of her mouth were, "What's done is done. What's important is that we face the future together."

"What future?" Consuela demanded. "What are you talking about? We have no future. We're contestants on a television show." Then she whirled around and pointed to Bernie and Libby.

"And why are you two in charge?" she demanded. "If

anything, the police should be investigating you! You were the ones who were going through Hortense's files looking for the ingredients."

Bernie was just about to say something but Libby got there first.

"How can you lie like that?" she demanded. "Aren't you embarrassed? You were the one going through the files, not us."

Consuela tossed her hair and appealed to the other contestants.

"I'm not lying," she told them. She gestured toward Libby and Bernie. "How do we know you didn't steal the list?"

"Yeah," Reginald said. "I think Consuela deserves an answer. How do we know that the investigators don't need to be investigated?"

Bernie was not happy to see that Pearl and Brittany started clapping. She was about to frame her answer when Eric Royal walked through the door. Bernie was relieved to see that he'd gotten a haircut and that he was wearing a tweed jacket, blue shirt, and brown and blue tie, instead of the ensemble he'd had on the day Hortense was killed.

"It doesn't matter," Eric told them.

"How can it not matter?" Reginald cried.

"I'll explain in a moment," Eric said. "But first I suggest we all spend a moment of silent meditation. Hortense and I liked to do that before all our shows."

"We should meditate on Hortense," Jean La Croix called out. "It is only right."

Consuela rolled her eyes. "Oh please," she said.

"No. It is a good thing to do," Jean La Croix insisted. "She was a great lady."

"She was a bitch," Consuela said.

La Croix put his hand to his throat. "Where I come from, it is considered bad to speak ill of the dead."

"Come on," Consuela said. "You hated her as much as anyone else, and you can stop with the phony accent."

"Looks who is talking," La Croix replied. "The only time you ever set foot in the Dominican Republic was when you took a cruise."

"Well, the only time you saw Haiti was when you were watching the Travel Channel in Attica."

"You lie!" La Croix screamed.

Uh-oh Bernie thought as she watched La Croix heading toward Consuela. She was thinking, Emergency room, here we come, when Estes started bellowing. La Croix froze.

"That is enough!" Estes yelled. "I will not have this type of behavior on my show." He looked around. Bernie was interested to see that La Croix, Pearl, Consuela, Reginald, and Brittany were looking at the floor. "Good," Estes said into the ensuing quiet. "We have some changes that Eric wants to go over with you, and since we have"—he consulted his watch—"only eight minutes left, I suggest you pay attention."

"Changes?" Pearl exclaimed. "What changes?"

Estes glared at her. "If you'll be quiet, you'll find out."

"Oh dear," Pearl said. "I don't do well with changes. I don't do well at all."

Brittany put her hands on her hips. "Why are we changing the format at this late date?"

"Yes," La Croix said. "For once I must agree with the queen."

"Excuse me," Brittany snapped. "Did you just call me a JAP?"

La Croix shrugged. "No. I'm calling you damned lucky to get away with what you did. I certainly wouldn't have. I don't have a daddy to help me out."

Bernie could see that Brittany had paled slightly under her make-up.

"And what does that mean?"

"You know what I'm talking about. And if you don't want everyone else to know, you'll shut up."

"What *are* you talking about?" Bernie asked.

Neither Brittany nor La Croix answered. Bernie followed their gaze. They were both looking at Estes. He was making snarling noises, and his color had become the most alarming shade of crimson. It would make a wonderful dress color, Bernie thought, but she was fairly positive it wasn't a good skin color.

"Shut up!" he bellowed. "Everyone just shut up."

There was dead silence in the room again.

Bernie watched the director's assistant step in.

"We've got three minutes to airtime," he cried.

It's going to be an interesting show, Bernie thought. An interesting show indeed.

At which point her sister's cell phone began to ring. She answered it. "Okay, Dad," she said after a moment went by.

"What was that about?" Bernie whispered after Libby hung up.

Her sister explained.

"So that's what La Croix was talking about," Bernie said.

Libby nodded. "I don't see how I can do what Dad wants me to."

Bernie glanced at the clock on the wall. They had two minutes to go. "Go ahead. So you and Brittany will be a little late walking onto the set."

"I don't know," Libby told her.

"Go on. What's the worst thing that can happen?"

"Estes can yell at me."

"Exactly," Bernie said.

Chapter 19

Libby looked at the camera staring back at her as the opening credits for the *Hortense Calabash Show* rolled across the monitor. She'd totally forgotten. Was she supposed to look at camera one or was it camera two or three or did it matter? Except, weren't they all focused on different parts of the room? But they could move around, so it probably didn't matter. Or did it?

For the life of her she couldn't recall what Eric had said. She must be getting early Alzheimer's. Or mad cow disease. Actually, she knew why she couldn't remember. She was too busy digesting what her father had asked her to ask Brittany. It was incredible. She just wished her dad had called after the show. She didn't need any distractions now. She caught Bernie giving her a worried glance. She tried to give her a smile. Then she took a deep breath. Okay, she told herself, forget everything. Forget about Brittany. Forget about the murder. Concentrate on what's happening now.

She could feel beads of sweat forming on her forehead. Should she wipe them off? Shouldn't she? If she didn't, the sweat would start running into her eyes and that would make her eyes tear, which in turn would make her eyeliner and mascara run, and she'd look like a raccoon.

But how could she wipe her forehead without looking like a total dork? Especially since she didn't have a Kleenex with her, and she couldn't go get one out of her backpack. She'd have to use her shirtsleeve, which was totally unacceptable.

Bernie never perspired when she got nervous. At least she never did it in places people could see. Why did she? No one else in her family had this problem except her. Libby started to fan herself with her hand and stopped herself even though she wanted to continue. But it was so hot under the lights. She couldn't stand the heat.

She should have worn something cooler; she'd meant to, but the only thing she had in her wardrobe that didn't make her arms look fat and her waist too big was this long-sleeved, wool-blend, light blue blouse. Her T-shirts were, as Bernie put it, beyond redemption, so she couldn't wear those, and her other white shirts were stained and frayed.

She should have gone clothes shopping. She should have bought that shirt Bernie had wanted her to get, Libby reflected as she glanced at Bernie, who was wearing the black pants she'd gotten in Paris and a pink V-neck silk sweater. *I should have gotten the shirt even if it was over two hundred dollars*, Libby thought. Bernie was right. It would have been worth the price. Libby clicked her tongue against her teeth as she studied her sister.

Bernie always looked relaxed and in control, just the way she did now. *Why can't I be like that?* Libby wondered as she snuck glances at everyone else. Why do I just want to go home and eat chocolate? She was sure no one else in the room felt that way. Everyone else in the studio looked calm and collected. Just like Bernie.

Except for Pearl, that is. Pearl was having a meltdown.

She was busy buttoning and rebuttoning her cardigan. Suddenly Libby liked Pearl a whole lot better than she formerly had.

Libby found her gaze straying to Estes. His color had returned to normal, which was good because for a few minutes there she'd thought they'd be calling Marvin's father to come and take him away. Which, considering Estes' size, would have been a hard job. How did one get four hundred pounds of dead weight on a stretcher anyway? Libby wondered. She shuddered briefly. It sounded like the beginning of a bad joke.

But in any case, she didn't have to worry about that. Right now Estes was up in the production box, or whatever it was that Bernie had called it, talking to the guy sitting in front of the console with all the levers and dials on it. Libby forgot what he was called too. Engineer? Production manager? Production assistant? Who cared? She was too nervous to remember anything.

I am going to make such a fool of myself, she thought. Especially with this new format.

Why, oh why was everyone judging the outcome? Having Hortense as the judge was bad; having the other panelists act as judges was worse. They were going to say terrible things about her cooking. Why shouldn't they? It certainly wasn't in their interest to say anything nice. And as if that wasn't bad enough, she and Bernie were the first contestants. And tomorrow if she and Bernie won, they were going to cohost the show. Great. Libby could feel her temples starting to throb.

Tomorrow they were contracted to deliver two dinners for eight and twelve, respectively, as well as twelve dozen cookies for the Holiday Spirit Day at the Longely Library, not to mention the potato pancakes for twenty for the Jewish Center. At least she'd already made the applesauce and three-quarters of the cookies.

But that wasn't even counting all the salads, muffins, scones, soups, and breads they had to make for their regular customers. Libby shook her head. It looked as if she and Bernie were going to be working through the night.

They'd have to finish up everything that needed to be done, because Amber and Googie certainly weren't going to, although Amber had promised she'd get a head start on tomorrow's soups. Maybe she could pay Amber and Googie to stay up and help her. Or maybe she could cajole Marvin into helping, even though the thought of Marvin in the kitchen was enough to make her shudder. *I must have been nuts to agree to this*, Libby told herself. Her mother never would have. She would have just faced Bree down.

So what if they lost Bree's business? Big deal. So they'd tighten their belts a little. It wasn't anything she hadn't done before. At least she wouldn't be making a fool of herself for everyone in the country to see.

Which included her dad. And Clyde. And Rob. And Brandon and the guys down in R.J's. And Marvin. Probably even Marvin's dad was watching. She'd never be able to show her face again. Then Libby realized that Eric was talking. It would probably be good if she listened, she decided as she tried to focus on what he was saying.

She watched Eric rub his hands together as he stood in the center of the room in front of one of the Viking stoves.

"Okay, all you people out there," he said. "Welcome to the *Hortense Calabash Show*. Today, in fact all this week, we have something special planned for you. Unfortunately, Hortense can't be with you this week. She wanted to; in fact, she was dying to, but an unforeseen medical emergency has arisen that she's been forced to contend with."

That's one way of putting it, Libby thought again as Eric repeated the same line that he had earlier in the day.

Eric kept rubbing his hands. "So I guess you'll have to put up with me and my cohosts instead," he continued.

As Libby watched him, she realized that Eric looked different somehow. It wasn't the clothes, although that helped. Or the new haircut and glasses. So what was it? A moment later, Libby had the answer.

It was Eric's posture. Eric was standing up straighter. He looked more self-assured. As if removing Hortense from his life had given him his confidence back, Libby mused. Judging from what she'd seen of Eric and Hortense together, it probably had had that effect, Libby decided. Was that reason enough to kill someone? Sounded like it could be to her.

Eric smiled.

Libby decided he needed to get his teeth whitened.

"But don't worry," he intoned. "Hortense made out the list herself and I'm checking it twice." He stopped for a moment. "Get it. Checking it twice. Naughty or nice? No? Just a little Christmas humor, folks. But be assured I am following Hortense's list to the letter."

The list, Libby thought. She'd forgotten about the list. As far as she knew, no one had found it yet. Then she noticed that Estes was frantically drawing the flat of his hand against his throat. Libby looked at the teleprompter. Nope. Eric's last comments weren't there.

Obviously, Estes wanted Eric to keep to the script. Or maybe he just didn't like what he was saying. She brought her attention back to Eric. She could tell from the way he was standing that he'd gone back to reading from the teleprompter again.

Eric smoothed down his tie.

"I bet all of you out there in TVland want to know what our special ingredient is." He paused for a moment for dramatic effect. "Well, our special ingredient for today is"—another long pause—"venison."

"Venison?" Libby repeated out loud.

Eric shot her a dirty look. "That's what I just said," he told her.

"Oh my god," Libby mumbled as Eric continued reading off the teleprompter. "I am so screwed."

Chapter 20

Libby tried to focus on Eric as she found herself wondering what Hortense would think of Eric's performance. Not much, she was willing to wager. Whatever you could say about Hortense, she'd had presence. Which Eric did not. She turned her attention back to him.

"Venison was a staple of our forebears," Eric was saying. "Many people still make use of it today in this world of prepackaged food. It is also known as deer meat, although the term is sometimes applied to elk, moose, buffalo, and caribou as well.

"The game we are using comes from the white-tailed or Virginian deer, the species most commonly hunted in the United States." Eric drew a breath and continued. "Deer has always played an important role in the human diet, as archaeological evidence shows. In fact, in many societies it has been the primary protein source."

Libby looked at Eric. He was still reading off the teleprompter, still giving everyone a lecture on deer as a food source. The lecture sounded just like one of Bernie's, Libby couldn't help thinking. The way he was talking made it sound as if everyone ate the stuff. But she'd never cooked venison in her life, let alone eaten it, and she was willing to wager her sister hadn't either.

Eating Bambi just wasn't an appetizing idea to either one of them. She remembered when her father had gotten some venison steaks from Clyde, and her mother had refused to let him bring them in the house.

"It's barbaric," her mother had said.

"It's life," her father had replied.

"Not in my kitchen it isn't," her mother had retorted, and that had been that.

Libby's only consolation was that Reginald Palmer wasn't looking too happy at this moment. Maybe he didn't know much about cooking game either. That gave her a little hope. Not much, but a little.

She'd thought that Eric would choose something like partridge or quail or wild turkey or even that old chestnut, a goose. She thought he'd choose something Christmasy. Or literary like Hortense would have done. Maybe something out of *The Twelve Days of Christmas.* Something like a partridge for a partridge in a pear tree. Or a goose out of Dickens' *Christmas Carol.* She'd been ready for those. She wasn't ready for *Little House on the Prairie.*

As she and Bernie moved to their cooking station, Libby's mind was whirling, trying to remember what she knew about venison. Libby turned to her sister. She was about to say, "Tell me you've cooked this before," when she remembered they were miked. She coughed instead.

Bernie looked at her and raised an eyebrow. Libby nodded toward the mike. Bernie covered hers up. Libby did the same.

"What do you know about venison?" she whispered.

"It has no fat," Bernie told her.

Libby noticed she was being careful to keep her voice down too.

"Which means it gets tough."

Libby was just about to add something about the meat

getting dry when she realized that Eric was walking in their direction. Great, she thought as he reached them. The next thing she knew, he was standing between them.

"Well," he said as he, in Libby's opinion, shamelessly mugged for the camera. "Here we have the two Simmons sisters, the movers behind A Little Taste of Heaven."

Libby forced herself to smile.

"What are you gals planning?" Eric boomed. "Can you give us a hint?"

Libby froze. Hortense had never done anything like this. Libby felt as if she was on one of those pregame spots, the kind before the football game, where the announcer goes, "So, coach, what's the game plan?" and sticks the mike in his face.

Eric leaned in closer to Libby.

"Come on," he coaxed. "Give us a hint."

What should she say? She didn't have a game plan. She didn't have anything. She opened her mouth to speak, but no words were coming out of her mouth. This was even worse than she thought it would be. She could feel her stomach clenching. Everyone there, all the guys in the camera crew were watching her. Those cameras were like big eyes, staring at her. She looked at the clock on the studio wall. It felt as if a half hour had gone by. She couldn't believe it was only thirty seconds. She felt as if she wanted to sink through the floor.

Libby, focus, she told herself.

She was just about to say something when Bernie stepped in.

"Well, Eric," she said, using her best TV voice, "as you know, venison tends to be on the dry side, so the usual preparation for this kind of meat is to grind it up and make it into sausage or marinate it or braise it."

Eric nodded. "But both of those take time," he pointed out.

Libby almost expected him to say, "Back to you, Chet."

"Yes, they do, Eric," Bernie replied.

From the tone of her voice, Libby wouldn't have been surprised if her sister slapped Eric on the back.

"I guess that's a problem my sister and I will have to solve," she said.

Eric raised his eyebrows. "And how are you going to do that?"

Bernie gave out a girlish little chuckle. "Now that would be telling, wouldn't it?" And she reached over and chucked him under the chin.

Libby started to smile as she watched Eric freeze. He obviously hadn't expected Bernie to do that. But a moment later he had himself in hand.

"Well, good luck," Eric said to both of them, and he moved off to talk to Reginald.

"You okay?" Bernie mouthed.

Libby nodded. She'd regained her equilibrium. "Thanks."

"No problem."

"I know how we can marinate the meat if we need to." The idea had come to her while Bernie and Eric had been talking.

"How?" Bernie asked.

"We can heat it in the marinade and let it sit. That'll speed up the process."

She'd done it last week with coq au vin, when she'd forgotten to marinate the chicken. She had to say, the dish had turned out pretty well.

"Very good," Bernie said. "We're going to kick ass," she whispered in Libby ear.

"I hope so," Libby replied while she looked down to see what else they'd been given to work with.

In no particular order they had cranberries, dried chestnuts, leeks, potatoes, red wine, walnuts, endive, fennel, chicken broth, three oranges, eggs, sugar, butter, fresh thyme, oregano, sage, salt and pepper, pork fat, a bar of dark chocolate, and a pint of milk.

Libby half listened as Eric went through and named each ingredient for the audience. He pointed to the clock on the wall.

"Ladies and gentlemen," he read off the prompter, "our contestants have one hour to make a three- or four-course Christmas dinner. The special ingredient must be used in at least two of those dishes." He turned to Libby, Bernie, and Reginald. "Are you ready?"

Reginald and Bernie nodded.

Eric nodded back.

Libby could feel her heart thumping in her chest.

"Good," Eric said. "On your mark, get set, go."

Libby took a deep breath and focused on the ingredients on the table.

"What do you think?" Bernie said.

"I think we should shoot ourselves now."

"Besides that," Bernie said.

Libby closed her eyes and opened them.

"Okay." Suddenly, her mind wasn't blank anymore. She didn't know how or where the ideas were coming from, but they were there. "How about we do a composed salad. We'll oven roast the endive and fennel and use that as a base; then we'll layer it with thin quick-seared slices of venison, and finish it off with a sprinkling of chopped glazed walnuts and a drizzle of a red wine reduction."

Bernie bit her lip.

"I'm a little worried about the rare venison part. It might be a little gamey if it's rare."

Libby realized she was picking on her nails again and stopped. "So what would you suggest?"

"That we grind up the meat with the pork fat and make it into sausage instead."

"We don't have any casings."

"We could use endive leaves."

Libby thought it over. "I like the idea, but I don't think

the presentation is going to look very nice," she concluded. "And in this case, presentation is half the battle."

Bernie was silent for a moment. Then she said, "You're probably right. How about if we scatter a few strips of orange zest over the venison? That should help balance off the taste."

Libby nodded. That would work.

Bernie moved her ring up and down her finger. "The salad reminds me of a seared duck breast salad."

"Exactly," Libby said. She looked at the clock. Two minutes had already gone by since Eric had announced they were starting. They couldn't afford to waste much more time planning. "And then for the main course," she said, thinking out loud, "we could cut the venison up into small chunks, lard the cubes with the pork fat, and marinate them in the red wine, sage, oregano, and thyme.

"After which we could sauté them quickly and let them finish cooking with the presoaked chestnuts in the wine and the chicken broth."

"Chestnuts usually take an hour and a half of soaking to soften," Bernie said.

"Not if we presoak them in hot water and break them into smaller pieces. Then we'll cook down the liquid almost to a glaze consistency."

Bernie was nodding her head. Libby could tell she was liking her ideas.

"Let's add some small rounds of sautéed potatoes and some braised leeks to finish the dish," Bernie added.

Libby drummed her fingers on the table. They needed something for color contrast. They'd already used the orange zest, so that was a no-go.

"How about we fry some sage leaves and use that as a topping?"

After all, the Thai used fried cinnamon leaves as a topping on their food all the time.

"I like it," Bernie said. "I like it a lot. We could use chestnuts for dessert."

"Except we've already used them in the venison," Libby reminded her.

"So what? We can use ingredients more than once."

"True, but let's do this instead." And Libby explained what she had in mind. "I'm thinking we should do something with the cranberries. We can make a compote with the cranberries, oranges, and sugar and serve that over a custard flavored with fennel seeds and—"

"Chocolate."

"Chocolate curls," Libby said "Large chocolate curls. We'll use them the way we'd use rolled cookies."

Bernie nodded her approval.

Another good thing about the chocolate rolls, from Libby's point of view, was that they didn't take long to make, and they always impressed people. Suddenly Libby realized that she wasn't nervous anymore. She was too busy thinking about what order she and Bernie had to do things in, or as Julia would have put it, she was busy planning her order of battle.

Okay. First they had to cut up the venison, lard it, and get it in its marinade and heat it up, after which they had to break up the chestnuts and put them to soak. Then they had to prep the leeks and the fennel and pop them in the oven.

After that, they had to peel the potatoes and make the custard, because the custard had to cool. Next they'd do the cranberries, then they'd melt the chocolate and spread it out on a layer of wax paper to harden. Then she'd use a vegetable peeler to make it into curls.

Libby closed her eyes and rested her fingers on her temples as she tried to picture how everything fit together. She just hoped they had enough burners. She thought for a moment.

Yes, they did. Of course, she could always bake the custard. But that would mean they'd have to go in the oven now, and she wanted the temperature on high, high for roasting the fennel and the leeks. No, she decided, she'd do better sticking to her original plan and make the custard on top of the stove. It was safer that way.

Libby turned on the oven.

"Do you think we need a fourth dish?" Bernie asked as she started cutting up the venison into cubes and slices.

"No," Libby said. "I think we'll be fine with what we've got."

And she meant it too. For the first time since she'd stepped into the studio, she felt like she was in control.

Chapter 21

Sean looked around R.J.'s before settling back between Rob, Marvin, and Clyde. Originally the three of them had suggested sitting in a booth. Even though they denied it, he knew it was because they thought it would be easier on him.

But he was damned if he wasn't going to hunker down at the bar like he used to, damned if he wouldn't walk in here under his own power instead of in a wheelchair. Even if he did walk slow, even if it did take him a while to get where he was going. Otherwise, what was the point?

This was the first time he'd set foot in the bar since he'd gotten sick, and it felt good. It felt real good. It felt good to be out of his room. It felt good to be back. He hadn't realized how much he'd missed the place.

How he'd missed the peanut shells on the floor and the dart games and the pool table and the tacky holiday decorations and the people chatting each other up and the smells of frying food and beer. He'd spent many a Friday night happy hour here talking with his buddies when he got off duty. He'd even tried to get Rose to come join them, but she'd always refused. Called it his time with the guys. Said she wasn't going to interfere with that. He shook his head. That woman had a lot of good sense. It would be hard to find another one like her. In fact, he was fairly certain he couldn't. Not that he was interested. Not that he was looking. He had his girls and that was enough for him.

Sean decided he was glad Clyde had prevailed. Clyde had been right. Clyde was right about a lot of things. Heaven knows, if he'd listened to him a little more closely he might still have his job. Or maybe not. With political firestorms you never knew which way the flames were going to go.

But this one thing he was sure about. It was definitely better watching the *Hortense Calabash Show* on a big, high-def screen with a group of guys than it was watching it at home alone. Normally the TV at R.J.'s would be set on a sports or news channel, but not tonight. Tonight everyone was watching his daughters, Libby and Bernie, cooking. It was an amazing world they were living in.

It was too bad Rose couldn't see it as well, Sean thought as he watched Rob take a sip of his beer.

"They're going to win," Rob said.

Sean took another swallow of his Bud. "Of course they're going to win," Sean told him. Could there be any doubt? They were his daughters, weren't they?

Sean noticed that Marvin was shaking his head.

"I don't know," he said. "This Reginald fellow is pretty tricky. Look at what he's doing."

Sean could see what Marvin was pointing to. He watched Reginald oh so casually walking by Libby and Bernie's station. His neck was craned in their direction.

"He's looking to see what they're cooking," Marvin muttered.

Sean shot him a look. "Don't worry. My girls can take care of themselves."

"But it's not fair," Marvin observed.

Clyde snorted. "Welcome to the world." He ate a peanut and leaned forward a little. "Look at what the miscreant is doing now."

As Sean watched, he saw Reginald "accidentally" slip and bump into Libby's shoulder.

"No," he cried as she almost dropped the pot she was carrying.

But she didn't. Somehow she managed to hold on to it.

"That was a foul," Clyde said.

"It certainly was," Sean agreed. "He should be penalized for that move."

That son of a bitch. He hadn't liked Reginald Palmer from the second he'd been introduced on screen. In the old days, if someone had tried something like that with his girls, he would have found himself on the wrong end of some really bad luck. It was amazing how karma worked.

Sean smiled as one of the guys down the bar called out, "You go, girl," to the television screen.

Someone else hooted and hollered. "Yeah," he yelled at the screen. "You show him a thing or two," as Bernie "accidentally" stamped on Reginald's foot.

Sean laughed as he watched Reginald trying not to grimace as he hobbled back to his station.

Clyde shook his head. "Who woulda thunk? Cooking as a blood sport."

"Well, it certainly can be," Sean said, thinking of what had happened to Hortense. You couldn't get much more lethal than that.

He swallowed down the last of his beer. This was so good. Nectar of the gods. Maybe it was because it was the first one he'd had in ages. Bernie's cocktails were all right, but a straight-up brew was what he craved.

He'd asked her to buy him a six-pack from time to time, but she'd always come home with this strange stuff that people—unfathomably, in his opinion—paid huge sums of money for, so he'd stopped asking. Who would want to drink something like apricot ale or an eggnog porter or a raspberry stout? What had happened to plain old beer?

And he couldn't exactly tell Bernie that he didn't like her selection. First off, it would have been rude, and secondly, there was always the fact that he wasn't supposed to be drinking anyway. Not really. According to the doctors, it wasn't good for his condition.

Ha! Screw his condition. What the hell did the medical establishment know? They were real good at telling you what not to do, but they weren't so good at telling you what would make you better. Recently Libby had been trying to enforce that particular prohibition. She'd probably skin him alive if she found out what he was doing. But who was going to tell her? Certainly not Clyde or Rob.

Then Sean's glance rested on Marvin.

Ah, yes.

He'd forgotten about him. Sean sighed as he looked at him cracking peanuts open and eating them. He'd have to have a word with him, Sean decided as Marvin brushed peanut shells from his shirt and watched them fall on the floor. He'd have to make sure they were on the same page, as it were.

Sean turned back to the TV. Bernie was glazing the walnuts, dipping them in sugar syrup, and then carefully laying them out on wax paper to dry. He had to say she was doing a great job.

"So what do you think?" Clyde said.

Sean answered without taking his eyes off the set. "I think I'm sorry I'm not going to have a chance to eat the meal they're cooking."

"No," Clyde said. He dropped his voice. "I'm talking about the other thing."

"Oh, that thing," Sean said, his eyes still glued to the screen.

"Yes. That thing."

"What about it?"

"Who do you think is the one . . . ?"

"That killed Hortense?" Brandon said.

Sean looked up at him. He'd forgotten how big the guy was. He was really huge. Plus he had enormous hands. When Sean had been on the force, he'd seen the result of some of his work. But that had been a while ago. He'd calmed down since then.

"I don't know what you're talking about," Sean told him. He felt he should at least make a minimal effort at denial.

Brandon grinned. He wasn't buying it, but Sean had known he wouldn't.

"Sure you don't," he said.

"Really," Sean insisted.

Brandon's grin grew even wider. "We have a pool going. Care to wager a small amount of money on the guilty party?"

Sean laughed. "Thanks, but no thanks." He wondered how much longer Bree was going to be able to keep a lid on this thing. Not much longer, he wagered.

"Here." Brandon pushed the can of beer he was holding across the counter to Sean. "On the house. A welcome back present. Although"—he softened his voice—"don't tell Libby I gave you this."

"Not too likely," Sean replied. "So why do you think that Hortense is dead?" he asked Brandon.

Brandon snorted. "Easy. Bree Nottingham's cleaning lady told me. She heard the great lady, as she likes to think of herself, talking on the phone."

Sean threw up his hands. It was ridiculous to even try and pretend. "So who is the odds-on favorite in the pool you got going?"

Brandon scratched his chin. "Right now we have Reginald out in front, followed by Consuela and La Croix, with Brittany and Pearl bringing up the rear."

"What about Estes and Eric?"

"Eric. Estes." Brandon slapped his forehead with the palm of his hand. "I forgot about those two. How could I be so dumb? I gotta put them on the board. This is going to mess up everything."

Sean laughed as Brandon went charging off.

"You think I should blow him in for illegal gambling?" Clyde asked.

Sean nodded. "Yeah. Call up right now and have the guys come down and raid the place."

Marvin's eyes widened. He looked at Clyde. "You wouldn't do that, would you?"

"He's kidding," Sean told him. He shook his head. Even though Libby said he did, as far as he could see, Marvin had no sense of humor at all.

"So who's your favorite?" Clyde asked him.

Sean thought his answer over. "I'd have to say Brittany."

"Brittany?" Rob voice was incredulous. "Why Brittany? The only thing she seems capable of doing is talking on her cell phone."

Clyde jumped in before Sean could answer. "Well, she's capable of a few other things," he said.

"Like what?" Rob demanded. "I can't see her booby-trapping an oven."

Sean popped a peanut into his mouth. "First of all, it's not that difficult, and second of all, you should never underestimate the power of a woman," he said, remembering the time his wife had managed to break into his safe so she could throw out the pictures of his old girlfriend.

"All right," Rob conceded. "Maybe what you say is true. Maybe she can booby-trap an oven. But why would she want to?"

Clyde looked at Sean.

"Tell him," Sean ordered.

"Well," Clyde replied, "she did get a whole heap of people sick with salmonella poisoning."

"She seems like such a nice lady," Marvin said.

Sean heard himself groan.

"Even though one thing has nothing to do with the other," Marvin hastily concluded.

"No, it doesn't," Clyde agreed. "It has to do with sanitation. This happened at a Bar Mitzvah at Congregation Concordia out in Jersey. Sent three people to the hospital. The admitting nurse's sister worked for Hortense. Word gets around.

"I figure maybe she was using that information to make Brittany do whatever she wanted. After all, if anyone found out, Brittany would be ruined. No more book sales for her. People don't usually buy cookbooks from people who have sent other people to the hospital with food poisoning."

"But how do you know Hortense was blackmailing Brittany?" Rob asked.

"He doesn't," Sean told him. "It's just a working theory. Actually, I'm hoping Libby asked Brittany if Hortense was blackmailing her."

Marvin put his beer glass down and wiped his mouth with the back of his hand.

"Why should she do that?" he inquired.

"Because I asked her to," Sean told him. "I called her up right before she went on the air."

"And you expect Brittany to admit to something like that?" Brandon asked.

Sean looked up. Brandon was drying his hands with a dish towel. He didn't remember Brandon moving so quietly. Quite the opposite.

"That would give her a motive."

"No," Sean answered. "I don't expect Brittany to admit anything. I just want to see what her reaction is."

Brandon shook his head and moved down the bar to wait on someone who was signaling him.

"Did the admitting nurse's sister tell you too?" Marvin demanded.

Sean took a sip of his new beer. "The Internet is an amazing thing," he noted. "If you know where to look. Actually, it's a matter of public record."

"Like with Boomer . . ." Clyde said.

Marvin wrinkled his nose. "Who is that?"

"Jean La Croix," Sean said. "It's on record that he served time in Attica and that he worked for Hortense in an early release program when he got out."

"Poor guy," Clyde added. "He must have thought he was walking into a good thing. He must have thought he could just smooth his way through everything."

"Yeah," Sean said. "He didn't realize he was spending time with someone that would make Ma Baker look nice."

"Who's Ma Baker?" Marvin asked.

"A well-known criminal," Sean answered. "Don't they teach you anything in school these days?"

"Personally," Clyde said, "when all is said and done, I'm liking Reginald for this. According to my sources, Hortense got him kicked off whatever that fancy food magazine is called for taking bribes. From what I understand, it was a good gig." Clyde paused to eat another peanut. "That might make a man cranky."

"True," Sean answered. "But let's not forget La Croix. Hortense could have ruined his reputation. How many people do you think would be buying stuff from him if they knew he learned how to cook in Attica instead of Paris? All those Brooklyn ladies would be running in the opposite direction."

Clyde grimaced.

"You don't agree?" Sean asked him.

"I'm not so sure, Cap. These days people in Brooklyn are pretty liberal."

Sean was about to reply when Marvin broke into the conversation. "So why don't you question him?" he asked.

"Because," Sean explained, "we have no evidence, and since we have no official power—"

"Bree Nottingham not withstanding," Clyde added.

"We just have to watch and wait and see what develops."

Clyde ate another peanut.

"While we're on the subject of people with lots to lose, there's always Consuela."

"And Pearl. Don't forget Pearl," Sean reminded him. "Charging people twelve dollars a pound for reconstituted mashed potatoes. That's almost fraud." He took another sip of his beer. "The problem as I see it is there are an embarrassment of suspects or as Bernie would say, 'A surplus of suspects.' What we need is another angle."

Clyde brushed the mound of peanut shells in front of him onto the floor. "I wonder if Hortense kept records?"

"Hasn't Lucy looked?" Sean asked.

"Not as far as I know," Clyde replied.

"Interesting," Sean said.

"Isn't it though."

Sean smiled at Clyde. Clyde smiled back.

This is why Bree had called his daughters in. Lucy did a slipshod job. Always had, always would. In most investigations of this kind, you started with the victim and worked outward. Media stories to the contrary, strangers didn't kill most people. People they knew did. And it was usually for one of three reasons: money, love, or revenge.

Sean stroked his chin. He really needed to get a better razor. He'd ask Bernie to get him one the next time she went out.

"The question is how to get to them?"

"I think you left your glasses in the house," Clyde said.

"I think so too," Sean agreed.

"But you don't wear glasses," Marvin said. "I do. Oh," he said when Sean didn't reply. "I get it."

"Very good." Sean took another sip of his beer.

Of course, they could just let things go and see what developed. Or they could be a little more proactive. Over the years, Sean had always found that the proactive approach worked better for him. His dad always used to say, "If you wanted to get the apples down, you had to shake the tree." Or was it, "You had to crush the grapes to get the wine." It didn't matter. The idea was the same. Sean consulted his watch. If they left now, they'd have time to carry out what he had in mind.

"No point in telling Lucy. I'm sure he's busy with his holiday preparations."

"True, true," Clyde said. "Got to make the house look nice and wrap all those presents." He nodded toward the TV set. "And everyone there is busy with the show."

Sean nodded.

"Probably will be for a while," Clyde continued.

Sean nodded again.

"I'm thinking Rob and I should take a drive up to the estate."

Marvin raised a hand. "And me," Marvin said. "I can help too."

"No," Sean said. "You stay here and keep Clyde company. I need you to report on what Libby and Bernie did so that I can talk to them about it."

Marvin hung his head. "Fine," he mumbled.

Oh God, Sean thought. Give me a break.

"Libby will never forgive me if something happens to you."

Marvin didn't say anything. Sean tried again. "Neither will your dad."

Marvin shrugged his shoulders. "So what," he muttered. "Who cares?"

Great, Sean thought. Just great. Marvin. Just what he wanted to deal with. A sensitive soul. He and Clyde exchanged looks. He knew he should just tell Marvin goodbye and get going. But somehow he couldn't. After all, the kid had stolen his dad's hearse for him. He did owe him something.

And Libby would get upset if she found out that Sean had excluded him. Although maybe not from this. Maybe she'd be upset if she included him. That was the trouble with Libby. She was so emotional. You never knew what was going to set her off. But this he did know: He was going to regret what he was about to say. He said it anyway.

"All right," he told Marvin. "Let's move."

Marvin beamed. "Super," he cried as he jumped up.

Amazing, Sean thought as he watched him get his leg tangled up in one of the barstool legs. Both he and the barstool hit the floor.

"Good going," one of the guys down toward the end yelled.

Everyone else in the place clapped and hooted and hollered.

"You okay?" Sean asked Marvin as he got up.

Marvin didn't say anything. He just picked up the stool and dusted himself off.

"Are you okay?" Sean repeated.

"I'm fine," he mumbled.

Sean noticed that Marvin's ears had turned as red as Santa's suit.

Sean turned and looked at Clyde. He was standing there shaking his head.

I am losing my mind, Sean thought as he and Rob and Marvin headed for the door. The only consolation he had was that this time Marvin wasn't driving.

Chapter 22

"Maybe this isn't such a good idea after all," Rob said to Sean.

"It'll be fine," Sean assured him, even though he was beginning to have doubts about the wisdom of his plan himself. Maybe they shouldn't be doing this. On the other hand, he couldn't think of another way to get the information he needed.

Sean looked at Hortense's mansion through the light veil of snow that had begun to fall. His perceptions were off. The place was bigger than he'd remembered. Like twice as big. He sighed. Well, they'd just have to move faster, that's all. But between his slowness and Marvin's clumsiness . . . he hated to admit it, but now he was a little worried.

But it was still going to be an easy in, easy out deal. That hadn't changed. They were going to use the studio entrance and go from there into Hortense's office and master bedroom, both of which, according to Clyde (Sean didn't ask him how he knew; maybe he should have), were located in the west wing of the house, as opposed to the studio, which was in the east wing.

Sean didn't expect anyone to stop them. Why should

they? Everyone was in the studio filming the cooking show. And if there was a security man posted, they could always turn around and leave. Or as his dad liked to say, "No harm, no foul."

"I still don't understand what we're looking for," Marvin grumbled as Rob parked his car behind the curve that led into the parking lot.

He was doing that per Sean's instructions. No point in being seen if you didn't have to be, Sean reckoned.

"Marvin, it's simple," Sean told him, trying to keep impatience out of his voice. "We're looking for anything that looks suspicious."

"But how will we know?"

"Tinkerbell will point the way."

Marvin blinked.

Great, Sean thought. *Now I have to apologize again.* He took a deep breath and told Marvin he was sorry. Libby would never forgive him if he didn't. And he did have a tendency to be intolerant. And sarcastic. After all, Marvin's question was fair. Maybe, Sean told himself, he was annoyed with himself because, if truth be told, he really didn't know what they were looking for either, at least not in the definitive way that Marvin wanted to hear.

This was strictly a fishing expedition. If he was still on the force and applied for a search warrant on these grounds, the DA would throw his ass out the door. But he wasn't on the force.

Sean took another deep breath while he figured out what he was going to say. "Okay," he finally told Marvin after a couple of seconds had passed. "We're looking for anything that has anything to do with Consuela or La Croix or Pearl or any of the other people on the show."

"You mean like employment records or health records?" Rob asked.

Sean nodded. "Or bills or insurance forms or IOUs or anything that has anyone's name on it," he added.

Given the circumstances, it was the best way for them to go. Not that they were doing anything wrong. After all, Lucy had invited them to investigate. And this was a murder scene. Except Lucy wouldn't see it that way. He'd see Sean as having shown him up.

Too bad he hadn't gotten Sean's message. That was the trouble with technology. It had a tendency to malfunction. Sean chuckled. It was terrible the way things disappeared in the . . . what was the word Bernie used? Ah, yes. The ethernet.

Sean glanced at his watch again. It was getting up there. They had to hustle.

"You know," Marvin told him as Rob got Sean's wheelchair out of the backseat of his SUV, "I saw this movie once where the bad guy had this little black notebook, and on each page it had the name of a person, and next to it, it had the amount of money the man was blackmailing them for and how much they'd paid him. It was a ledger."

"Sounds like someone with a very orderly mind," Sean remarked.

In his experience, people didn't write down those kinds of things, at least not like that, not even people like Hortense. They tried not to make it easier for the cops if they possibly could.

"Maybe we'll get lucky," Marvin said. "Maybe we'll find something like that."

"Maybe," Sean said. He hoped they would, but he wasn't counting on it.

"What'll we say if we meet somebody?" Marvin asked.

"We'll say we've come to pick up Hortense," Rob said.

"She's in my father's basement," Marvin pointed out.

"I was just joking," Rob said.

"Oh." Marvin stopped for a moment, thought, then said, "So what will we say?"

God give me strength, Sean thought as he patted his jacket pocket to make sure he hadn't dropped his wallet.

He always seemed to be doing that these days, that or losing his reading glasses. Getting old was a distinct pain in the ass.

Sean brushed the snowflakes out of his eyes. "What we'll say is that we're here to see Libby and Bernie."

Marvin nodded. "That's good. That's very good."

"I know," Sean told him. "That's why I said it."

After all, he should be good at this stuff, Sean thought. He'd been doing it for long enough. As he watched Marvin, he could see another thought was occurring to him, always a bad thing.

"They can't arrest us, can they?" he asked.

Sean noted the hint of panic in Marvin's voice. He decided lying would be kinder.

"No, of course not," he told him, even though technically they could be taken in for breaking and entering—but that was a big "could." He motioned for Rob to unfold his wheelchair.

"Come on, guys, let's get going."

Marvin punched the air. "We're on a mission. Well, we are, aren't we?"

Sean held back his sigh. "No," he corrected. "We're on a job." Too much exuberance in these kinds of situations led to carelessness, which led to mistakes.

Marvin nodded, but he looked so crestfallen that Sean heard himself saying, "Come on, Marvin. You can't take everything I say so seriously."

"Yeah," Rob added. "He's just a grumpy old man."

Marvin grinned. Then he and Rob started walking toward the house. Ordinarily Sean would have left someone in the vehicle, but he needed both Rob and Marvin. After all, three people could look through things a lot faster than two people could, a third faster to be precise.

He felt that old familiar jolt in his belly as he came to the door of Hortense's house. The adrenaline surge wasn't unpleasant. It wasn't unpleasant at all. In fact, he'd liked it. Okay. He loved it. His wife had called him an adrenaline junkie, and she'd been right. That's why he'd continued being a street cop long after he could have taken himself off of patrol.

He tried the door. It opened. Which was good, but in case it hadn't, he'd stopped by his house and gotten the old set of lock picks that he'd taken off a kid called the Loose Goose twenty years ago. Preparation for things was key. He guided the wheelchair inside and motioned for Rob and Marvin to follow him.

Okay, Hortense, Sean said to himself. Let's see what you got cooking.

Chapter 23

Sean looked around Hortense's bedroom. It was in line with what he'd seen of the rest of the house sizewise, he decided. What anyone would want with this much space was beyond him. The room was as big as some of the bowling alleys he'd been in and just about as cozy. Even the fireplace looked as if it belonged in a European castle. And those andirons. Was Hortense planning on deforesting the town?

The fact that everything was white certainly didn't help the warmth factor. He knew from Bernie that white was a cold color. Jeez. Even the Christmas decorations were white. White candles in the windows, a white wreath near the mantle, white lights strung around the walls.

He felt as if he was in the lobby of a fancy office building. Although, he had to say he did like the plasma TV screen hanging on the far wall. He wouldn't mind having one of those in his house. He was sure the girls wouldn't mind either. Unfortunately, even if he could afford it—which he couldn't—something like that was too big for his room at home. Actually, it was too big for any place in his house.

"I feel as if I'm in the North Pole," Rob whispered.

"Yeah. All we need are the elves," Marvin whispered back.

Sean nodded. Given the snow falling outside, Sean could understand why Rob felt that way. White outside. White inside. It was like Antarctica. If he wasn't careful, he'd get snow blindness. He took another look around. Given the size of the room, the place really had very little furniture, just a four-poster bed draped with some sort of white gauzy material that he didn't know the name of. But Bernie would. Not that it mattered.

Sean studied the bed for a moment. It was large enough to accommodate three adults comfortably, possibly even four. Sean couldn't imagine sleeping in something that huge. A person could get lost in there and have to hike out. As for the embroidered comforter, he wasn't sure, but it looked like white silk.

Personally, he liked something you could wash. He wondered if you could even dry clean this thing. Probably not. Probably when it got dirty Hortense would just throw it away and get something else. He took in the rest of the furnishings. Two night tables, two dressers, and a settee. All of them built to scale. But big as they were, there wasn't too much to look through in this room and that was good.

He sniffed. Among the scent of evergreens he caught the faint scent of stale liquor and remembered about Hortense's drinking. His eyes roamed around the room again. He was betting Hortense had her bottles stashed somewhere and that somewhere was one of two places, under her bed or in the closet.

"Hey, Rob," Sean said. "You want to do me a favor and look under the bed for me? See if there are any cartons." He felt gratified when Rob pulled one out.

"There are lots more under there," Rob informed him.

Sean lifted an empty bottle of Gray Goose out of the

carton. Even if it wasn't evidence, it was nice to know he hadn't lost the magic. He wondered if there were more empties in the closet. He motored over to it and opened the door. It was larger than his bedroom.

And it was filled to the gills. Evidently, Hortense had had enough clothes and the stuff that went with them to outfit a department store. In fact, the closet looked like a department store, or rather it looked like one of those boutiques Bernie was always buying her stuff from.

Everything was in apple pie order. All the shoes were shelved, as were all Hortense's bags. Hortense's clothes were arranged by season and category. It would take hours to go through everything, Sean reflected. But his gut told him that what he was looking for wasn't in here. It was in her office. From her TV show and looking at her house, Sean had gotten the impression that she was the kind of woman who lived by the adage, "A place for everything and everything in its place."

Nevertheless, he'd give the shebang a once-over just the same. People thought police work was exciting, but it wasn't. It was just tedious. And methodical. You got on a trail and you checked everything on it. That was the drill. Always had been, always would be. He told Rob to take the closet, Marvin to take the dressers, while he took the nightstands.

If Hortense had anything of interest, Sean reasoned, it would probably be in there. Through the years, he'd found that most people use their nightstands as a combination medicine holder and loose change, telephone number, and odd note repository. But there was nothing of interest in Hortense's nightstands, nor in her dresser drawers, nor in her closet. Sean was not surprised.

"What now?" Marvin asked.

Sean pointed to the door in the middle of the wall. "Now we go into her office. Maybe we'll have better luck here." He looked at his watch. They were going to have to hurry. The show would be over soon, and he wanted to be out and gone before that happened.

Hortense's office was considerably smaller than her bedroom. Sean estimated it was a quarter of the size. Unlike the other rooms, this one was strictly utilitarian. There were bad reproductions of Degas' ballet dancers on the walls, plus a calendar from the gas station near R.J.'s.

The desk, two file cabinets, a shelf full of cookbooks, and a couple of chairs all looked as if they'd come from somewhere like OfficeMax. Even the oriental rug on the floor looked cheap. Sean thought about what Libby had said about the green room and how Hortense never spent money on things that didn't show. Maybe that principle was operating here.

Sean took the near file cabinet, told Rob to take the far one, and gave Marvin the desk. He struck pay dirt almost immediately. The third folder in the top drawer was labeled CONTESTANTS.

"It's about time something went my way," he muttered to himself as he took the folder out of the file cabinet. He was just about to open it up when he heard the sound of running feet.

"Who is that?" Marvin cried.

Sean turned and faced him. Marvin looked as if he was going to faint. "Lower your voice," he hissed. "Otherwise they're going to hear you."

"Sorry," Marvin whispered.

Sean tried to reassure him. "They're probably going someplace else."

Marvin shook his head. "No, they're not."

Sean listened for a moment. Marvin was right. Whoever was coming, was coming this way.

This was not good. But it could be dealt with. Sean pointed to the door they'd come through.

"Let's go back into Hortense's bedroom. We can get out that way."

Rob and Marvin both nodded. They were right behind him when he turned the doorknob. Nothing happened. He tried again. Still nothing.

Rob stepped in front of him. "Third time's the charm," he said.

Sean gave him some room, and he did the same thing Sean had done with the same results.

"Try your hip," Sean told him. Sometimes doors got stuck.

Rob did, but nothing happened.

"It's locked," Marvin said.

Sean just looked at him. The kid had a genius for stating the obvious.

"Well, it is," Marvin said. He had a mulish expression on his face.

"I know that," Sean retorted. Somehow the door had swung shut, locking itself behind them, and none of them had noticed. "Why don't you guys go out the window? There's no point in all of us getting into trouble."

Rob folded his arms across his chest. "Forget it," he said.

"I'm sticking too," Marvin said.

"Hey, you need to get the folder out of here," Sean told them.

Marvin and Rob just shook their heads.

This is what came of working with amateurs. "You're not helping," he told them.

Marvin put his hand on his shoulder. "We're with you to the end."

"We're not talking about my landing in a death camp here," Sean replied. But even as he said it, he realized it was probably too late anyway. He needed to look for somewhere to hide the folder.

He could always jam it in one of the books or behind the shelf.

Or he could return it to the file cabinet, which was the most logical course of action.

But if he did any of those things, he probably wouldn't be able to get it back because the odds of him returning here to reclaim it were zero to none. And as for hiding the file on his person, that wouldn't work either if whoever was coming decided to search him.

No. There had to be another way. But what? That was the question.

"What are we going to do now?" Marvin whispered.

Sean shushed him. He had to think. But his mind was blank. Nothing was coming. He was telling himself to focus when Marvin bumped into his wheelchair.

"I'm so sorry," he whimpered as Sean grabbed the seat to keep himself from sliding out.

Sean grinned. The seat. Of course. That was it.

"I love you," he told Marvin.

"I don't get it," Marvin said.

"You will." Sean levered himself up.

The seam that held the two pieces of fabric together that formed the seat of his wheelchair was frayed, frayed to the point where it was starting to unravel.

"What are you doing?" Rob asked.

Sean tried to grasp the thread, but his fingers wouldn't work.

"Pull on that for me," he told Marvin.

Marvin did. The hole got a little larger.

"More," he told Marvin.

Marvin pulled again. More thread came out.

"That should do it," Sean told him.

Hopefully the pocket would be big enough. He took a deep breath and prayed.

He pushed the file into it and sat back down just as the

door burst open. Two Longely policemen, guns drawn, came through the door.

"Don't move," the first one yelled.

"Ah, Longely's finest," Sean said. He started up his wheelchair.

"I said don't move," the first cop repeated.

Sean lifted up his hands and smiled.

"So, guys," he said, "how are things hanging?"

Chapter 24

Libby set a cup of tea and two gingersnap cookies in front of her father and tried not to glare at him.

"What's in the tea?" he asked.

"Tea," she replied. "What else would there be?"

"How about a drop of whiskey?"

Libby sucked in her breath. *I will not say anything to him,* she told herself. *I absolutely will not.*

Her father looked up at her. Trying to look piteous, Libby thought.

"I've had a hard day," he said.

Libby could hear Bernie snorting behind her. "Really? So have I."

"You could be a wee bit more charitable."

"And you can stop with the phony Irish accent. Fine," she growled when he didn't reply. "If you want to kill yourself, be my guest." And she went downstairs, got the bottle of Jameson's out of the liquor cabinet, went back upstairs, and slammed the bottle down in front of him. "Satisfied?"

He gave her his the whole-world-is-against-me stare.

"How was I supposed to know the rooms were alarmed?"

"Nothing's ever your fault, is it?" Libby asked him. She

knew she was tapping her foot, but she couldn't help it. "Thank heavens we were done taping." At least for that, Libby thought. The alternative would have been unthinkable.

Her father smiled. "Hey, did I ever congratulate you on your victory? With everything that happened, I don't think I did."

Libby didn't say anything because if she did, it would be something really not nice.

"Giving me the silent treatment, huh?"

She caught herself before she said, "Yes, I am." She was damned if she was going to reply this time.

She watched her dad as he poured a shot of whiskey into his tea and stirred it. She noticed that his hands were barely shaking at all, but if he continued to drink, they'd start again. Well, it wasn't her business. If he wanted to make himself into a cripple and shorten his life, so be it. He looked up at her again.

"So the police came. So what?" he said to her. "It isn't a big deal."

"It's a big deal to me." Libby realized she was shouting and lowered her voice. "You should think about other people once in a while," she continued, even though she knew she sounded like a broken record.

"I do," he answered. "That's why I was doing what I was. You and your sister were the ones who got me into this, remember?"

His comments made Libby even madder. Especially since she couldn't argue with them. Her father took a sip of his tea, then indicated the bottle of Jameson's with a nod of his chin.

"Maybe you should have a shot of this too. It'll calm you down."

It probably would, Libby thought. But she wasn't going to do it on principle.

He shrugged. "Suit yourself."

"Marvin was terrified," she told her dad.

He took another sip of his tea. "Marvin loved it."

"No. He didn't."

"He most certainly did."

"I've got to agree with Dad here, Libby. Rob thought it was fun."

"Good for Rob."

Libby watched while Bernie walked over to where her dad was sitting and poured a slug of whiskey into her glass from her dad's bottle.

"Nobody asked you," Libby told her.

"Sor-ry," Bernie said.

Then her dad started in again. "Marvin likes the excitement," he said.

As if she didn't know her own boyfriend.

"Even though he gets scared, he likes it," her father continued.

These people just didn't get it.

"That's the point. I don't want him to like it," Libby responded.

"Why not?" her father asked as he took another sip of his tea.

"Because . . . " Libby stopped. She almost said, "Because I don't want him to drive me crazy like you and Bernie do," but that would have been rude. She finally she came out with, "Because I don't want him to get in trouble."

"A little trouble is good for the soul," her father responded. "A man who's never in trouble is a poor man indeed."

"You just made that up, didn't you?"

"It's true just the same. So," her dad continued, "are you at least going to tell me Brittany's answer to my question?"

"She started crying," Bernie said.

"At least let me tell it," Libby told her.

"I'm sorry. I thought you weren't talking."

"Well, I am."

"Okay. What did she say?" he dad asked.

"She said it was an accident."

"And what did she say when you asked about Hortense blackmailing her?"

"She started crying louder."

"Anything else?"

"No. We had to be on the air."

"But she recovered pretty quick," Bernie said.

"Yeah. She did," Libby said, although she didn't want to agree with Bernie.

Her dad raised his eyebrows. "Suggestive," he said. "Very suggestive. And speaking of that . . ."

She watched as he got up from his wheelchair and reached between the pieces of material that formed the seat.

"What are you doing?" she asked as he groped around.

"This," he said, coming out with a file. "I'm doing this."

Bernie moved closer. "What is it?" she asked her dad.

"I haven't looked at it yet," he said. "But it came from Hortense's file cabinet."

"Neato," Bernie commented. She grabbed the file out of her dad's hand.

In spite of herself, Libby moved close enough so she could look over Bernie's shoulder.

"This is interesting," Bernie said as she flipped through the pages. "Very interesting indeed. Don't you want to see it?" she asked her.

"Later."

Libby glanced at the clock. She was sure it was interesting, but she still had to get her work done, and as of now, she was officially three hours behind schedule. No, actually it was more because she hadn't factored in the time it would take the bread dough to rise, and rye dough was notoriously poky in that regard.

"I've got to go down to the kitchen," she said.

There was a knock on the downstairs door.

Libby looked at her sister. "I hope it's not Bree Nottingham. I don't think I could deal with her now."

"It's not. It's Rob and Marvin," Bernie explained.

"We can't go out now," Libby wailed. "There's too much to do."

Bernie closed the folder. "I know how much there is to do. I've asked them over to help."

"Help what?"

"Help cook and bake."

Libby groaned. "But they don't know how."

"So," Bernie said. "We'll teach them. We're not talking about brain surgery here."

"I don't know," Libby said. Over the years she'd found that it was usually easier to do it herself.

"Well, I do," Bernie said.

Her dad leaned over, took the folder back, and began paging through it.

"This really is interesting," he said as Bernie left to go get Rob and Marvin.

Chapter 25

Libby looked around the kitchen and thought, *I love this place. I love the way it smells; I love the way the cabinets look*. She loved the fifty-pound bags of flour stacked on the floor next to the industrial mixer she'd gotten on sale. She unbuttoned her sweater. It was nice and warm. In the summer the kitchen was so hot she felt as if she would faint, but tonight, when it was eighteen degrees outside, it was delightful.

Plus, the warmth would help the bread dough to rise faster. Which was a good thing. Especially since the bread should have been in the oven by five o'clock this afternoon. Six o'clock at the latest. Of all the Christmas breads in the world, why was she saddled making Swedish limpa? There was over a cup of rye flour in each loaf of bread, which, given the time schedule they were operating on, was bad news because, in general, rye flour took longer to rise than wheat or white flour did.

I should have picked another holiday bread to make instead, Libby decided. Something with all white flour. Heaven knows there were enough recipes to choose from. She could have made something like stollen or something Italian like Panatone. Not that she really could.

Strictly speaking, Swedish limpa wasn't even a Christmas bread, but her mother had started the tradition of making it over the holidays when she'd opened the store and people had come to expect it to be there. Libby realized that she'd never asked her mother why she'd chosen that particular bread as her eyes strayed to Marvin. He had flour on his shirt and in his hair and vanilla icing on his breast pocket. He was cute, but his rolling technique left a lot to be desired.

"No, no," Libby told him.

"No, no what?" Marvin replied. "I'm doing what you told me to."

"Not exactly. Here." And she took the rolling pin out of his hand and showed him. "You apply steady pressure, and you try not to stretch the dough with your hands, because that activates the gluten and makes it tough."

"So they'll be tough cookies. What's wrong with that? What about Bette Davis?" Bernie commented as she dumped another cup of rye flour into the mixer.

Rob looked up from peeling potatoes. "Ha-ha," he said. "Very funny."

"I thought it was," Bernie retorted.

Libby put down the rolling pin and went over and peered into the industrial-size mixer.

"I hope the dough isn't too sticky," Libby told Bernie.

"It'll be fine," Bernie reassured her. "I'll just add some more white flour if it is."

Libby wanted to tell her that making dough was an exact process, not some sort of slapdash affair, as Bernie would say, but she didn't; because if she did, it would just lead to their usual discussion about following recipes exactly versus throwing in a handful of this and a handful of that and how baking was different from cooking in that regard. She wasn't in the mood for that, especially not at this time of night.

In fact, Libby thought as she watched Bernie reach for

her mug of the mulled wine Libby had made when all of them had come down into the kitchen, all she wanted to do was go upstairs, take a bath, and go to sleep. But that wasn't an option. Not even close to one.

"Nice," Bernie said appreciatively after she'd taken a sip. "Very Christmasy."

"It's the orange and tangerine peel," Libby told her. She'd dried and made her own peel last winter. By the time she'd finished, she was afraid she'd given herself carpal tunnel syndrome, but the results had justified the effort.

Bernie nodded absentmindedly as she turned off the mixer. Then she dusted the counter with flour and started scraping the dough for the Swedish limpa bread out of the bowl with her spatula. Bernie had been right about one thing, Libby decided as she watched her. It was nice working with Marvin and Rob, even if they weren't doing things in the manner she would have.

For example, Rob was taking half of the potato off with the peel, not to mention the fact that there were little pieces of potato peelings all over the floor. What a mess. Libby took a deep breath and tried to channel Bernie. She had to stay positive. She had to remember that Rob and Marvin were doing the best they could. That it was nice of them to help out. She had to remember not to criticize.

As she decorated the Christmas cookies, Libby's mind drifted back to what they'd found in the file folder her father had snatched from Hortense's mansion. She was still having trouble believing what was in it, but there it had been in black and white.

"I guess Pearl wins the pool," Rob said.

"What pool?" Libby asked as she distributed some white sprinkles on the outer edges of the branches of the evergreen tree cookies. "What are you talking about?"

Rob explained.

Libby shook her head. Something about it didn't seem right.

"Guys really do have to quantify everything, don't they?" Bernie observed as she sprinkled more flour on the dough.

"I resent that," Rob said.

"But it's true," Bernie shot back.

Libby shut her eyes for a moment.

"What's the matter?" Marvin asked.

"Nothing," Libby said, which was a big fat lie. She was feeling totally overwhelmed.

"It'll be fine," Bernie said. "You'll see."

"I hope so."

But Libby wasn't so sure. All the things she had to do kept swirling around in her head like handfuls of windblown confetti. She was beginning to wonder how she was going to survive the holidays. Of course, she reminded herself, she thought that every year. But this time was worse, way worse.

Being involved in the contest as well as the murder investigation had put her over the top. Normally those two items would be enough to fill her day; now they were a part of her day. Actually, not that she'd say this to anyone, but she was sorry that she and Bernie had won the cook-off against Reginald.

It would have been better if they hadn't. That way she would have had one less thing to worry about. And she still had the store and all the parties, and she hadn't even started her Christmas shopping yet, much less made up her list or sent out cards. Maybe she'd just give food to everyone this year. That would be easy.

And then Libby thought about what she'd read in the folder. If either Pearl or La Croix was in fact the person who had killed Hortense, that would be another thing off her plate. The investigation would be over, and she could go back to devoting all her attention to what she needed to do because the thing with a business like hers was that it demanded constant attention. You could never take a day off.

But then Libby felt terrible for thinking that. Especially since her dad and Bernie thought Pearl was responsible for Hortense's death. Of all the contestants, she liked Pearl the best. Maybe because she was the most like her. Well, there was no maybe about it. She was the most like Pearl.

Libby cleaned some pieces of dough off the edges of her cookie cutter and put them with the other scraps on the side of the rolling board. Her mother had taught her never to waste anything, and it was a teaching she still tried to adhere to.

"Well, I don't believe it about Pearl," Libby said. "I think La Croix is the guilty party."

Marvin looked up from the work board. "Your dad does."

"My dad's been wrong before," she said.

"He doesn't think that."

Libby laughed. "He just won't admit it. There's a difference." She leaned over Marvin and scrutinized the dough. "One more roll and it'll be done," she told him. "You don't want the dough to be too thin. It shouldn't be thinner than a quarter of an inch."

As Libby watched Marvin nod, she felt a sudden rush of affection for him. He always tried so hard. He really was a good soul. Even if her dad couldn't always see it. But that, Libby decided, was his problem. And then she realized she hadn't turned the oven on. How could she have forgotten to do that? She was totally, completely fried, she decided as she went over to remedy the situation. She was turning the oven on when she heard a crash.

She whirled around. Marvin was picking up one of the metal mixing bowls off the floor.

"Sorry," he said. "It just slid off."

Libby put her hand over her heart. It was still beating

fast. For one second she'd thought the oven was exploding.

Bernie frowned. "Are you all right?"

Libby nodded. What had happened to Hortense must still be bothering her. Jeez. Why couldn't she let things go like Bernie could? Nothing ever seemed to bother her. Libby took a deep breath. *The oven is my friend*, she told herself.

And it was. She used it several times a day. It's just that until Hortense's death, she'd never thought of it as a weapon.

"Libby."

She turned toward Rob.

"Why don't you think Pearl did it?" he asked.

She was glad to answer. It took her mind away from ovens. "I just can't picture her doing something like that."

"Why?" Bernie asked. "She did before."

"No, she didn't."

"Close enough," Bernie said.

"It was an accident," Libby said.

"Actually, the courts called it 'criminally negligent homicide,' " Marvin said.

"I know what the courts called it," Libby told him. "I was with you when we found out, remember? She was a kid."

Bernie went over and ladled some more wine into her mug. "She was fifteen."

Libby shook her head. She knew the facts as well as Bernie, but she just wasn't convinced. "It just doesn't seem like her style. It seems like something La Croix would do."

Bernie took a sip of her wine.

"She threatened Hortense."

"I bet other people did too."

"Maybe. But she's the only one who wrote her threats down and mailed them to Hortense. 'Dear Heavenly Housewife,'" Bernie recited, " 'If you do not cease and desist, I will make sure that everything blows up in your face.' And it did. You can't deny that."

"But that could just be an expression she was using," Libby protested. "She might not have meant that in the literal sense of the word."

Bernie ignored her and went on. "Listen, we know from the files Hortense was keeping that she'd already gotten sixty thousand dollars out of Pearl by threatening to expose her lack of taste buds. And we know that Pearl was up against the wall, financially speaking."

"You could say that about La Croix and Consuela as well," Libby objected.

"Yes," Bernie finished. "But they didn't kill anyone."

"We've been through this already," Libby protested. "She tried to commit suicide by turning the gas on; then she changed her mind and closed the oven door, but she forgot to turn off the—"

"Something I find hard to believe," Bernie interjected.

"So when the baby-sitter came in and lit up her cigarette—blammo."

"How could the baby-sitter not have smelled the gas?" Rob protested.

Bernie ran the tip of her finger around the mug's edge. "Well, there's that too. I mean, Libby, come on. Don't you think that's suggestive? Haven't you heard the expression about lightning never striking twice in the same spot?"

"But it can," Libby argued. "There was a story in the paper two months ago about a man who got struck by lightning twice." She hurried on before Bernie could interrupt her. "And as for being a criminal, how about La Croix? He was in prison. He was paying off to Hortense as well."

"He was in jail on a burglary charge," Bernie said. "Burglary and homicide are two different animals entirely."

"So now you're an expert on criminal activity as well,"

Libby retorted, even though she knew her sister was probably right.

Libby watched Bernie's face as she moved her silver and onyx ring up and down her finger. They'd been going for almost fifteen hours now, and Bernie's eyeliner and shadow were still in place. How does she do it? Libby wondered. We both use the same products, and hers lasts and mine comes off in twenty minutes. It just wasn't fair.

"You know what interests me," Bernie said.

Libby shook her head to clear it. "What?" she replied, even though she knew it was a rhetorical question.

"What interests me is how Hortense got Pearl's police records. They were supposed to be sealed."

"I think *supposed to be* are the operative words," Rob said. "If you know the right person, you can get anything you need."

"I'll grant you that, but who did Hortense know to ask?"

Rob looked at Bernie. "She probably Googled her. The story would be there if it was in the papers."

"You're a genius," Bernie told him.

Rob grinned. "I like to think so."

Marvin cleared his throat. Libby turned toward him.

"What?" she asked.

"I just wondered what we were going to do next."

Libby pointed to the dough. "How about rolling out another piece?"

"No," Marvin said. "I meant about the investigation."

"Good question," Bernie said as she went back to kneading the dough for the Swedish limpa.

Libby could see that it was becoming shiny, which was a good thing. She could feel the small knot of tension in her neck easing.

"Because I have a suggestion. I think one of us should talk to someone who was involved in that thing with Pearl," Marvin continued. "You know, like a neighbor or a policeman. Someone like that."

"It's a good idea, but how are we going to do that?" Libby asked. "After all, this thing with Pearl happened about twenty years ago."

"Twelve," Bernie corrected. "It was twelve years ago."

"Whatever." Sometimes Bernie could be beyond annoying, Libby thought.

"I bet your dad's friend knows someone who can tell us something about the incident," Marvin went on.

"You mean Clyde?" Libby asked.

Bernie clapped Marvin on the back when he nodded.

"You're brilliant, " she told him as she brushed a bit of flour off the back of his shirt.

Libby bit her tongue. It was a great suggestion; she just didn't want to do it because it meant yet more work. She closed her eyes for a moment, then opened them again. Maybe she should have some of that mulled wine after all.

"And when do you propose we do that?" she asked her sister.

"Tomorrow before the taping."

"Excuse me," Libby said. "But in case you've forgotten, we have two parties to get ready for."

"I'll go," Bernie said.

Libby went over and ladled some of the wine into a mug. She took a sip. Bernie was right. This was good.

"If Clyde has a lead."

"I bet he will," Bernie said. "He knows everything."

"And then what?" Libby asked.

"And then we'll see," Bernie said. She patted Libby's arm. "Cheer up. If we're lucky, we could be done with this whole business."

"That would be wonderful," Libby told her. "Absolutely wonderful." And then right after she said it she felt guilty, because if that were true, it was going to be because Pearl was the guilty party.

Chapter 26

"This must be the place," Bernie said to herself as she parked the car in front of O'Brien & Sons Hobby and Train shop and turned off the van's headlights.

This was one of the things she hated about this time of year, Bernie thought. It got so dark so early. Of course it could be worse. She could be in someplace like Nome, Alaska, where they got four hours of sunlight a day.

But still. Even though it was a little after five, it felt like midnight; but then maybe it felt like that because she'd gotten three hours of sleep the night before. Bernie rubbed her temples with the tips of her fingers.

As her guru back in L.A. kept telling her, the trick was to stay in the now and not think about everything else she had to do. Just focus on what you have to do next, she told herself. Not that that would be hard to do—if she could stay awake to do it.

According to Clyde, Jean Claude O'Brien had been the first officer on the scene of Pearl's "accident." When Bernie had looked up his name on the computer, she'd found a listing for a Jean Claude O'Brien three towns away.

The name wasn't all that common, so she figured he was her guy. A little further research had showed that he had opened a hobby shop, at which point she'd checked out his Web site. Luckily for her, there'd been a picture of him and his son standing in front of their storefront.

When she'd shown the picture to Clyde, he'd confirmed it was the guy he'd been talking about. Sometimes the Web was a wonderful thing. Clyde had wanted to call him, but Bernie had decided she'd rather surprise him. Now as she looked at the gift she'd brought him, she wondered about the wisdom of her choice.

Bernie sighed as she assessed the store window. She and Libby had done a better job on A Little Taste of Heaven's. O'Brien's decorations were rather perfunctory. There was a train going around and around, a plastic Santa, and four elves. Not very imaginative. Of course, maybe she felt that way because she hated model trains.

Had ever since her dad had run over her pet chameleon with one. The tail had been on one side of the tracks and the lizard on the other. Actually, the lizard had been fine. Evidently they shed their tails whenever they got nervous, some sort of survival mechanism, but it had taken her father hours to convince her of that. Her mother had not been amused, but if truth be told, she usually wasn't.

And then there was that guy in Venice Beach who had turned one room of his apartment into a perfect replica of some historic railroad site in Rhode Island. Or maybe it was Vermont. She wouldn't have cared so much, but the apartment had only two rooms. That was a relationship that hadn't lasted too long. She'd had to duck under the trestles to get to the bathroom.

One day she'd had one glass of wine too many and accidentally destroyed a major road. Bernie started to laugh thinking about it, although at the time it hadn't been so funny. God, she hadn't thought about Ned in years. She was wondering what had happened to him when her cell phone rang. It was Libby.

"No," she told her when she'd fished her phone out of

her pocketbook. "I haven't forgotten to pick up the sugar, and yes, I know I have to be at the studio soon. That's why I'm dressed the way I am."

Jeez, Bernie thought as she stashed the phone in her jacket pocket. Give me a break. Like she was going to forget something like that. She walked into the store. Jean Claude O'Brien came toward her. He sure didn't look like any Irishman she'd ever seen. Or Frenchman. Actually, he looked Puerto Rican.

"Anything I can help you with?" he said.

Bernie handed him the basket she was carrying. It contained three fancy plastic bags filled with chocolate chip, gingersnap, and oatmeal cashew cookies, a jar of strawberry jam that Libby had made last summer, and three walnut-oatmeal scones. When in doubt, come armed with food. That was her motto.

He frowned. "What's this?" he asked.

"A present from Clyde Schiller over in Longely."

Bernie was not happy to see that instead of thanking her, much less oohing and aahing over the basket, O'Brien just took it and put it down on the counter. That was not the way things like this usually went.

"Haven't heard from him in a while," O'Brien said. "Is he still doing the same thing?"

Bernie nodded.

"I hear Lucas is chief of police now."

Bernie nodded again.

"Good going. That other guy who was there before him . . ."

"Sean Simmons," Bernie said.

"He was a net loss."

Bernie couldn't restrain herself. She knew she shouldn't, but she said it anyway. "That man is my father."

O'Brien shrugged. "Doesn't change the truth."

Bernie could feel herself flush. "You have no right to say that."

"It's my store. I can say what I want. I'm sorry you don't want to hear it, but I call 'em as I see 'em."

Bernie leaned over and grabbed the basket. "Good for you."

"That's not very nice," O'Brien said.

"You're not very nice," Bernie replied, and she marched out the door.

"Talk about a total waste of time," Bernie muttered to herself as she turned the key in the ignition of Libby's van. The damned thing wouldn't start. Bernie slapped the dashboard with the palm of her hand. "Don't do this to me," she cried. She was turning the key again when she realized that O'Brien was by her window. She rolled it down.

"What do you want?" she snarled.

"How come you came over here in the first place?"

"What do you care?"

O'Brien lifted his hands up in a gesture of peace. "Listen. I'm sorry about what I said back there. Me and your father have some history."

"So?"

"So. It's Christmas. I'm trying to be nice."

"Well, you're not," Bernie snapped.

O'Brien shrugged. "If that's the way you want it." And he turned to go.

It was the way she wanted it, Bernie decided as she watched him trudge back toward his store. She didn't need to hear what he had to say.

But the trouble was she did.

What was her father always telling her about not letting the personal get in the way of the job? He'd probably be telling her that now if he was here. No *probably* about it. That's what he *would* be telling her. She took a deep breath. All right, Bernie, she told herself. It's time to grow up.

"Wait!" she cried.

O'Brien turned back toward her.

"I have a question for you."

O'Brien nodded. "Shoot."

"Clyde said you were the person to ask."

"I'm waiting."

"It's about Pearl—"

"The dead baby-sitter," O'Brien exclaimed. "How could I forget. That baby-sitter was the first dead person I'd ever seen."

"Do you think Pearl—"

"Did it on purpose?" O'Brien asked.

"How did you know what I was going to say?"

"It was the question everyone was asking."

"And?"

O'Brien scratched his cheek. "I thought she did, the ADA thought she did, but her parents were rich and had a good lawyer, so she got off with probation and some serious shrink time." O'Brien shrugged. "That's the way these things go sometimes. Why do you want to know?"

Bernie made a vague gesture. "Oh, I'm thinking of writing an article," she lied.

O'Brien grinned. "I didn't know you were a writer."

"In my spare time."

"I see."

Bernie decided O'Brien had a cat-ate-the-canary smile on his face. She wondered why as he gestured toward the basket on the front seat.

"Any chance of getting that back?"

Bernie reached over and handed it to him. "Merry Christmas," she said.

"Same to you. And by the way, good luck on the cooking show."

"What?" She wasn't sure she'd heard O'Brien right.

He pointed to his watch. "You should be getting moving shouldn't you? You're going to be on the air soon."

"But how—" Bernie began.

O'Brien cut her off before she could finish. "My wife's been watching the show on TV. So where's Hortense?"

"She broke her pelvis."

"I thought it was her hip."

Damn me, Bernie thought as she watched O'Brien's grin grow even bigger.

"Following in your dad's steps, are you?" he said.

"Not at all," Bernie replied. She tried the van again. This time it turned over. She put it in gear and shot out of there.

When she got around the corner, she reached into her bag, pulled out her cell phone, and called Libby.

"It's her," she told her.

Chapter 27

Libby watched Pearl for a moment as she flitted around the green room. The woman hadn't stopped moving since she'd walked in the door. First she'd rearranged the chairs that were lined up against the wall so they were exactly a quarter of an inch apart, then she'd done the same thing with the chairs around the conference table, and after that she'd gone to work on the food table. She'd gotten done with the bagels and the muffins and was now reorganizing the jam by flavors.

Libby turned to Bernie. "Don't ever call me obsessive-compulsive," she told her sister.

Bernie laughed. "I won't."

"I can't imagine what living with her would be like."

"I know." Bernie leaned in closer. "Do you think she ever stops?"

"No. Being like that must be exhausting."

Bernie moved her ring up and down her finger. "Not to change the subject or anything," she went on, "but what do you think about getting a DVD player for Dad?"

Libby nodded. "Good idea. Then I'll get him a DVD burner."

Bernie shook her head. "God, look at Pearl's clothes."

Libby clicked her tongue against her teeth. Her clothes were amazing. And not in the good sense either. The bright green sweater with the line of bells across the top and the red and green plaid skirt that Libby couldn't help noticing made Pearl's hips look bigger than her own were definite showstoppers. She and Estes were running neck in neck in the bad taste department. Libby shook her head. What was wrong with her? She usually didn't care about things like that.

Bernie nudged her. Libby turned back toward her sister.

"Whatever do you suppose possessed her to wear that?" she asked.

"She probably thought it was festive." Libby wiped a drop of sweat away from her forehead with the end of her napkin.

It was too hot in here. There were just too many people crowded in this room, Libby decided. They were taking up all the air. Either that or she was nervous, although Libby couldn't figure out why she should be.

She and Bernie weren't scheduled to cook today. Which was good. On the other hand, they *were* going to cohost the show with Eric Royal. This was the price of winning yesterday's contest. She was just glad that Bernie was with her, because Libby hadn't even thought about what she was going to say. She liked to be prepared, but there'd been too much going on.

Bernie shook her head. "She looks like she's wearing wrapping paper, and cheap wrapping paper at that. I mean, why do people have to dress in themes?" Bernie continued. "They're not shop windows. And Christmas is the worst. All those sweaters with reindeer and snow-flakes. Feh."

"I wouldn't go that far," Libby told her.

"Well, I would."

Libby sighed.

"What's the matter?" Bernie asked her.

"Just thinking," Libby replied.

"About Pearl?"

"Yup," Libby admitted.

Bernie stroked her arm. "It's hard when the criminal turns out to be someone you like."

"Thanks," Libby replied. She smiled at Bernie. Maybe they did bicker a lot, but when it came down to it, Bernie always knew what she needed to hear.

"Maybe she won't be guilty after all."

"Dad thinks she is." She was about to say something else when Consuela started talking.

"Will you stop that," Consuela said to Pearl, who was in the process of lining up all the coffee cups on the table so that their handles faced the same way.

Pearl froze.

"I'm not doing anything," she stammered.

"Yes you are. You're annoying me," Consuela told her.

Brittany stepped forward. "I second that."

Libby could see Pearl looking at her.

"Am I annoying you too?" she wailed.

Libby shook her head. She felt terrible. "Not at all."

"Then you're as crazy as she is," Brittany told her.

"Now, that is not necessary," Bernie shot back.

I should stick up for myself, Libby thought as Brittany rounded on her sister.

"I'm just making an observation," she told her, at which point her cell phone started ringing.

"Talk about annoying," Bernie said. "Shouldn't that thing be off? Or why don't you get one surgically implanted in your ear and save us all the bother of hearing it."

"Excuse me."

Libby watched Brittany stick her neck out. "I need to talk to my people."

"Your people?" Bernie scoffed. "You don't have any people."

"I most certainly do," Brittany told her.

Bernie put her hands on her hips. "Yeah? Like who?"

"I don't have time for this stupidity," Brittany retorted.

"Then you should look at yourself," Libby told her.

But Brittany didn't hear her comment. She'd already turned her back on her and Bernie and was talking into her phone. *Typical of me*, Libby thought as she observed Pearl looking around the room. *When I finally decide to talk, no one listens.*

Libby nodded in Pearl's direction. "She looks as if she's going to cry," she said to her sister.

"Doesn't she though," Bernie agreed.

Pearl spread her arms out and appealed to everyone. "I just want to make things even. What's so wrong with that?" she asked.

La Croix looked at her and shook his head in disgust. "What's so wrong is that you are flitting around, going here, going there." He did a pantomime of Pearl's actions with his hands. "You are making it impossible for me to concentrate."

Consuela snorted. "What a load of nonsense. You have nothing to concentrate on."

"This is not true," La Croix shot back. "I must retain my focus so that I may be in tune with the harmony of the universe."

Brittany rolled her eyes as she put her cell back in her bag. "Spare me. You're not the one that's going on next. I am."

"So what?" La Croix said. "You have nothing to think about."

"I have my menu to consider," Brittany told him.

La Croix's eyebrows shot up. "You can't plan that. Unless, of course, you already know the ingredients you are going to use."

"And how would I know that?" Brittany demanded.

"Perhaps because you are"—La Croix paused and made what Libby's mother would have called a rude gesture—"doing this with Eric Royal."

Libby watched as two spots of color appeared on Brittany's cheeks.

"How dare you?" she demanded. "I've never used sex to get what I want in my life, and I never will."

Reginald Palmer turned around from the Christmas tree in the far corner and came forward. "Maybe that's because no one wants you, my dear," he suggested.

Brittany whirled around and faced him. "At least I'm not a whore."

"Excuse me," Reginald said. "And what, exactly, did you mean by that?"

"You know exactly what I meant," Brittany told him.

"No, I don't."

"You and Hortense were quite the item."

"I don't know what you're talking about."

Brittany laughed. "Oh please. Everyone knows you were sleeping with her. She owned you."

I didn't know, Libby thought. She looked at Bernie. Bernie looked back at her and gave an imperceptible shake of her head. Evidently Bernie hadn't known either. This is getting more interesting by the second, Libby thought as Reginald started talking again.

"That's ridiculous," Reginald said. "That's the most ridiculous thing I've ever heard."

"Maybe it's ridiculous, but it's true," Brittany said.

Reginald stepped in front of Brittany. Libby could see that he'd made his hands into fists.

"Take it back," he said.

"Like hell I will," Brittany said.

Reginald raised his hands. "I said take it back."

He had a tone in his voice that Libby didn't like. Before she realized what she was doing, she'd stepped between them.

"That's enough," she said.

Reginald glared at Brittany, who glared back. For a second, Libby thought she was going to get punched, but then both Reginald and Brittany stepped away from each other.

"At least I haven't poisoned anyone," Reginald said.

"That allegation was entirely untrue," Brittany cried.

Reginald smiled. "Was it? That's not what I heard. That's not what I heard at all. Good thing you have a rich daddy who can buy your way out of things like that and save your ass. How much did he spend? A couple of million? Must have been at least that—maybe more." He wagged a finger at her. "Salmonella. Tsk-tsk. But I guess that's what happens when someone like you gets into a business they know nothing about. It's a good thing your daddy has the money to buy all your books. Otherwise they'd never sell."

"That's a lie," Brittany told Libby as Reginald walked away. "Everything he said is a lie. He's just jealous because he can't get any business." Then Brittany's phone started ringing.

"Shut that off," Reginald bellowed as Brittany stepped away to answer it.

The hell with the phone. Libby wished she could shut Reginald, Brittany, and La Croix off with the press of a button. She couldn't remember when she'd been in a place with so many disagreeable people.

Libby closed her eyes and massaged the nape of her neck. She hoped that Bernie had some aspirin on her because between the heat and all the arguing, she was getting a terrible headache. Maybe she should go to the bathroom and splash some water on her face—at least it would be quiet in there. She was trying to decide when she heard Pearl calling her name.

She opened her eyes. Pearl was standing beside her, wringing her hands.

"Oh dear," she said. "Oh dear. I don't want anyone to fight on my account."

"They're not," Libby tried to assure her.

"But I think they are. And now I have to cook, and I'm so upset I can't concentrate on anything."

Bernie leaned over and patted her on the back. "It'll be fine," she assured her.

"I don't know what I'm going to make," Pearl wailed.

"You'll figure it out," Libby assured her. "We did."

Pearl bit her lip. "I need to find my knives. Where did I put my knives?" And she wandered off.

When she was out of earshot, Libby turned to Bernie and whispered in her ear, "This is the person you think is guilty of murder? Get real. She couldn't kill a cockroach without apologizing."

"You should know that just because someone is mild on the outside doesn't mean they can't have an explosive temper," Bernie whispered back. "Appearances can be deceiving."

"I never thought I'd hear you admit that," Libby said.

"You know what I mean. And let's not forget what O'Brien told me."

"That's his opinion. Just because he said it doesn't mean it's true."

"Given his job, I think you have to assume he knows what he's talking about."

Libby shrugged. "Maybe you're right," she admitted. But as she watched Pearl scurry around looking for her knives, no matter how hard she tried, she just couldn't see her for this. "Anyway, we still don't have any proof."

"No, we don't," Bernie agreed. "But that isn't our job. Maybe Lucy will get her to spill her guts by rearranging all the silverware and not letting her straighten it up until she confesses."

"Ha-ha," Libby said. "Very funny."

"I thought it was."

Libby was about to tell her sister that sometimes her

sense of humor was way off base when Eric Royal and Estes came through the green room door.

"They don't look happy," she said to Bernie instead.

"They never do," her sister replied.

Estes blew his nose. Then he clapped his hands together and everyone quieted down.

"All right," he said. "Everyone listen up. We have ten minutes to airtime, and I want to go over some things with you. First off, Consuela and La Croix will be cooking against each other—"

"But I thought I was supposed to be on," Pearl cried.

"You were, but we've changed the roster," Estes said.

"But you can't do that," Pearl protested.

"Of course I can," Estes said. "I can do anything I damn well please. I'm the producer."

"But I got myself ready to do this today."

Estes smiled. He's like a dog baring his teeth, Libby thought.

"Eric and I decided that La Croix and Consuela will make a more interesting pairing showwise."

"But that's not fair," Pearl cried. "I'm ready now."

Estes glowered at her. "I don't care what you're ready for. This is the way it's going to be," he informed her. "Understand?"

"But—"

"I mean it."

"It's not fair."

"This has nothing to do with fair. This has to do with what's good for the show."

"But I expected—"

Estes pointed to the clock on the green room wall. "We don't have much time, okay? I have to go through a number of things. Now I want you to shut up. Go even out some things, empty some ashtrays, dust the floor moldings. I don't care what you do as long as you don't say another word to me until I'm done talking to everyone. Do you understand?" Estes spoke the last three words in such a loud voice that Libby wanted to cover her ears with her hands.

"Well, do you?" Estes yelled.

Pearl nodded. Libby tried to figure out the expression on Pearl's face. Was it hate? Rage? Embarrassment? All of them? She couldn't be sure.

"What did you say?" Estes said to her.

"I said yes," Pearl whispered.

And then Libby heard her mutter something else as well.

She turned to Bernie. "Did she say what I thought she said?" she asked.

Bernie nodded. Libby was not pleased to see that she had an I-told-you-so expression on her face. It would be weeks before Bernie stopped talking about this one.

Estes pointed a finger at her. "Hey, you be quiet too."

Libby bit her lip. "Sorry," she said as she contemplated what she thought she'd heard Pearl say. Maybe Pearl meant "I'll kill you" as a figure of speech.

Or maybe Bernie was right after all. She watched as Pearl walked over to the Christmas tree. A few of the lights were obviously askew. She just can't resist, Libby thought as Pearl put her hand up toward the lights. It must be such a burden to be like that. She was bad, but she wasn't that bad. At least she didn't have to have her bagels in neat little rows and her coffee cup handles facing the same way.

She was half listening to Estes yammering on about adhering to the schedule as she watched Pearl reach over and grab one of the Christmas lights. She shrieked and started twitching. Sparks flew.

"This is not good," Libby heard herself saying as Pearl collapsed on the floor. "This is not good at all."

Chapter 28

"I'd say that 'not good' is a massive understatement," Bernie muttered to herself as she pushed her way past Consuela, La Croix, and Brittany to get to Pearl. "Move," she yelled. But no one budged.

Consuela was screeching, La Croix was muttering, Reginald was shaking his head, and Brittany was already talking on her cell.

Unfrigginbelievable, Bernie thought as she listened to Brittany saying, "You'll never guess what just happened." Just unbelievable. She'd almost reached Pearl when Eric Royal stepped in front of her, blocking her path.

"Don't," he said.

"What is your problem?" she demanded. "Let me through."

Eric Royal pointed toward the floor. "That's my problem."

"Oh," Bernie said as she spotted the puddle of water by the base of the Christmas tree.

"Oh indeed. I don't need you getting electrocuted as well."

"Maybe you should pull the plug."

"I don't want to get shocked."

"You won't get shocked."

"We should wait for the police."

"No, we shouldn't," Bernie said, and she stalked over to the outlet and pulled the plug out. "See," she said, turning to Eric Royal, "nothing happened."

She hurried over to Pearl. The poor lady still had the string of Christmas lights clutched tightly in her hand. She clearly wasn't going to be worrying about evening up the silverware anymore. Bernie bit her lip as she surveyed the scene. The puddle of water might have come from someone accidentally overwatering the Christmas tree, but somehow Bernie didn't think so.

As her eyes moved over the scene, she noticed a ring of keys lying almost underneath Pearl's body. *Hmm*, Bernie thought as she caught sight of the initials PW on it. Pearl's keys. Who else's could they be?

She must have had them in her hand and dropped them, Bernie thought as she reached over and picked them up. She expected someone to say something, but no one did. That's because they haven't noticed in all the confusion, Bernie concluded. Then before she realized what she was doing, she found herself slipping the keys into her pocket. As her father would have said, "Never look a gift horse in the mouth."

She was patting her pocket when her sister joined her.

"Maybe Eric's right. Maybe we should leave this for the police," Libby suggested.

"I'm not doing anything," Bernie said as she pried Pearl's hand open.

"What do you call that?" Libby asked.

"I call it trying to figure out what's going on."

The bulbs on the string of lights seemed intact. There wasn't a loose wire. And then she saw it.

"Look," she said to Libby.

"What?"

"There." And she pointed to the bare wire on either set of the bulb. "See. Someone cut the protective covering away. No insulation."

"Nice," Libby said.

Bernie was just about to agree with her when Estes came charging over.

"This is terrible, just terrible. I feel as if this set is cursed." He rubbed his nose with the back of his hand.

"That's one way of looking at it," Bernie said.

Estes glared at her. Bernie glared back. If they were going to have a staring contest, she was damned if she was going to be the one to turn away first. Finally Estes did.

"This is an extremely unfortunate accident," Estes growled.

"I think someone did this on purpose." Between the condition of the wire and the water on the floor, Bernie couldn't see any room for doubt.

Estes rubbed his nose with the back of his hand again.

"Always with the accusations. Do you do this because it makes you feel important?"

"That must be it. It's nice to know that in addition to your other talents you're a shrink too." She pointed to the cord. "If you bother to look, you'll see that someone cut the protective covering off the wire."

"That's ridiculous," Estes scoffed. "The cord was frayed. Like I said, this show is cursed. Maybe I should get an exorcist in here."

"An exorcist. What a good idea."

"Sometimes these things help."

Bernie was about to tell him that the knife marks on the wire were clearly evident when Eric Royal tapped Estes on the shoulder.

"We're going live soon," he said. "What do you want me to do?"

"Get everyone on the set," Estes told him.

"You sure?" Eric Royal asked.

"Absolutely."

Estes clapped his hands. "Everyone take your places, please."

Libby pulled Bernie aside as she was walking out of the green room. "I can't believe we're going on the air," she told her.

Bernie snorted. "Obviously you haven't worked in the industry."

"But—" Libby began.

Bernie put up her hand to stop her. "If you had a dinner for seventy-five and one of your workers died, what would you do? Exactly," she said when Libby didn't answer. "You've heard the expression, 'The show must go on.' Well, this is what it means."

Bernie looked around the set. The show was not going well. Actually, that was an understatement. Maybe this was a bad luck show after all. Maybe they needed to get a feng shui master in here.

So far, Consuela had jammed the knife she was using to open oysters with into the palm of her hand. Blood had spurted out everywhere, including into the oyster stew she was preparing, which in Bernie's humble opinion didn't help its appearance any, but then Bernie had never been a big fan of oysters, or clams either, for that matter. Never had been, never would be.

You could dress oysters up all you wanted, but they still looked like mucus to her, and as if that wasn't bad enough, they had an unpleasant slippery texture going down. And as for cooked, the only good thing about oyster stew was the cream. Cream always made things taste better, and in this case it made the stew look better too. Of course, it didn't look better with spots of blood floating around in it, but that was a different matter.

And as if that wasn't bad enough, Consuela had spilled oil over the front burner of the Viking stove she was using and started a small fire. It wasn't anything that big, but one of the crew had had to run in and put it out with a fire extinguisher, which ruined the mushrooms she'd been sautéing in the pan on the front burner. No. Life had not gone well for Consuela.

La Croix hadn't faired much better. He'd scalded the back of his hand when he took the Oysters Rockefeller off of their bed of salt, after which he'd dropped the plate, tried to catch it, and got hot rock salt on his pants and hands.

Bernie decided his scream must have discombobulated the viewers out there in TVland. But maybe they liked that sort of thing. She noticed that most people liked to watch disasters, and this show was shaping up as one gigantic one. She wondered if Estes was sorry he'd insisted the show go on. He certainly didn't look very happy.

But then he really didn't have much choice, Bernie thought as she watched Brittany get up from her seat. Now that's odd, Bernie decided as Brittany started to sashay down the stairs. I wonder what the hell she's doing. Then she looked at Estes. He was red in the face again, kind of a purplish red. Not good. Better to watch Brittany instead, Bernie decided. Watching Estes just made her nervous.

By now Brittany was between the two prep tables. She paused to smile at the camera, then half-turned to Eric.

"My dear man," she trilled. "I hope you don't mind, but I'm just dying to see how Consuela's Rock Cornish game hens are coming."

Given the circumstances, *dying* was probably a bad word choice, Bernie decided as she watched Eric summon up a twitch of a smile. He cocked his head and came out with a nervous whinny of a laugh.

"But, Brittany," he said, "you know the judges aren't supposed to go down to where the contestants are cooking."

He's doing fake-reasonable, Bernie decided. She wondered if he was fooling the viewers. Because he wasn't fooling her.

Brittany shrugged and kept going.

Eric directed his gaze at camera two.

"I guess the excitement's gotten to her," Eric said. "Isn't that right, Bernie?"

"Oh yes," Bernie replied. Taken by surprise, she came out with the first words that came to mind. "The excitement here is palpable."

She could hear Libby tittering next to her. She kicked her shin. Libby jumped.

"What was that for?" Libby said out of the corner of her mouth.

Bernie covered her mike with the palm of her hand. "Behave," she told her. "Dad is watching."

Libby covered her mike with her hand. "I am. What the hell do you think has gotten into Brittany?"

Bernie thought about that for a moment. "Maybe she's drunk," she finally suggested.

"Or in shock."

Bernie moved her ring up and down while she watched Brittany weaving back and forth as she walked. Her mother's expression, "drunken sailor," came to mind. "I think I'm going with my suggestion," she told Libby, although after she'd said that she realized that Brittany hadn't had time to drink anything, so maybe Libby was right after all.

Finally Brittany got herself over to the table Consuela was working on. She leaned over her, ignoring Estes's frantic motions from the production booth to get back to where she belonged. As Bernie watched, Estes started gesturing to Eric Royal to do something, but he seemed to be frozen. He just nodded and smiled and ran his fingers up and down his jacket lapels. Bernie went back to watching Brittany.

She was gesturing at the Rock Cornish game hens. "Those look nice," she told Consuela. "Are you planning to glaze them?"

"It's none of your business," Consuela snapped as she elbowed her way by her.

Consuela must be frantic, Bernie thought. She certainly had been yesterday and that was without someone dying ten minutes before they had to go on the air. Actually, put in that context, it was a miracle they were doing as well as they were.

Brittany arched her back and fluffed her hair. "No need to get rude," Brittany told Consuela. "I was just hoping you'd have some tips for our viewers."

"Who died and made you El Jefe?" Consuela demanded. And with that, she took a big bunch of parsley and a cleaver and started chopping.

Brittany smiled. "Everyone gets nervous around this time," she confided to the camera.

Bernie groaned. If she were Consuela, she'd be doing something with that cleaver right about now, and it wouldn't be something nice.

"Is this the way they do it in New Jersey?" Brittany asked.

Consuela didn't reply.

Brittany leaned against the table. Somehow her hip knocked against the platter that the Rock Cornish game hens were resting on. Everything went tumbling to the floor.

Consuela picked up her cleaver and advanced on Brittany, who was walking backward. She banged into La Croix, who unfortunately was carrying his second attempt at Oysters Rockefeller.

As Bernie watched, the metal platter flew out of his hands, went airborne, did a spiral, and came down. Suddenly there was rock salt and Oysters Rockefeller sliding down Brittany's shoulders.

Consuela started laughing. Brittany gasped and ran off the stage. Bernie turned to Eric. She was interested to see what he was going to say to try and rescue the situation, but he had apparently been rendered speechless. He kept opening and closing his mouth, but nothing came out. Well, Bernie thought, this is certainly turning out to be a night to remember.

She stepped in front of Eric and began talking. Someone had to host, and it looked as if it was going to be her by default.

Sean turned his gaze away from the television. What a giant cock-up tonight's show had been.

"I can't believe what I'm seeing," he said to Clyde while he watched Marvin make his way out of the men's room and walk back to his seat.

"You can say that again," one of the guys down the bar called out. "This is better than *America's Funniest Home Videos*."

"I'm sure Bernie and Libby aren't laughing," Sean said to Clyde as Brandon slapped another beer down in front of him.

"You could probably use this," he told him.

"I probably could," Sean agreed. After tonight's episode of the *Hortense Calabash Show*, he could probably use two more beers.

"What I want to know," Brandon asked Sean, "is what happened to that Pearl dame? Why isn't she there with the other contestants? She's supposed to be cooking, isn't she?"

"Yes, she is," Marvin said.

Sean turned to look at him as he slipped into his seat.

Marvin pushed his glasses up his nose with his finger. "One thing about beer," he observed, "it makes you want to pee." Sean realized he had to be frowning at him because the next thing Marvin said was, "Did I say something wrong?"

Sean sighed. He certainly couldn't tell him that his presence was annoying him. Instead he said, "You know, Marvin, you can get kits in the convenience stores to fix your glasses with. That way they won't keep sliding down."

Marvin nodded. "I know. But I keep on dropping the screws. They're so small."

Sean took a sip of beer. He didn't even know why he'd bothered to make the suggestion. The kid was a whackadoo. That was all there was to it.

"So what did I miss?" Marvin asked.

"A lot."

Sean could see Marvin was waiting for him to explain, but in his opinion if you want to know something, you don't go off and take a piss at the time it's happening. You stayed and watched. But that was just him. Instead of answering Marvin, he took another a sip of his beer and considered Bernie's attempts to restore some semblance of order to the program. Bernie was giving it a valiant effort, but considering what was going on, he wasn't sure that anything short of a couple of shots fired into the ceiling would do.

"So where do you think Pearl is?" Brandon repeated.

Sean looked up at him. "I take it this has to do with the board?"

Brandon grinned. "Something like that," he allowed.

Sean took another sip of his brew before speaking. His wife had always accused him of liking to know things that other people didn't. He had to admit it was true. It was one of the things he missed about not being chief of police.

"She isn't there because I think she got herself arrested," Sean told Brandon.

"You're kidding," Brandon said.

"Nope, I'm not."

"For Hortense's murder?"

"It would appear so."

Sean had to say the kid looked suitably impressed.

"Pearl was arrested?" Marvin repeated.

"That's what I just said," Sean told him. Maybe the kid needed a hearing aid too.

Brandon scratched his chin. "Damn," he said. "Who would have thought it was her? I was betting on that French fellow. I was sure he was the one."

"Personally, I had my sights on that Reginald Palmer," Clyde said.

"I liked him for this too," Sean said.

Brandon slapped the bar. "I'm out fifty bucks." He cupped his hands and brought them to his mouth. "Hey, guys," he yelled, "guess who the murderer is? It's Pearl."

Sean shrugged as Clyde lifted an eyebrow. "They're going to read about it in tomorrow's paper anyway," he said.

"I didn't say anything," Clyde retorted.

"No. But I know what you're thinking."

And he did too, Sean thought as he grabbed a handful of peanuts and settled back into watching the cooking show. Eric Royal was now saying that due to the unfortunate events that had transpired that evening, they were thinking of doing another run tomorrow night with the same contestants but with a different surprise ingredient, and this time steps would be taken—he emphasized the phrase "steps would be taken"—to ensure that everyone remained in their seats.

"Pearl? Give me a break," one of the guys down at the other end of the bar was yelling.

"Why? Because she's a woman?" his date retorted.

He snorted. "Oh, save me from this feminist crap."

"It's not crap," his date was shrieking when Marvin's cell phone rang.

Sean could hear Marvin talking, but he wasn't paying

much attention to what he was saying, because he was trying to watch the end of the show, which was proving to be extremely difficult with everything that was going on at the bar.

"Hey," he yelled. "Can we have it quiet in here?"

Guess he hadn't lost the old magic, he thought as everyone settled down. He went back to watching the show. Eric Royal was talking about the meaning of the Christmas feast when Marvin started tugging on his sleeve. Sean moved his arm away. Not that he'd say anything, but he didn't like having his personal space invaded.

"Mr. Simmons. Mr. Simmons."

"Sean," Sean automatically corrected. How many times did he have to tell the kid not to call him that? It made him feel like his father.

"Okay, Sean," Marvin said.

"What?" Sean said, not even bothering to try and keep the irritation out of his voice.

"It's about Pearl."

"I already told you about Pearl," Sean said. Jeez, all he wanted to do was watch Bernie. Was that too much to ask?

"She's dead," Marvin said.

Sean kept both eyes fastened on the screen. "Who's dead?" he asked.

"Pearl."

Sean half turned to face him. "What do you mean dead?" he asked him.

Marvin gave him an apologetic smile. "You know. Dead."

"There was an accident?"

"No. I think someone murdered her."

"Murdered her?" Brandon echoed.

Marvin nodded. "At least that's what my dad said."

Sean took another gulp of his beer. If Pearl hadn't killed Hortense, who had? Unless of course Pearl had killed Hortense and someone had killed her? That seemed like an unlikely scenario. No. One person had killed both women. Had to be.

"What do you think?" Clyde asked him.

"I think we have a mess on our hands, that's what I think," Sean said.

Chapter 29

Bernie looked at Bree Nottingham and sighed. Then she sighed again.

Bree was pacing back and forth on the white tile floor in front of the counter, the floor Bernie had just mopped. Now she was going to have to clean the darn thing again, because there were spots of salt and dirty snow all over it. Why her mother had ever picked the kind of floor that showed every speck of dirt was something Bernie had yet to fathom. But she had and given Libby's resistance to change, they were stuck with it.

"Would you like a scone?" she asked Bree. "Perhaps a cup of coffee?"

Heaven only knew she could sure use one. Just looking at Bree pacing the way she was made her feel tired and out of sorts and sloppy. It was a little after seven in the morning and Bree was perfectly dressed in her perfect black ski jacket with ruching on the sleeves, back pants, and matching blue and white striped cashmere hat and scarf. Not to mention that her nail polish was perfect. The woman was inhuman.

Thank heavens I put on some mascara and my hair is up, Bernie thought. *Otherwise I'd look like total crap.*

What with the police and all, she and Libby hadn't gotten back from the studio until well after midnight, and they'd had what their dad liked to call a *debriefing*, which in her opinion was an odious word, and then they'd had to go down to the kitchen and start in on the cooking and baking for today. That was the problem with murder, Bernie reflected.

Well, one of the problems. Murder ate up time—and resources. Not the act per se, but all the attendant stuff that went on after it. And now, on top of everything else, in an hour or so they were going to have a line out the door as everyone in town came to get the "real story." The fact that Pearl's death hadn't hit the papers yet didn't matter. Everyone would have heard some version of what had happened. Somehow everyone always did.

The question was, how much longer could Bree keep it out of the local paper, let alone the national ones? Personally, Bernie expected to see a spread in the tabloids by tomorrow morning at the latest, and it wouldn't surprise her if she saw something in the papers today.

"I just can't believe it," Bree said again.

"Neither can I," Bernie replied.

She rested her forearms on the counter and watched Bree continue to pace. *I'm getting old*, she reflected. When she was in her twenties, she used to be able to stay up five nights in a row on two or three hours of sleep a night, but not anymore. Now she needed her sleep. Even worse, when she didn't get it, her eyes looked as if they were sinking into her head.

"There goes millions of dollars down the drain," Bree said. "My investors will never build on the Randall Estate."

"Well look on the bright side—"

"There is no bright side. I was this close to closing the deal"—Bree put her thumb and her forefinger together—"and now I'm going to have to start all over again." She tapped her finger against her chin. "Although maybe not. Maybe I can still salvage this mess."

"At least Pearl didn't die on camera. Now that would have been really bad."

"True." Bree picked an invisible speck off her jacket. "I just hope there's no television in heaven," she said. "Because Hortense would have a fit if she saw what happened on her show last night."

"You really think Hortense went to heaven?"

Bree glared at her.

"Sorry," Bernie murmured. "I forgot she was your friend." She stifled a yawn. "Well, I think everyone did very well considering; except for Brittany, of course. I mean, it's hard to be at your best cookingwise when someone has just gotten fried in front of you."

Bree stopped pacing, faced Bernie, and extended her arms into the air. "Why do things always happen to me?" Bree lamented.

Bernie straightened up. She was getting a kink in her back. "Funny, but that's what Estes said when Hortense died."

"I don't care what that grotesque man said," Bree replied.

"I'm not sure that's a good word for Estes," Bernie reflected. "Morbidly obese would probably be more accurate. The word *odious* might also be applicable. The word *grotesque* originally comes from the Italian word for grotto and refers to an art style where people and animals intermingle with animals and plants to take on fantastical shapes. It also—"

Bree held up her hand. "Stop," she told Bernie.

"Fine."

If Bree wished to remain ignorant, that was her problem. Bernie walked over to the coffeepot and poured herself a cup. She had to have some, she decided as she stirred in a teaspoon of raw sugar and a little bit of heavy cream into her cup. Otherwise she'd fall asleep standing up on her feet. She took a sip. Sumatran. God, it was good. Coffee and chocolate. Where would the world be without them? Well, actually the world had been without them for a long time. Bernie was glad she hadn't lived back then.

"Sure I can't get you some?" she asked Bree, indicating her cup with a nod of her chin.

"I'm positive," Bree replied. "Coffee creates wrinkles."

"I didn't know that," Bernie replied. "I thought wrinkles were created by genetics combined with interaction with the environment."

Bree shot her a dirty look. Bernie shut up. She was too tired to do anything else.

"When I hired you and your sister to solve Hortense's death, poor Pearl's unfortunate demise was not what I had in mind."

"If it's any consolation, neither did we," Bernie said. She felt like pointing out to Bree that her use of the word *hire* connoted payment of some kind and that Libby and she were doing this as a favor. But she didn't since that would only prolong the conversation.

Bree glared at her. "I expected better," she told her.

Bernie half turned as she heard Libby coming out from the back. She was carrying a tray of cranberry-orange muffins.

"So you're firing us?" Libby asked.

Bernie couldn't help but note the hopeful tone in her voice.

"Of course I'm not firing you," Bree said. "But I warn you, if you don't get it right this time, there will be consequences to pay."

"Such as?" Bernie asked her.

Instead of answering, Bree Nottingham stormed out the door.

"Like we're not paying the consequences already," Bernie said as she watched Bree getting into her BMW.

"What do you think she meant?" Libby asked her sister.

Bernie shrugged. "I don't know, and I don't care."

She followed Libby into the back. Libby was taking the chocolate chip muffins out of the oven. The smell of butter and chocolate and cinnamon overwhelmed her.

"Don't," Libby said as she reached for one. "I don't think we have enough. Have one of these instead." And she handed her a mint chocolate brownie with a chocolate glaze on the top.

They were warm too. Not as good as a muffin, but good enough. Bernie took a bite.

"What kind of chocolate did you use?"

"Valhorna."

"Very good. Very good indeed."

Libby smiled at the praise, but her smile only underlined the circles under her eyes. *She looks the way I feel*, Bernie thought as she studied her sister's face. Actually, she probably looked that way too.

"It would have been nice if someone had left a fingerprint on the wire," Libby said.

"Yes, it would have been."

Actually, Bernie thought, it had been a question of having too many fingerprints. According to Clyde, everyone in the place had handled the cord. She glanced at her watch. If she wanted to catch the 9:05 into the city, she'd better get a move on, because she still had to roll out the dough for the sugar cookies and make the sausage and lentil soup.

Libby looked at her. "By the way, did you ever find out how Brittany got that glowing review in the *Times?*"

Bernie put her hand over her mouth. "I forgot. I'll take care of it," she promised. She took another bite of her brownie and washed it down with a swig of coffee. She licked some of the chocolate glaze off the tips of her fingers.

Libby frowned. "It's embarrassing. We were there for both murders and neither of us saw anything."

"That's because there was nothing for us to see. Both murders were set up before we came in."

Bernie watched Libby think about that for a while.

Finally she said, "But what if Estes is right? What if Pearl's death was an accident?"

"Libby, you saw the wire and the puddle of water. How could that be an accident?"

Libby was silent for another moment. Then she said, "But how did whoever did this know that Pearl was going to touch the wire?"

"Think about that."

"I am thinking," Libby said.

"And . . ." Bernie prompted.

"And . . ." Libby said.

Bernie could see from the expression on Libby's face that she had gotten it.

"The lights weren't evenly spaced," Libby said.

Bernie nodded. "Exactly."

"No one else would have noticed—"

"Or, more to the point, if they did, they wouldn't be compelled to fix them."

"Because they don't have OCD."

Bernie nodded again. "But Pearl would."

"In fact," Libby mused, "she wouldn't have been able to help herself."

"No, she wouldn't," Bernie agreed.

"So all the murderer had to do was pour some water on the floor and wait."

"Right again."

Libby reached over and broke off a corner of Bernie's brownie and ate it. "But what if someone had noticed the water and mopped it up?" she said.

"Then I suppose whoever the killer is would have tried another time."

"Why not just shoot her?" Libby asked.

Bernie ate the last of the brownie and wiped her fingers off on the dish towel lying on the cutting board.

"For that matter, why not shoot Hortense?" Libby continued. "Why go to such elaborate lengths to pull off this crime?"

"Maybe because whoever did it couldn't get near Hortense or Pearl?"

"If it's the same person."

"Libby, of course it's the same person. Probability alone would indicate that they're linked together in some way. I mean, what are the chances of two people being killed in a short period of time, in a small group of people, and not be connected? We're not talking about Manhattan here."

"True," Libby said. "I can see people wanting to kill Hortense. I mean, she wasn't a nice person."

Bernie laughed. "I don't know why you're saying that. Just because she blackmailed people and got them fired and had a foul temper. What's not to like?"

"Exactly," Libby continued. "But Pearl was merely annoying. She was scared of her own shadow. Why would anyone kill her?"

"I don't know," Bernie said.

"Maybe she found something out she wasn't supposed to know," Libby suggested.

"That's as good a reason as any," Bernie allowed.

"Do you think there'll be anyone else?" Libby asked.

"You mean as in another victim?"

Libby nodded. "Maybe even one of us."

"That would suck," Bernie said.

"Suck big time," Libby agreed.

Chapter 30

Bernie got off the Metro-North and walked through Grand Central Station. *I love this place since the city has redone it,* she thought. *I love the ticket sellers' windows; I love the marble; I love the main ticket area with the constellations painted on the ceiling.* And now with the Christmas tree up and the lights on it twinkling, the place looked even more festive than it usually did.

While she walked out onto the street, Bernie was thinking that when she was done she'd have lunch at the Oyster Bar. Even though she didn't like oysters, she loved the atmosphere of the place, and they did make a mean shrimp scampi. The place was worth eating in, even if it was a bit expensive. Every time she went down there she felt as if she were being transported back into the thirties.

She stepped off the curb and hailed a taxi. Libby, she knew, would take the subway. But what the hell. Bree was paying their expenses, and even if she wasn't Bernie would have taken a cab anyway. She loved seeing the lights in the city this time of year, which was why she asked the driver to go down Park Avenue.

Then she sat back and enjoyed the ride. She was of the firm opinion that it was the little luxuries that made life bearable. Take the boots she was wearing, for instance. They were Italian. Brown suede. Pull on. The heel was just right. Every time she looked at them she wanted to smile, just the way she wanted to smile at the trees decorated with white lights on Park Avenue.

Even though it was still early and Lexington and Seventy-fifth Street wasn't a tourist locale, Bernie noted that the street was still more crowded than it would usually be at this time of the day. The holidays seemed to energize people.

Maybe I can do a bit of Christmas shopping as long as I'm down here, Bernie mused. *If everything goes according to plan, I should have the time.* Especially since the store she wanted to go to wasn't more than six blocks away. She was thinking that she could get Libby a new bag.

She'd had the one she was carrying for as long as Bernie could remember. It was definitely time for a change. Something that wasn't black or dark brown. Something that didn't look like a satchel. Something smaller. Possibly in pink or light green. Well. She'd see what Porto had.

The taxi stopped in front of Pearl's place. Bernie paid the driver, took the shopping bag with the blouse she planned on returning to Bloomingdale's if she had time, and got out of the cab. She took a deep breath. This is it, she thought as she went into the brownstone next to the store. She hoped her plan worked. She hoped she'd gotten here before the police had roped everything off. Of course, she could have asked Clyde to find out, but he would have asked her why, and she didn't feel like telling him, because he would tell her dad.

He definitely wouldn't approve of what she was doing, Bernie thought as she stepped into the vestibule and looked at the names listed on the intercom. Pearl's wasn't there. *I should have expected that*, Bernie thought. Lots of times people didn't bother changing the names on the intercom. Sometimes it was laziness, and sometimes they just didn't want their names out where people could read them. In Pearl's case, Bernie was willing to wager it was the latter.

Bernie twirled her ring around her finger. Improvisation always was her strong suit, she told herself as she headed out the brownstone door and went into Pearl's place. She guessed she was going to see how good she was. Bernie looked around as she walked in. She was the only customer in the place, probably because they'd just opened. Bernie wished A Little Taste of Heaven could afford the luxury of opening around ten, but they couldn't. They did almost one-quarter of their business before eight in the morning.

The girl behind the counter surprised her. Bernie assumed the wait staff in a place like this would be strictly prep, but the girl behind the counter was totally downtown with her pink hair done up in braids, her nose ring, and the heart tattoo on the base of her throat. She was definitely not the kind of help she expected to find in an uptown, expensive establishment like this.

Maybe she's just filling in for the day, Bernie thought as the girl smiled at her. Either that or things on the Upper East Side were getting funkier. One thing was for sure though—she couldn't put someone like that in back of the counter in her and Libby's store. She'd never hear the end of it if she did.

"Hi," Bernie said.

"Hi," the girl replied. "What can I help you with?"

Bernie took a deep breath and started in with her spiel. She just hoped that her assumptions about the police were right and this trip wasn't going to be a waste, but she guessed she'd find out soon enough.

"This is so embarrassing," Bernie said.

The girl waited, a slightly panicked look on her face. Clearly, she didn't want to deal with anything that wasn't in her job description. Bernie leaned forward slightly.

"You know what Pearl is like." she confided.

The girl waited. She didn't say anything. Bernie didn't know if that was a good sign or a bad sign.

"Well, I promised I'd return her cookbook."

Bernie lifted a shopping bag with her blouse to demonstrate. It wasn't as if the girl was going to look or anything.

"Okay," the girl said, looking slightly confused.

Bernie was relieved to note that nothing in the girl's demeanor indicated that she knew that Pearl was dead.

"Well, she gave me the key to the apartment."

"Okay," the girl said again. She pulled on one of her braids.

"The key to where she lives."

"I understand. And?"

"I've forgotten the apartment number."

"It should be on the intercom next door."

"I've already looked. It isn't there."

The girl nodded.

"So do you think you could tell me what it is?"

The girl shrugged. "I don't know what it is."

Bernie wanted to shake her. "Do you know who does?"

Instead of replying, the girl turned and yelled into the kitchen. "Hey, Sandy, do you know Miz P's apartment number?"

A moment later, Sandy came out front. Bernie decided he looked typical kitchen crew with his buzzed cut, multiple tats, and stretchers in his ears.

"She's not there," he said as he wiped his hands on the apron he had tied around his waist.

"I know." Bernie dug the keys she'd lifted off of Pearl out of her bag. "That's why she gave me these." And she rattled them.

Sandy looked at her and thought. Finally he shrugged his shoulders. "What the hell," he said. "It ain't my lookout. It's 2B."

Bernie thanked him and walked out the door.

* * *

Pearl's apartment was smaller than Bernie expected. She estimated that the tiny two-bedroom apartment was one-third the size of her father's flat and probably three times as expensive. In addition, it was dark. All of the windows in it faced the back alley. Kinda like *Rear Window*, Bernie thought as she watched a Jack Russell terrier running around chasing snowflakes in the garden of the brownstone across the way from her. Then the dog's owner came out.

She was watching the woman trying to get the dog inside when she heard a noise. Bernie put her hand to her mouth. Then she laughed as she realized the noise was coming from the store down below. But if she could hear the people downstairs, they could hear her. She'd better try and be quiet. And fast. She didn't think Sandy would check up on her, but she'd rather not have to explain things to him.

She took a quick look around. The apartment was immaculate. Not that she'd expected anything less. The wood floors gleamed. So did the windows. The wood furniture had been polished to a high gloss. Even the Christmas ornaments shone.

The Christmas tree was one of those aluminum ones—no chance of needles on the floor. The lights spiraling down it were arranged exactly one-half inch apart. Bernie bet that if she took a ruler, she'd find the space between each and every one of them was equidistant.

The same was probably true of the blue Christmas lights that festooned the door into what Bernie presumed was Pearl's bedroom. Yup, Bernie thought, taking a look at them, whoever had killed Pearl had known her special form of craziness. He'd known it very well and had capitalized on it.

Bernie sniffed the air. It had a slightly stale smell to it. She wondered when the last time Pearl had opened the windows had been. She would have loved to have cracked one open. It was so hot she felt as if she were suffocating, but she reminded herself it would be better if she didn't touch anything she didn't have to. That's the trouble with New York City apartments, Bernie decided as she took off her jacket and threw it on the sofa. You pay a fortune, and you can't regulate the heat.

The word *heat* made her think of the police, which made her think of her dad. She'd just told him she was going to talk to Pearl's employees. Somehow she'd forgotten to mention that she'd stolen the keys to Pearl's apartment. Well, *stolen* was a harsh word. She'd borrowed them. It wasn't as if Pearl would be using them again.

Bernie reflected that she didn't exactly know what she was looking for, but that was okay. She was counting on the fact that someone like Pearl kept meticulous records. Maybe there was something in them that would give her a clue for the motive behind Pearl's death. She hoped so, because motive was all they had left to go with.

They couldn't do a time-of-death line—the wire could have been tampered with at any time after the last show or the start of yesterday's. In addition, there wasn't any physical evidence of note—no fingerprints, no special knife, no fiber samples that they could send to the lab to have analyzed—at least nothing Lucy's men had turned up, so they were stuck with trying to find a motive for the two crimes.

"Find the motive and you might find the answer," her dad had said. "Concentrate on Pearl and work back from there."

And that's what she was doing. She decided to start her search in the kitchen because, according to her dad, you had to look through the whole place. At least the place was small. It shouldn't take her a lot of time to go through everything.

The kitchen was like a ship's galley. The phrase "A place for everything and everything in its place" popped into

Bernie's mind as she opened the cabinet drawers. Everything in them was arranged alphabetically. In the refrigerator, all bottles, food, and produce were evenly lined up. The glasses in the cabinets were all stored in their own little plastic bags. The dishes had separators between them.

"Nothing here," Bernie said out loud as she walked into the living room. It turned out there was nothing in there either. Next she went into Pearl's bedroom. There had to be something here that pointed to a motive for Pearl's murder. Some hint. Something. But there wasn't.

Bernie sighed. Pearl's office was next. If she was going to find anything, this was where it was going to be, she told herself. Bernie sat down at Pearl's desk and opened up the drawers. Absolutely nothing of interest unless seeing paper clips stacked up in neat little piles could be considered fascinating. So much for that, Bernie thought as she tackled the file cabinet.

She started thumbing through the files. There were files for insurance, files for repairs, files for her taxes, recipe files, a file labeled BOOK REVIEWS, files for each employee. Bernie pulled those out and gave them a quick once-over. Nothing jumped out at her as she flipped through them. She put the file back and opened one up called EXPENSES.

Nothing there either as far as she could see, but she decided it wouldn't hurt to take another look at them in a more leisurely fashion. In fact, Bernie thought that could hold true for Pearl's tax forms and employee files. She took them out and put them in her shopping bag too. *At least I did something*, Bernie thought as she got up to go.

She was collecting her coat from the sofa when Pearl's phone began ringing. A moment later the answering machine picked up. A cheery voice floated out in the air from the kitchen telling Pearl that she'd won a free all expense paid vacation to Orlando, Florida. And all she had to do to collect was call this number toll free.

"She's not calling you back," Bernie said to the answering machine as she headed for the door.

She was almost there when she realized something. The answering machine. She'd forgotten to check out the messages on it. How pathetic was that! She went over and pressed the PLAY button. The first three messages were from Pearl's accountant, laundry supply company, and dentist confirming her appointment for the next day. But the last call was from Consuela.

"We need to talk. We need to talk now," she said.

Bernie pressed REPLAY. Interesting. Did Consuela sound desperate? Scared? Angry? Bernie couldn't decide. She played it one more time. Maybe angry. She was just about to call her dad and play the tape for him over the phone when the doorbell rang.

Bernie froze for a moment. The doorbell rang again. And again. She had to get it.

She opened the door. Sandy, the guy from Pearl's shop, was standing there. Uh-oh, Bernie thought.

"What the hell are you doing here?" Sandy demanded.

"I told you. I'm returning a book to Pearl."

"That was twenty minutes ago."

"Well," Bernie ad-libbed, "I was just looking at her cookbooks."

What a stupid thing to say, Bernie thought as Sandy said, "Pearl doesn't have any cookbooks."

"Yes, she does."

I hope I sound convincing, Bernie thought, but she guessed she didn't sound convincing enough, because the next thing that Sandy said was, "Show me."

"You'll have to ask Pearl about that," Bernie told him as she began edging around him and out the door.

Sandy put his arm across the entrance to the door. "No. I want you to show me."

"Hey," Bernie said, "don't make me call the cops."

"You're kidding, right?"

"No." Bernie decided that the correct word for the expression on Sandy's face was *incredulous* as she ducked under his arm. "No. I'm not."

Then she was out into the hall and heading down the stairs. Don't run and don't look back, she kept telling herself. She expected to hear Sandy behind her and feel his hand on her shoulder, but she didn't. Maybe he's calling the police, Bernie thought. But then she was out on the street. A taxi pulled up on the corner and a woman got out. Bernie ran to get it.

"Union Square," she told the driver as she got in.

It wasn't until the cab was pulling away that she realized she'd left her shopping bag with her blouse and the documents she'd collected from Pearl on the sofa.

Chapter 31

Sean hung up his phone and looked out the window at his neighbor across the street, who was trying to string Christmas lights on the bushes in front of his house and doing a bad job of it from what he could see. Ned had been trying to get them lit for the last two hours, and he seemed to be just as far along as when he started. Of course, throwing the lights across the yard probably hadn't helped matters any.

Sean stared at the phone for a moment. *Bernie, Bernie, Bernie. Why are you always doing this to me*? He could tell from her tone of voice she'd just done something she wasn't supposed to. And from what she'd told him about the message on Pearl's answering machine, he could guess what it was. He wanted to kill her for not listening to him. But then, when had she ever?

He reminded himself things could be worse. At least he didn't have to go down to the city and bail out his youngest daughter. At least she was in a taxi heading toward Union Square to speak to Brittany instead of in a holding cell. As Rose used to say, "Things could always be worse." He'd pointed out on more than one occasion that things could also always be better. His wife had not been amused.

But the question remained: What to do about the message Bernie had heard on Pearl's machine? There were two possibilities. He could either do nothing or he could ask Consuela what was going on. Actually, there was no choice. During the course of his being the Longely chief of police, he'd always observed that it was better to shake the tree than wait for the apple to fall. At least then you weren't standing there when it fell on your head.

And at least if he talked to Consuela, he wouldn't have to sit here and watch Ned trying to put those dratted lights on his bushes. It was making him crazy. He wanted to go down there, rip them out of his hands, and show him the way to do it. Three years ago, he would have. Now, of course, with things being what they were, he couldn't.

He took a bite of one of Libby's lemon squares and chewed slowly. She said she'd made them with Meyer lemons, which she'd carefully explained to him weren't really lemons at all. They were hybrids and had originally come from India or somewhere in that part of the world.

Their claim to fame was that their juice was less acid than that of regular lemons. Libby had wanted to know if he could taste the difference, but honestly he couldn't. These lemon squares tasted the same as the ones she always made.

As he took another bite, he found his mind drifting back to the problem at hand, which was whether he should or should not go talk to Consuela. The first obstacle was geographic. Consuela was in Hoboken, New Jersey, and he had no way to get down there unless someone drove him. Since everyone else was busy, that someone was going to be Marvin. Strike the probably. Was going to be Marvin. But no matter what, he wasn't going in that hearse again. Why court bad luck? There was enough of it out there already.

The second obstacle was that he was uninformed as to Consuela's whereabouts. For all he knew, she might not be in her store. She might be out doing errands. Of course, that situation was an easy fix. All he had to do was make a couple of phone calls. He picked up the phone and punched in the number for information.

Twenty minutes later, he knew that Consuela was going to be in her shop until 4:30 in the afternoon. He went back to considering his ride possibilities. He'd sworn to himself after the last time that he'd never ask Marvin to drive him anyplace, ever again. Marvin on the Jersey Pike. Now there was a thought to chill a man's blood. He reminded himself he'd gone into crack houses, faced down deranged husbands waving 9-mm Glocks around, and disarmed a crazed bank robber wielding a butcher knife.

But if he was being honest here, the thought of driving with Marvin scared him more than any of those. It was Marvin's total lack of focus that did it, but as Clyde would have said, "Drastic times call for drastic measures." He took a deep breath, picked up the phone, and dialed Marvin's number. Sometimes a man had to do what a man had to do. Anyway, he was damned if he was going to sit around while some moron was running around his town and knocking people off.

Several thoughts were running through Bernie's mind as she exited the taxi in front of the Union Square Barnes & Noble. The first one was that she probably shouldn't have called her dad and told him about the message on Pearl's answering machine, because now she was going to have some explaining to do.

Well, not exactly explaining. She was positive her dad had figured out exactly what she'd done. What she'd have was—she stopped for a moment while she figured out the exact word—a lot of placating to do. She really hadn't had a choice though. She couldn't go see Consuela herself. She just didn't have the time.

But someone had to and with Libby pretty much

trapped in the kitchen until the taping, that left her father. Of course, there was always Rob. He'd leave his job if she asked him to, but she was reluctant to do that except in times of extreme emergency. Well, in times of emergency, "extreme emergency" being a redundant phrase since by definition emergencies were extreme.

Oh well. Bernie started playing with her ring as she walked around two smokers partially blocking the store's entrance. The best thing she could do now was put her dad and Consuela out of her mind and concentrate on what she was going to say to Brittany. Earlier this morning she'd finally gotten an e-mail back from Amanda Worthy. Evidently she'd been on vacation in Sicily with her boyfriend. Poor baby. Being in publishing was a tough racket. Especially if you were a trust-fund baby so you didn't need to live on the pitiable earnings the industry traditionally paid.

What Amanda had said was interesting if somewhat disheartening, at least in relation to the book business. Brittany's cookbook had gotten the glowing review it had because the woman who reviewed it was a friend of Brittany's father. Another illusion shattered, Bernie thought.

But she still wanted to speak to Brittany. She'd had a motive for murdering Hortense since Hortense was blackmailing her. But what about Pearl? Could she have a reason for wanting to get rid of her as well? Bernie didn't know, but she intended to ask the question and observe Brittany's reaction.

Bernie shook her head to clear it, then opened the doors and went inside the bookstore. A sign posted at the entrance to the store informed her that Brittany's signing was taking place on the fourth floor. Bernie took the escalator up. It didn't take her long to spot Brittany. She was sitting at a table, copies of her cookbook piled around her in neat stacks, sipping coffee out of her paper cup, and talking on her cell.

She's spotted me, Bernie thought as she saw Brittany's eyes widening fractionally.

"Hi," Bernie said.

"Gotta go," Brittany said into her cell. Then she clicked it off and rested it on the table. "What a pleasant surprise," Brittany said.

Bernie smiled. "Well, I was passing by and saw your name in the window and decided to stop and say hello."

"My name isn't in the window," Brittany said.

Bernie shrugged. "I didn't mean that in the literal sense." As she studied Brittany's face, she could see signs of fatigue. Even Brittany's eye concealer couldn't hide the circles under her eyes, and her jaw line looked a little droopy, as did Brittany's shoulders.

Brittany waved her hand around in the air. "You got me at a slow period. Twenty minutes ago the line was so long it was almost out to the escalator."

Bernie unzipped her jacket. "It must be gratifying writing a best-selling cookbook and all."

"Oh, definitely," Brittany answered.

"So how do you do it?"

"Do what?"

"Write a best-selling cookbook."

Brittany giggled nervously. "You know, a little of this and a little of that."

"Like sugar and spice and everything nice?"

Brittany giggled some more. "Something like that. So, are you ready for tonight?"

Bernie nodded. Evidently the last thing Brittany wanted to do was talk about the cookbook. "At least Libby and I aren't cooking."

Brittany let out with another nervous giggle. "I don't know what happened to me last night."

"You were in shock."

Brittany giggled again. "People thought I was drunk."

Bernie remained diplomatically silent.

"But seeing Pearl like that." Brittany shook her head. "It threw me."

"It would throw anyone," Bernie agreed. "It certainly threw me."

"She was such a nice lady," Brittany added.

"Evidently someone didn't think so," Bernie pointed out.

Brittany cocked her head. "Why do you say that?"

"Ah . . . duh . . . because someone killed her."

Brittany tittered. "I suppose that's true. I hadn't thought of it that way."

"Well, we don't usually kill the ones we like. We reserve that for the ones we love . . . and hate."

Brittany took a sip of her coffee and put her cup down. She began fiddling with her pen.

"So who do you think killed Pearl?" Bernie asked.

Brittany shook her head. "I can't imagine who would do such a thing."

"Not even a random, stray thought, a shred of an idea," Bernie insisted.

"Well, I don't know." Brittany scratched her cheek with her nail.

Bernie could see it was chipped. A sign of stress perhaps?

Bernie continued pressing. "Surely you must have some idea?"

"No. Honestly I don't."

"That's funny," Bernie told her. "Because if I was doing the thinking, I might think that you had something to do with it."

"Me?" Brittany shrieked. Then she clapped her hand over her mouth and looked around. No one was there. "Are you out of your mind?" she hissed. "People like me don't do things like that."

"Really?" Bernie replied. She especially liked the "people like me" part.

"Yes, really. Why would I do something like that?"

Bernie wanted to say, "That's what I was hoping you'd tell me," but she didn't. It would be a novel approach, but she wasn't sure how successful it would be. Instead she launched into her spiel. "First of all, you had a good reason to kill Hortense."

"I did not," Brittany said.

"She was blackmailing you," Bernie pointed out. "And don't bother to deny it. It's an open secret."

Brittany smirked. "I guess you don't know as much as you think you do, because my daddy's lawyer was getting ready to sue Hortense for libel. He'd already had a chat with her. If she said anything else about that thing that happened at the temple—"

"That thing," Bernie interrupted. "That's an interesting expression, given the circumstances."

"That thing," Brittany insisted. "This is America. People get second chances here. Anyway," Brittany hurried on before Bernie could interrupt her, "Daddy's lawyer was going to take her to court, but he was so mad, he was going to do even worse—"

"Hire a hit man?"

Brittany snorted. "Don't be a moron. He was going to feed stories to *Page Six* and the *National Enquirer* about the fact that she liked Whoppers and ate baked beans out of the can with a plastic fork. He even got pictures of her doing that."

Bernie burst out laughing. "You're kidding, right?"

Brittany looked offended. "No. Of course not. Ask Daddy if you don't believe me."

"That's okay," Bernie said. After all, who could make up something like that? "It's ridiculous." A libel suit was one thing, but releasing that kind of story to the media was something else entirely.

Brittany drew herself up. "Not if you're Hortense Calabash, it's not. Not if your brand depends on never going near that kind of stuff. It would be like . . . like . . . an Orthodox rabbi eating roast pork."

"I suppose you're right," Bernie conceded. She could hear Brittany's father's instructions to the PI. "Trail her until you get her going into a fast-food joint, the worse the better. I want shots of her eating a Big Mac." The world was becoming very weird.

"I mean," Brittany continued, "the only reason my daddy paid Hortense in the first place was because he thought it would be cheaper than paying our lawyer, even though he told me he knew he shouldn't. 'People like that are greedy,' he said. 'Nothing is ever enough for people like that.' And he was right. It wasn't."

Bernie was about to reply when she saw a woman heading toward Brittany. Two women in fact. No. Three. Book buyers, Bernie thought. She sat there as Brittany nodded and smiled and said things like, "Thank you for coming. Of course, I'd love to sign your book. Whom should I make it out to?"

"Now," she said to Brittany when they were gone, "that still doesn't answer my question about Pearl."

"Why should I kill Pearl?" Brittany demanded.

"Maybe she was demanding money too?"

Brittany snorted. "You really don't know a lot, do you?"

"Enlighten me."

"With pleasure. If you did know anything," Brittany said, "then you'd know there isn't a reason in the world why I would want to kill Pearl. She's the person who's responsible for my book sales. She's the one who wrote the glowing review in the book review section."

Bernie frowned. The woman must think I'm a moron.

"Unless I'm mistaken, the person who wrote the book reviews is called Lulu Brandt."

"That was the name she wrote under. She started doing it when she was younger to make some extra money, and she kept on doing it."

Bernie closed her eyes. She could see the folder labeled REVIEWS in Pearl's file cabinet. But she'd assumed they'd been reviews Pearl was collecting. But they weren't. They were copies of reviews she was writing.

"I thought the woman who reviewed your book was a family friend," Bernie finished lamely.

"She is. Pearl and my dad went to high school together."

"You and she didn't seem that friendly to me when you were on the set."

"Well, I didn't know who she was. My daddy never told me." Bernie realized she must have raised an eyebrow because Brittany said, "He doesn't tell me lots of things. You know how guys are."

"Yes, I do," Bernie said, thinking about all the stuff her dad had tried to keep from her over the years. *Tried* was the operative word. But she'd wanted to know. She had a suspicion that Brittany didn't want to. "So if I call him, he'll confirm what you're telling me?"

Brittany nodded. "Oh, absolutely."

"Who is he?"

"He owns F&B, one of the biggest ad agencies in the country."

"I know who they are," Bernie told her. Everyone did. Besides, she'd done some work for them when she'd been in L.A.

On the way out of Barnes & Noble she called Libby. "I think you can cross Brittany off our list—at least in the motive department." As she clicked off, she consulted her watch. It was too late to go back uptown to shop for Libby's Christmas present. And then she had an idea. She'd get Libby some really good aged Balsamic vinegar, the kind that cost a hundred bucks a bottle; that and some farro should do the trick.

She'd been talking about making a tart with it recently, and it was still fairly hard to find. Bernie had had polenta made with farro when she'd been in Tuscany several years ago, but it was only recently, that the grain was showing up in restaurants in New York City.

The Romans had eaten it. They'd done more than eaten it; it had fed the Roman legions. Historians had traced the grain back to Mesopotamia. Maybe she and Libby could work up a whole menu around it. It had a nice nutty flavor and a pleasing crunch. They used it in Italy in soups and salads, and if she wasn't mistaken, she'd even seen a few desserts featuring it. Yes. Libby would definitely like that better than a new handbag. And what was even nicer, Bernie thought, was that she could order the farro and the vinegar online.

Life is good, Bernie decided as she stopped at a newsstand to buy a copy of the *New York Post* and a pack of gum before heading uptown. As she was paying, she saw a key ring with a picture of the Statue of Liberty waving to two tourists. Since Rob had just started collecting Statue of Liberty stuff, she decided she might as well get that too. She liked getting surprises for people. It was fun.

Chapter 32

By Sean's calculations, he and Marvin were about ten minutes away from Consuela's place. He was just about to tell Marvin that when his cell rang. He picked it up. It was Libby.

"Are you sure about that?" Sean asked Libby when she was done telling him what she'd phoned him to say.

"Sure about what?" Marvin asked, turning his head to look at him.

"Van! Van!" Sean yelled as the Taurus Marvin was driving started drifting into the other lane.

"Sorry about that," Marvin told him as he got back into his lane.

Unfortunately, that wasn't enough for Libby. That fact that Marvin had apologized might have given his daughter a clue about who was right here, but given what she said next, it obviously didn't.

"Libby, I'm not yelling at him," Sean explained. "I'm speaking emphatically. Yes. It's very nice that he's driving me. No. I don't need to apologize. He's not offended." Sean sighed. "Marvin, are you offended?" he asked him.

Marvin shook his head.

Sean held out the phone. "Say it."

"Do I have to?"

"Absolutely," Sean said.

"It's okay," Marvin said. "I'm fine."

"See," Sean told his daughter. He shut his eyes briefly as Marvin passed a truck in the left lane with less than an inch to spare. If you didn't see it, it doesn't exist. "Everything is fine. Really. It's all just peachy. Love you, too, darling." And he clicked off. "Now that was interesting," he mused. "It just confirms what we already know."

"What?" Marvin asked.

Sean realized he'd spoken out loud. "That Consuela owes a great deal of money."

"How do you know that?" Marvin asked as he cut in front of a BMW and decreased his speed to fifty miles an hour.

You could use this kid as a primer for what not to do on the road, Sean reflected. He could feel a headache coming on.

"What?"

"How does Libby know that?" Marvin repeated.

Sean shook himself. "Before I left I asked her to ask around. Confirm what we heard. The people she asked told her Consuela owes money to all the vendors. That's not good. You don't pay your vendors and you're out of business. They said she owes New York State taxes, too, but that could just be a rumor."

And with that Sean decided to close his eyes. If he was going to die, he didn't want to see it coming since there was nothing he could do about it in the present circumstances. After a few wrong turns and a ride down the wrong way of a one-way street, they arrived. That wasn't too bad, Sean thought as they stopped in front of the building that housed Consuela's kitchen. Okay. It was terrible. But Marvin's driving had gotten marginally better on the last leg of the trip.

He surmised this because the volume of honking had

gone down. And at least they weren't in Marvin's hearse. So that was a blessing. They'd borrowed Rob's Taurus. It was rusty, and the rear driver side door didn't work, but Sean didn't care. It was still better than Marvin's dad's death-mobile, as he'd taken to calling the vehicle.

"Watch it, watch it!" Sean yelled as Marvin narrowly missed a Ford Explorer that was pulling out in front of them.

Marvin grunted. Sean could tell he was still unwinding from driving on the Jersey Pike.

"I hope she's here," Marvin grumbled.

"She will be," Sean assured him.

He'd been surprised to learn that Consuela had two places: her shop and the place where she did most of her food preparation. They'd gone to the first place and had been sent to the second, which was a little bit outside of town. Maybe that was one of the reasons she was having trouble. She was paying two rents, two utility bills, liability on two places. Things like that added up real fast.

At least, Sean thought as he looked at the place, there's parking. Even though it was obviously commercial, the place was laid out like a strip mall. It was nothing more than a row of one-story buildings lined up next to one another with room for cars and trucks in the front.

"Do you want me to come in with you?" Marvin asked.

"No. I want you to stay in the car."

"But—"

"Seriously," Sean said.

"But what if she attacks—"

"Me with a dough hook?"

"No. I was thinking of a knife," Marvin told him, alluding to when La Croix had come running out of the store.

"That was a cleaver," Sean corrected.

"Who cares? It was big, and it was sharp. Libby would never forgive me if anything happened to you."

"Nothing is going to happen to me," Sean assured him.

"That's what Bernie always says," Marvin noted.

Sean decided it would be better not to answer.

"What's your plan?" Marvin asked.

"I don't know. I'll figure something out when I get there."

"You mean you don't have a plan?"

"No," Sean snapped. "I don't." He got out of the car. Marvin got out too. The kid was incorrigible. "What are you doing?"

"Helping you get your wheelchair out of the backseat."

"Thanks. But I can do it on my own. Really," Sean said.

Marvin flushed and got back in the vehicle.

Damn this thing, Sean thought as he finally managed to wiggle the chair out of the backseat, set it on the ground, and open it up. He hated it. Of course, without it he wouldn't be going too far. His legs were simply too unpredictable. One minute they'd be fine, the next minute they'd give out. He hated having to use the chair, but without it he'd still be in his house watching the Home Shopping Network. He managed to pull the door open and go inside.

He counted five people working in the kitchen. The place was way bigger than the kitchen for A Little Taste of Heaven, not to mention better equipped. It had more ovens, more stoves, more sinks, more prep tables. No one seemed to be talking much. Everyone was intent on their tasks. Four out of the five people working were wearing headphones, moving their shoulders in time to the music they were listening to.

Consuela was running an expensive operation. She needed lots of business to keep it going. He knew what Libby did with what she had, and he knew what it cost her. This operation looked as if it cost Consuela a great deal more. He was trying to put a number on it when he realized Consuela was approaching him.

"I remember you," she said.

Sean nodded.

"You're Libby and Bernie's father."

Sean bowed his head slightly. "Guilty as charged. Sean Simmons at your service."

"You're the guy they arrested for breaking into Hortense's files."

"That was a misunderstanding."

Consuela folded her arms across her chest and started tapping her foot; then, before he had a chance to speak, Consuela started in. "Well, it didn't look like a misunderstanding to me," she told him. "What do you want? I mean, I know why you're here. You want to ask me questions about Pearl's death, don't you? Well, I have nothing to say to you. I don't have to talk to you, and I won't. So you can just turn that thing around and wheel yourself right out of here."

Wow, Sean thought as Consuela turned on her heels and began marching away, she's got quite a mouth on her.

"My daughter tells me you're in a lot of trouble, financially speaking," Sean called after her.

Consuela whirled around.

Bingo, Sean said to himself as he looked at Consuela's expression.

"That's a filthy lie."

"That's not what my daughter's sources say. They say you have to pay cash up front for every delivery you get."

"I'll sue you and your daughter for libel."

"Darlene, I hate to say this, but you can't sue for libel for something that is true."

"My name is not Darlene."

"Darlene Brown. Bernie remembers you. And I had the guys at the station run your name through the system. They came up with some interesting stuff." Which was a big fat lie, but you never knew what you'd get when you threw something like that out there.

"Listen." Consuela shook her finger in his face.

"No. You listen," he said as he grabbed Consuela's wrist and pushed it aside.

Suddenly one of the cooks was standing beside Consuela.

"You okay?" he asked her.

She nodded.

"You want me to get rid of this guy?"

Consuela fixed her hair. "There will be no need. He was just leaving, weren't you, Mr. Simmons?"

Sean nodded, although he wasn't ready to go just yet. "I'm going," he said. "You just want to tell me why you left the message you did on Pearl's machine before I tell the police about it?" Well, they probably already knew, but he wasn't going to share that information with Consuela.

Consuela leaned toward him again. "Because she said she'd lend me money. Satisfied?"

"Not really," Sean said. "But I guess this will have to do, Darlene."

"Why don't you just leave me alone?"

"I'd love to, but people are dying. Two people to be exact. I'd like to know why."

"You want to know why, ask Reginald."

"Reginald? Why should I do that?"

"Ask him what Pearl and he did the night they were in the pantry at The Best. Go on. Ask him."

"I will." And Sean left. He didn't fancy getting thrown out again. At least not when Marvin was watching.

"We have one more stop before we go home," Sean said to him after he'd stowed his wheelchair in the back of the Taurus and had gotten in. "We're stopping at Reginald Palmer's place."

On the way over he called Clyde and told him what he'd found out. Somehow that was easier than talking to Libby. Not only did Clyde ask fewer questions, he also didn't ask him to do things like stop at the store and pick up an extra carton of eggs or a gallon of milk.

"So," he said to Marvin, "what are you getting Libby for Christmas?"

Rose used to shop for the girls, and now that she wasn't here and he had to do it, he was always at a loss. It would be so much easier if they'd just tell him. All he wanted them to do was make out a Christmas list. But they wouldn't. Both of them were absolutely adamant on the point. They said it wouldn't be the same if they knew. He didn't get it. That way, he could get them what they wanted.

He was thinking how much easier things were when Rose was alive when Marvin turned toward him and said, "I'm getting Libby food. Chocolate to be exact."

Sean brightened. Sometimes Marvin did come up with some good ideas. There was no such thing as too much chocolate as far as Libby was concerned, and even better, he bet he could find that on the Web.

Sean had been doing some thinking about what Consuela had told him as he and Marvin headed back to Reginald's place. As far as he could see, there was only one interpretation. Reginald and Pearl had been sleeping together. According to what people were saying, Reginald had also slept with Hortense.

The man had strange tastes, Sean thought. Very strange. No doubt about that. But more importantly, he'd slept with both women and now they were dead. Suggestive? Possibly. Or it could be just plain bad luck.

"You think he's the one?" Marvin asked.

"Let's put it this way. I wouldn't be surprised." Sean was riding with his eyes closed.

"You think he's a serial killer?" Marvin asked.

Sean snorted. "No. Serial killers usually go about their business quietly."

"Maybe this is a different kind of serial killer."

Sean opened one eye. Things appeared to be proceeding

normally. He opened the other eye. "I think having a murderer running loose is enough to deal with."

"But in the movies—"

Sean cut him off. "This is not the movies."

"That's true," Marvin conceded. "Anyway, we don't really know he did this, do we?"

Sean conceded that they didn't. But Bernie had mentioned something about Reginald being near the Christmas tree before Pearl was killed. At least he thought she had. He took out his cell and punched in her number. When she came on the line, he asked her.

"Yeah. I told you. I remember he was moving away from the Christmas tree when Libby and I came in. We saw him. Why?"

Sean told her what Consuela had just said.

"Interesting," Bernie said.

"But still circumstantial," Sean noted, and he clicked off.

And that was the problem. Nothing that they were discovering was solid. Everything was circumstantial. It would be interesting to see what Reginald had to say, Sean reflected.

Not much as it turned out.

"I'd like to speak to you for a moment," Sean said to him once he was in Reginald's place.

He noted that Reginald put the teapot he'd been rinsing out down and dried it before replying.

"You're speaking to me now," he pointed out.

"In private."

"Take over," Reginald told the girl who was behind the counter. "I'll be back in a minute." Then he walked out from behind the counter and stood in front of Sean.

"I want you out of here," he told him.

"I haven't done anything," Sean protested.

"You must think I'm a moron. I know who you are and why you're here."

"And why might that be?"

Reginald snorted. "Listen, I have to be at the studio in another hour. I don't have time for these kinds of games."

"But you had time to have sex with both Hortense and Pearl and now they're both dead."

Reginald shot his cuffs. "So you're saying that I killed both ladies after I slept with them?"

"Am I?"

"Don't play cute with me. And since when does sleeping with someone mean you go and kill them?"

"I was hoping you'd tell me."

Reginald slicked his hair back with the palm of his hand. "I really have to go."

"One last thing," Sean said. "What did you and Pearl do in the pantry at The Best?"

"Consuela told you to ask me that, didn't she?" Reginald said.

Sean decided not to reply.

"That woman always has been a bitch," Reginald said. "She just can't stand to see people having fun. So Pearl and I got a little drunk when we were working together. So we got it on in the pantry. So what? Things like that happen all the time in the kitchen. Ask your daughters. They'll tell you."

Sean grunted. He wasn't going to ask his daughters anything about that. "Here's one thing they did tell me," Sean said.

"Only one?"

"You were near the Christmas tree right before Pearl got electrocuted."

"And your point is?"

"Maybe you were fiddling with the wire. After all, you were in a position to know how she'd respond to the lights being uneven."

"Me and everyone else," Reginald replied. "And as for fiddling with the wire, why should I do something like that where everyone could see me? Why didn't I come in and do it before everyone else arrived?"

"Maybe you did," Sean told him. "Maybe you were just checking up on your work."

"Listen, you can't have it both ways. And for your information, I liked Pearl. We had a little something going on and then it ended. And that as they say, is that."

Sean watched as he turned and went behind the counter. So what had he learned from this little expedition? Other than the fact that Reginald had slept with Hortense and Pearl, not much. Not much at all. Maybe he'd call Clyde and relay the information to him and see if he could do anything with it. But first he should call Eric Royal and clear up a point that was troubling him.

Chapter 33

Libby averted her eyes from the spot where Pearl had died. Even though Pearl was now resting in Marvin's father's funeral home, the memory of what had happened still shook her. She took a deep breath and told herself to calm down. But she couldn't. If she could, she wouldn't be here. Actually, she shouldn't be here because the *Hortense Calabash Show* was about to go live any moment, but she didn't think she could sit through it without some chocolate.

She really needed a taste of the 70 percent Lindt chocolate bar she kept stashed in her backpack for emergencies. Needed it bad. She had to face the fact she was a chocolate junkie. But, Libby decided, if she had to be addicted to anything, she supposed that there were worse things than chocolate.

Just the thought of the chocolate dissolving on her tongue helped calm her. But the question was, where had she put her backpack? She thought she'd left it resting against one of the table legs, but she felt so unsettled, or as her mother's Jewish friend would have said, so farblondjet, she couldn't remember.

Then she saw what Bernie disparaging referred to as her

hippy-dippy rucksack backpack leaning up against one of the chairs, and she sighed in relief. Thank God, Libby thought as she hurried over to it. She undid the buckle and reached in and came out with a notebook. What the hell? She hadn't put a notebook in there. She peered in. There were a couple of packs of Kleenex, a clipboard with paper attached, some pens, a small metal pill case, and an open packet of disposable cameras, with only one remaining.

"What are you doing?"

Libby whirled around.

Estes was standing right behind her.

"Looking for my chocolate," she stammered.

"Well, you're not going to find it in there," Estes growled as he grabbed the backpack from her.

Libby put her hand over her mouth as she realized she'd made a mistake. Even though this backpack was black like hers, there was a logo on this one that she hadn't seen because that side had been against the chair. And then she saw hers. It was by the table after all, only someone must have pushed it because it had slid down and was lying on the floor.

"You have to get out there," Estes said. "The show is about to start." He began pushing her toward the door.

Libby started toward her backpack. "I'll just be a second."

Estes' grip tightened on her arm. "No," he said.

"But my chocolate," Libby wailed.

"I guess you'll have to do without it," Estes told her as he pulled her out of the green room and toward the studio.

"Where were you?" Bernie whispered as Libby took her seat beside her. "Estes looks as if he wants to kill someone. I don't think I've ever seen him look so pissed."

"I'll tell you about it later," Libby whispered back.

She crossed her legs, realized that that made her thighs look big, and crossed her ankles instead. She just hated being on camera. And she hated the seat she was sitting in.

It was incredibly uncomfortable. The back had no support, and she had to make an effort to remember to sit up straight because when she slumped you could see her stomach, which looked like a roll of dough.

Ten minutes later she was still thinking about how much she needed that piece of chocolate while she watched La Croix chopping lobster meat into cubes so he could combine it with onions and garlic in the sauté pan before adding Cognac to the pan and flaming it.

"I don't think I'd use lobster as a stuffing for a capon. It seems like a waste," she said to Bernie. Maybe if she concentrated on what LaCroix was doing, she'd distract herself.

Bernie covered her mike with her hand. "Haven't you ever heard of oyster stuffing? They do it down south all the time. This is the same principle."

"I realize that," Libby said. "But I've never thought the concept of oyster stuffing is a good one. In my opinion, oysters are meant to be eaten raw or lightly stewed or not eaten at all. I'll be interested to see what a lobster bread stuffing tastes like." One thing was for sure, she reflected. It didn't sound good when you said it out loud.

"Me too," Bernie agreed. "Actually, now that I think about it, lobster just doesn't strike me as a good choice for a Christmas meal."

Libby pondered that for a moment. "It wouldn't be my first pick. It's impractical for a large family gathering both in terms of preparation and expense. But it is festive, and it's certainly easier to work with than the venison we got."

"Yes, but venison is more traditional."

"Lobster is quicker and hence, for a contest like this, easier."

"On the other hand," Bernie pointed out, "they have cardoons."

"This is true." Libby had read about them, but she'd never actually seen or cooked them. She wondered where

Eric Royal had gotten them from. She knew they were from the thistle family and that they were stalky like celery, but that was about it. Bernie had told her they softened as they cooked, and they had a flavor that was both bitter and sweet. At least she didn't have to contend with them.

She wondered if La Croix was going to use them as a base for his lobster sauté. It certainly looked that way. Well, she was curious to see what that tasted like.

She was interested to note that Brittany was doing a lobster sauté as an appetizer. She had removed the meat from the shell and was boiling the shells in water, which she would no doubt reduce to make a sauce. Libby wondered what she was going to use as a base.

Probably the Brussels sprouts Brittany was shredding. She'd give them a quick sauté, and then arrange them on the dish. Libby chewed her cheeks while she thought that through. The lobster and the Brussels sprouts both had an underlying sweetness to them. It might work if Brittany sautéed the sprouts really fast.

But she'd need something for contrast. Something acidic. Like the blood orange she had. That would work. Libby was so immersed in trying to figure out how to present the dish she'd constructed in her imagination that she startled as she realized that Bernie was speaking to her.

"The Italian Roman Catholics have that seven fish deal going on Christmas Eve, but I always associate Christmas with poultry or ham."

Libby nodded absentmindedly as she noticed Estes glaring at her. He made a stop-talking gesture by drawing the edge of the palm of his hand across his throat.

"I think Estes wants us to be quiet," Libby said to Bernie.

"I know what he wants. Personally, I don't see what difference it's going to make given the general mess of the situation. But we know that disasters sell, so I guess the ratings for this show are really high." Bernie moved her silver and onyx ring up and down her finger. "Although not as high as if someone got killed on TV."

"Don't say that," Libby chided. "Don't even think it."

"You're right. I apologize." And with that, Bernie uncovered her mike and sat back in her chair.

Libby tried not to think about what Bernie had just said, but she was probably right. She usually was about stuff like this. That's probably why Estes had insisted that the contest still go on. In her view, it hardly made any sense since one of contestants was gone, but Estes hadn't seen it that way, so here they were again. This was the third . . . or was it the fourth? night they were on.

There'd been so much happening that the days just blended into one another. Libby stifled a yawn. For a moment she watched Estes clean out his backpack. Then she started thinking back to the cooking gaffe she'd committed earlier that day.

She'd mixed up four fruitcakes. They'd had the usual ingredients, except this time she'd put in some very expensive imported glacé fruit that she'd gotten from France. The problem was that it wasn't until after she'd put the cakes in the oven that she realized that she'd left out the shortening. Which was not good. They were dry enough as they were. Somehow the cakes had held together when she'd unmolded them, but she wasn't sure how they were going to taste.

She'd asked her father to try some and give her his opinion, but when she'd left, the slices were still sitting on the tray next to his chair. He'd never been a big fruitcake lover anyway. He always claimed they made ideal doorstops.

Libby started biting her nails, realized what she was doing, and stopped. She just hated throwing out food, and, anyway, that glacé fruit had cost a fortune. Maybe she should just crumble them up and use them for something else, but what? Possibly as a base for a crust or maybe she could make a steamed pudding with them. Actually, the steamed pudding thing might work. If she wasn't mistaken, there was a recipe for something similiar in one of her cookbooks. The question was, which one?

She was trying to figure that out when her sister nudged her in the ribs.

"What?" she asked.

"Look at Brittany," Bernie instructed.

Libby looked. She couldn't see anything. "So?"

"Well, she's had that lobster meat in that pan for so long it's going to be inedible."

"Her timing's off," Libby said.

"Obviously," Bernie noted. "Maybe she has other things on her mind."

"Like what?"

"Like the fact that we're sitting here in this studio with someone who has killed two people."

"Why do you keep saying things like that?" Libby chided.

"Makes it kind of exciting, doesn't it?"

"Not to me," Libby told her sister.

Bernie leaned closer to her. "One thing I do know about everyone here," she told her.

"What?" Libby asked.

"We're the best cooks."

She's right, Libby decided as she looked at what La Croix was doing. He was actually boiling the Brussels sprouts. Not blanching them and then sautéing them, but boiling them. Now that was a crime.

They were going to be an ugly grayish green. And they were going to taste like cabbages. He should know better than that. Brussels sprouts were one of those vegetables that you either cooked right or didn't bother with, unlike carrots, which were a forgiving vegetable. You could pretty much do anything you wanted with them and they'd be fine.

"I'll tell you one thing," Libby said.

"What's that?" Bernie asked.

"I'm not looking forward to eating La Croix's Brussels sprouts."

"Neither am I," her sister agreed.

What Libby really wanted was her chocolate. But there was no chance of that now.

Chapter 34

Bernie spotted Marvin and Rob the moment she and Libby walked into R.J's. They were down toward the end of the bar where the dartboard was. She was amused as everyone in the place clapped and hooted and hollered as she and Libby walked toward them.

"This is embarrassing," Libby said to her.

"I think it's fun," Bernie replied as she stopped every couple of steps to curtsy and blow kisses.

"You would," Libby shot back.

"What's that supposed to mean?" Bernie demanded.

"That you like attention and I don't."

"You might if you were a little less uptight."

"Ah, our local celebs," Brandon said as Bernie and Libby took their seats next to Rob and Marvin. "Two Brooklyn Browns on the house. Any tips?" he said as he set the beers down in front of them.

"Tips on what?" Libby asked.

Bernie snorted. "What do you think? He's talking about the board." She saw Libby's blank look. "You know. The pool. The betting pool on who killed Hortense and Pearl."

"Right," Libby said.

Bernie turned back to Brandon. "No. No tips. We've made almost no progress on this investigation."

"That's not true," Libby protested.

"You're right," Bernie said. "We've managed to eliminate everyone's motive." She raised her beer bottle up. "To the holidays."

Everyone clinked their bottles together and drank.

"You don't mean that, do you?" Rob asked her.

"I most certainly do. As of this point, no one has a good motive for killing Pearl and Hortense—if they're to be believed. They're all little angels."

"That's the whole point," Marvin said. "What if they're lying?"

"Of course they're lying. Or omitting something, which is the same thing." Bernie tapped her fingers on the bottle. "The question is, what are we overlooking?"

Libby coughed. "Not to change the subject, but where's Dad, Marvin? How come he's not here? I thought he was supposed to come with you guys."

"He wanted to stay home," Rob told Bernie. "I think all that driving around with Marvin wore him out."

"Hey," Marvin squawked. "It's not my fault if her dad it super critical."

"Calm down," Rob said. "I was just kidding."

"Well, you drive him around and see how you like getting yelled at all the time."

There was an uncomfortable silence. Bernie caught Libby's eye. Libby nodded and started stroking Marvin's arm.

"Dad couldn't get along without you. He doesn't mean what he says."

"Well, he certainly sounds as if he does."

"You just have to learn to ignore him," Bernie said. "Like we do."

"You do," Libby corrected. "I never mastered the art."

"Anyway," Rob interjected. "Your dad said someone was coming over later."

Probably Clyde, Bernie decided. Aside from Rob and Marvin, he was the only person who visited her dad. Bernie looked up to see Brandon hovering nearby.

"What?' she asked him.

"So you really don't have any suspects?"

"We have lots of them. That's the problem."

Bernie closed her eyes for a second, then opened them again. She didn't want to talk about the case right now. It was too depressing. Especially since they seemed to be going backward. She'd thought Reginald was the killer, but her dad had disabused her of that notion. And she wasn't feeling any more confident with Brittany as a suspect. She'd called Brittany's dad and he'd confirmed everything that she'd said—not that he wouldn't, being her father and all.

Maybe tomorrow she'd ask Clyde if he could check into her father's bank records. If he actually had hired a lawyer and an investigator, there ought to be checks on file, and of course there was always La Croix. He was still her odds-on favorite. The fact that he'd come at her dad with a cleaver seemed to point to a certain . . . ah . . . instability in his character. Maybe she'd have Clyde check him out again too. Maybe he could come up with a new angle. The thought cheered her up slightly.

Rob nudged her. "Hey," he said, "did you bring me anything back from the city?"

"The Brooklyn Bridge."

"Seriously."

"I got you something for your collection."

"Neat."

Bernie reached into her tote bag. Where was it? This is what happened when you carried too much stuff around. Bernie took out her cosmetic case, her checkbook, her sunglasses, an extra pair of nylons, a nail file, a bottle of nail polish, her hairbrush, a small bag of cashews, a pack of sugarless gum, a small box of breath mints, her cell phone, the bills she was supposed to mail out, the copy of the *New York Post* that she'd bought and never gotten around to reading, and the instant flash camera she'd bought so she could take pictures of the studio and show them to her dad, which she'd also never gotten around to doing.

"It's amazing you're not permanently lopsided with everything you carry around," Rob said as he grabbed the paper off the bar. "I love *Page Six*," he explained.

Bernie turned and looked at him. He shrugged. "Guys like gossip too."

She went back to looking in her bag. She'd just found the key ring—somehow it had found its way into the pocket where she usually kept her cell phone—when he said, "Hey, isn't Estes the guy who's producing your show?"

"Yeah," Bernie replied. "Why?"

"Well, listen to this," Rob said, and he began to read it out loud.

Bernie grabbed the paper from him before he was half done and read the article herself, then she reread it to Libby.

"According to well-placed sources, Estes, the ex-porn producer who made the climb to TV may be heading back to his old haunts. Evidently, his cash cow the *Hortense Calabash Show* isn't as profitable as it once was. The renowned Heavenly Housewife seems to be taking a nosedive these days.

"Unless something is done quickly, rumor has it that the show is going to be pulled, and the powers that be aren't even waiting till the end of this season. Unfortunately for Estes, he's been banking on the money from it to dig himself out of the mighty big hole he's landed himself in with the Heavenly Housewife when they were an item."

"I can't believe they don't know that Hortense is dead," Rob said.

"I can't believe that Estes made porn," Marvin said.

Rob tossed a peanut into his mouth. "I can't believe you never saw *Jennie and the Jets*. It's a classic."

Bernie put down the paper. "And I can't believe he and Hortense were an item."

"Maybe he wasn't so fat then," Libby said.

"That's a weightest comment," Rob told her.

Bernie smacked his arm. "There's no such word."

"Anyway, we don't know if the article is true or not," Libby pointed out.

"No, we don't," Bernie agreed.

But some of the members of the crew might. It was worth a shot. Bernie reached for her cell.

"Who are you calling?" Libby asked.

"Eric Royal." But he wasn't there. "I guess he's gone home." She tried his cell. He didn't pick up. She left a message on his voice mail and was about to call her dad when she noticed the look on Libby's face.

"What's up?" she asked.

"Nothing."

"Give," Bernie told her.

"It's silly."

"Tell me anyway."

Libby pointed to the camera on the bar. "Estes had one of those in his backpack, not that that means anything. Lots of people have them. But it was a twin pack, and he'd already used one."

"So you're suggesting . . . " Bernie said, even though she knew exactly what Libby was thinking.

"Maybe he used the other one to blow up the oven," Libby said. "Not that it matters because there's no way to prove anything."

"They have serial numbers," Marvin said suddenly.

"What has serial numbers?" Bernie asked.

"The cameras. All of those cameras have serial numbers, and the ones in the package both have the same ones."

Rob leaned forward. "How do you know?"

Marvin shrugged. "My dad told me."

"Too bad we don't have the numbers," Libby mused. "Then we could compare the number of the camera that set off the explosion with the number on Estes' camera.

"I think Dad has the number," Bernie said.

"How could he have the number?" Rob demanded. "Given the circumstances, I'd think the camera would have been destroyed."

"It wasn't. I saw it. He got the serial number from Clyde. I saw him write it down in that file he keeps."

"We could call and ask him," Libby said.

"We could, but it's irrelevant if we don't have the serial number on Estes' camera?" Rob said.

"Good point," Bernie said. She started moving her ring up and down her finger.

"We could ask Clyde to do it," Marvin said.

Libby shook her head. "No, we couldn't. Clyde would need a warrant, which he couldn't get because there's not enough evidence. So Estes wouldn't have to give up the camera if he didn't want to. And anyway, the whole thing is ridiculous. It's probably not the same camera. I mean, why would he keep it?"

Bernie took a sip of her beer, even though she reflected that she'd probably be better off having coffee. "Maybe he doesn't realize it has a serial number. After all, you didn't."

"Possibly," Libby conceded.

Marvin tapped his fingers on the bar. "I think we should try and find out."

"How?" Libby demanded. "As far as we know, the camera is in his backpack, and his backpack is with him."

Rob took a sip of his beer. "Then we'll just have to figure out a way to separate him from it."

"And how are we going to do that?" Bernie challenged.

Rob put his bottle of beer down. "Give me a chance. I'm thinking."

Bernie watched Libby picking at her cuticles.

"Libby, if you have something to say, say it."

"Well," Liby began, "maybe we don't need to separate him from his backpack."

"How do you figure that?" Rob asked her.

"I saw him cleaning out his backpack when we were filming, so maybe he threw it in the trash. Maybe my seeing it made him nervous all of a sudden, and he decided to get rid of it."

Everyone was silent for a minute while they thought through the possibilities. Bernie was the first one to speak.

"Let's assume that Libby's right," she said slowly. "If she is, he could have thrown the camera in the trash, or he could have waited till he went outside and thrown it in the Dumpster. If I were him, I'd pick the Dumpster. Especially because tomorrow is trash day. Bernie looked at Libby. "What do you think?" she asked.

"I think it wouldn't hurt to look."

"Me neither," Bernie said, reaching for her jacket.

"Where are you going?" Brandon yelled after them as they headed out the door.

"To solve a crime," Bernie yelled back.

She and Rob went in Rob's Taurus while Marvin and Libby followed them in Libby's van. On the way, Bernie called Estes because, as she explained to Rob, if he was still at the studio, then maybe they should wait. But he wasn't there, so she left a message on his answering machine about having a question about tomorrow and clicked off.

She was watching the snow drifting off the trees lining the side of the road when Rob started talking. "You know," he said. "Here we are, four adults, and all of us are still living with our parents."

"Amazing, isn't it?" Bernie said.

Rob grimaced. "Pathetic is more like it."

"I'm not so sure," Bernie said slowly. "In the old days,

multigenerational households were the norm. I'm not so sure that's such a bad thing. However, if you want to change, the solution is simple."

"And what's that?" Rob asked.

"Easy," Bernie said. "All we have to do is get my father and your mother together. Then my dad could move in with your mom and you could move in with me."

"But what about Libby and Marvin?"

Bernie laughed. "Okay. So we need another house."

"Or we could build an extension onto the store."

"Hold that thought," Bernie said as they turned into Hortense's estate. "What the hell are they doing here?" she asked as she spotted two Longely police cars.

"I'd say unfinished business. You want to go back to the bar?"

Instead of answering, Bernie pointed to a crook in the road. "Pull off here."

A moment later, Libby rolled up behind them. Bernie got out of the car and approached the van. Libby rolled down her window.

"Now what?" Libby asked.

"We could go back to the bar," Bernie said.

"It's not an unreasonable suggestion," Rob said as he came up behind her.

"No, it's not," Bernie agreed.

"But you're not going to follow it," Rob said.

"This is true. I'm not."

Bernie rubbed her hands. She was getting cold standing there.

"The police aren't going to like this," Rob pointed out.

"If they see us."

Bernie looked around. If the moon wasn't out and if there wasn't snow on the ground, there wouldn't be a problem. But they were.

"You're determined to do this?" Rob asked Bernie.

"I am."

"Of course you are." Rob tapped his fingers against his thighs. "So what we need is a distraction."

"I know," Marvin said. "Libby and I will drive the van to the front door. We'll say that Libby left something inside and that we need to get in, and while we're doing that, you guys can go through the Dumpster."

"Going through a Dumpster is definitely not what I had in mind for this evening," Rob said.

"Come on," Bernie told him. "You're going to love it."

"No, I won't, but I'll do it anyway."

"Which is why I love you," Bernie said.

Rob grinned. "One of the reasons."

"Luck," Libby said as she put the van in drive.

"Same," Bernie told her.

"You think this will work?" Rob asked Bernie as they watched Libby drive up to Hortense's house.

"I certainly hope so." Bernie started walking. "Why didn't I wear decent boots?" she lamented out loud as she trudged through the snow. True, there wasn't a lot of snow on the ground, but since she was wearing light blue wedges, this was not good. Not good for her shoes and not good for her feet. Her toes were going to freeze off by the time she got back to the Taurus, and her fingers weren't doing very well either.

"I hate winter," she grumbled. "Hate it, hate it, hate it."

"Maybe you wouldn't mind it so much if you dressed for it," Rob pointed out.

"And succumb. That would be giving in."

"No. That would be smart.'

"Are you calling me stupid?" Bernie demanded.

"Pigheaded would probably be a better term."

Bernie would have hit him but her hands were so cold she couldn't make them into fists.

"Almost there," she said.

She turned and looked at Libby and Marvin. They were

talking to the policemen. No one was looking in their direction.

"Okay," Bernie said as they neared the Dumpster. It was a small one, smaller than the one that they had behind A Little Taste of Heaven. She opened the top that was designed to keep out the raccoons, cats, and dogs and looked inside. There were four large plastic garbage bags, plus a crumpled-up brown paper bag with grease stains on it.

"I think it's in here," Bernie said as she lifted it out.

"How do you know that?" Rob asked her as she started opening it up.

"Because the others come from the kitchen. This bag was probably something he had a slice of pizza in. It would just be easier for him to put it in here and toss it in the Dumpster and be on his way."

Bernie drew out the camera. "I can hardly wait to show Dad," she said.

He was going to be very pleased.

"Should we call him?" Rob asked.

Bernie shook her head. She wanted to surprise him.

Chapter 35

The cooking show was over, and Sean had to admit that he rather liked it without Hortense, although he had liked it with her too. Just not as much. Hortense had been unpredictably predictable, but with Eric Royal you never knew what was going to happen. He looked so nervous that you wanted to watch just to cheer him on.

Sean reflected that Libby hadn't looked as nervous as she had the first time she was on the show. Of course, she hadn't been cooking either. Sean was thinking about the face she'd made when she'd tasted the lobster and bread stuffing as he channel surfed. It was the same face she'd made as a little girl when his wife had forced her to eat liver.

He was thinking about how ironic it was that now liver wasn't good for you when back then it was when he heard the door downstairs open. Then he heard footsteps coming up the stairs. He put the remote down and listened. They weren't Clyde's; even his weren't that heavy, and they certainly weren't his daughters. He called out and Estes answered, which was a shock. It had taken him a few minutes to climb the stairs, which didn't surprise Sean, given the man's size. What did surprise Sean was that he was here. He felt a twinge of misgiving, but Sean told himself that was because he didn't like surprises. Experience had taught him that they were never good. As Estes came through the door, Sean thought of something else.

"Was the downstairs door open?" Sean asked him. "Usually my daughters lock it."

Estes took a handkerchief out of his jacket pocket and blew his nose. "I guess they must have forgotten."

"I guess they did," Sean agreed. But he wondered. Libby was a fanatic on that particular subject. He felt a faint stirring of unease in his guts.

"So the girls aren't here?" Estes asked.

Sean shook his head. "Is there something I can help you with?"

"I thought they were."

"Why would you think that?"

Estes blew his nose again. "I just assumed they'd come home after the show."

"Obviously they didn't. You should have called them."

"I tried. They're not answering their phones."

Sean felt another flutter of alarm. Libby might turn her cell off, but Bernie always had hers on. That left two possibilities: either the girls were injured or Estes was lying. Sean chose to go with the second possibility. If Bernie and Libby had been involved in some sort of misadventure, he would have heard by now.

"So what did you want to talk to them about? Maybe I can relay a message," Sean said to Estes.

Estes ignored his question and pointed to the table in front of Sean.

"Is that fruitcake?" he asked.

Not answering was not a good sign, Sean thought. It was not good at all. "Yes. Libby made it for me."

"You like fruitcake?'

"Not particularly."

"Mind if I have a slice?"

Sean shrugged. "Be my guest. In fact, let me call my daughters and tell them you're here."

"Remember, their phones aren't working."

Sean forced a laugh. "Oh yes. Well then maybe I should call my friend Clyde. He can find them for you."

"I think your phone might be out too," Estes said.

"Really?"

That's probably because you cut the line, Sean thought as he feigned surprise at what Estes was telling him. *I should have gone to R.J's*, Sean thought. I don't even have my service revolver in the house anymore, much less a twenty-two. He'd gotten rid of them when his hands started shaking so badly he couldn't hold them anymore.

He should have kept them anyway, because now he was alone with a guy who had most likely killed two people. Sean cursed himself. How could this man have escaped his radar? He hadn't even seen him coming. The only good thing was that Libby and Bernie weren't here. He just hoped the situation stayed that way.

Sean cleared his throat. "So what makes you say the phones are out?" he asked in a calm, even tone. He didn't want to get Estes upset. He didn't know what Estes had in mind, but he had the strong suspicion that it was going to be something that he wasn't going to like, so the longer he could postpone it, the better off he'd be.

As Sean watched Estes shift his weight from one foot to the other, he thought about how large Estes was. At least four hundred pounds. Maybe more. Then as Estes sniffed, then sniffed again, Sean realized something else. This man was coked out. How could he have missed that?

"I guess they had a malfunction somewhere," Estes told him.

Sean's eyes wandered around the room. He didn't see

his cell anywhere. He'd probably left it in Marvin's van. Of course, even if it was here, given that he walked like a ninety-year-old man, getting to it would be problematic anyway.

Estes took out his handkerchief, rubbed his nose with it, and put it back in his pocket. Then he reached over and broke off a piece of fruitcake.

"You called Eric," he said.

"Yes, I did. So how's the guy doing? He seemed a little stressed." When Sean had first joined the force, it had been hard to make polite chitchat in situations like these, but he'd learned.

"Eric is fine. He told me you were asking about how the show is doing without Hortense."

Sean nodded. He closed his eyes for a moment. If he could get to the bathroom, he could get Bernie's hairspray. That or any aerosol product and a match and you had a flamethrower. For the first time in his life he regretted not smoking.

"Why do you care?"

"It was just a question."

"Policemen don't just ask questions."

"I'm not a policeman anymore."

"No. But you still think like one."

Sean managed to get up. "If you'll excuse me," he said, "I have to use the little boys' room."

Estes smiled at him. Well, not exactly smiled, Sean decided. It was more like a snarl.

"Sit down," he said.

"I really have to go."

Estes pushed him back in the chair. "A little self-discipline is good for the soul."

"We're not talking about my soul."

"I am."

So much for Plan A, Sean thought. On to Plan B. Too bad he didn't have a Plan B.

Estes loomed over him. Sean looked up.

"You think I killed them, don't you?" Estes asked Sean.

"I have no idea what you're talking about."

"Then why did you ask about how the show was doing?"

"Because my daughters are on it."

Estes sniffed again. "You know," he said, "Hortense was a witch."

Sean grunted. He didn't want to hear this, didn't want to hear what he was positive was going to be Estes' confession. Because after that . . . well, he didn't want to think about after that. Estes went on anyway.

"You know," he said, "respect is an amazing thing. Now I get invitations to parties. Nice people ask me to their homes. They invite me out to restaurants. Before, they wouldn't look at me. And you know why? I'll tell you. Because now I'm respectable. And you know why I'm respectable? Because I'm successful. I'm a successful television producer."

"A very successful television producer," Sean echoed. Even at his healthiest and strongest he would have had trouble bringing this guy down without the aid of his weapon.

Estes smiled. "The *Hortense Calabash Show* was a success."

Sean nodded. He wondered how Estes was planning on killing him. Maybe he was going to sit on him. That would work

"An unqualified success," Estes reiterated. "But I forgot the number-one rule. I forgot you have to diversify. My grandmother always said, 'Never put all your eggs in one basket,' and she was right. I should have been working on several projects at once." Estes sniffed a couple of times, then started speaking again. "Americans always want new things. Better things. If you want to stay on top, you have to give them that. Hortense wouldn't admit that her numbers were slipping. I tried to talk to her, but she didn't want to listen. I mean, what could I do? Especially since she held an IOU on me."

"Yeah. Women. They can be like that. Totally unreasonable."

Estes let out a barking laugh. "You're a funny guy."

"Glad you think so," Sean replied.

What can I use to defend myself? Sean wondered as he scanned the space in front of him. There was nothing here. Just three days worth of newspapers and a stack of magazines. The plate the fruitcake was on. Maybe the fork on the plate. He could use that. But where would he jab it? It would have to be someplace in Estes' face to do any good. No. That wouldn't really work.

And then Sean's eyes fell on the can of Christmas snow that Bernie had been going to use to write on his windows before he'd stopped her. She was going to take it downstairs, but obviously she'd forgotten, because it was still next to his chair where he'd put it after he'd grabbed it from her. That might work. No. That would work. He blessed his youngest daughter.

All he needed now was a match. With luck he could get Estes to back up out of the room. With even more luck he'd trip and fall down the stairs. And even if he didn't, hopefully Sean would have enough time to get back inside his bedroom and lock the door behind him.

Then he could stick his head out the window and start yelling. If the gods were with him, Ned or someone driving by would see him. It wasn't a great plan. It probably wouldn't even work. But it sure as hell beat sitting there and waiting for Estes to do whatever he had in mind.

"The thing is," Estes continued, "you have to change with the times. If something doesn't work, you have to discard it and move on. That's the way the market is these days. It's impersonal. A force of nature. You have to get rid of what doesn't work to make room for what does."

Sean nodded. "I couldn't have said it better myself. You wouldn't have a cigarette on you, would you?" he asked.

"I didn't know you were a smoker."

Sean shrugged. "My daughters think I've given it up."

"Sure," Estes said. "Why not."

It's like he's giving me my last cigarette, Sean thought as he watched Estes go into his pocket and take out a packet of Camels and his lighter.

"That used to be my brand," Sean said as Estes handed them to him. Sean pointed to the piece of fruitcake Estes was holding. "Aren't you going to give that a try? You'd be doing me a favor."

Estes nodded. He took a bite. Then he took another. "A little dry," he said, but he kept right on eating.

Sean took a deep breath. What if he was becoming paranoid in his old age? What if he was wrong? What if Estes wasn't looking to kill him? What if he hadn't killed Hortense and Pearl? But if he hadn't, then what was all that business with the phones about? Why was he here?

And what was that business about getting rid of things that didn't work? Every instinct that he had gotten in his years on the force was telling him this man didn't wish him well. And if he was going to make a mistake, then so be it. Better to be wrong than dead.

Sean took another deep breath, put the cigarette Estes had given him in his mouth, and picked up the lighter. He allowed it to slip through his fingers.

"Damn," he said. "I can't hold on to anything these days."

Estes didn't even look at him. He was too busy eating Libby's fruitcake.

"Here goes," Sean muttered to himself as he bent over and picked up the lighter and the can.

He just hoped he could take off the top of the can and hit the spray button. Last year he wouldn't have been able to do that. But in the last two months the trembling in his hands had subsided, and he was gaining strength back in them thanks to the exercises he did five times a day.

He looked up quickly. Estes was still eating. Sean pulled at the top of the spray can. It moved slightly. He pulled some more. The top came off.

"Look what I found," he told Estes as he straightened up. Then he hit the button and lit the match.

An arc of flame came out of the can right near Estes' face. He took a quick step back. *I missed*, Sean thought. *Now I'm done for*. It took him a second to realize that Estes wasn't coming toward him, wasn't yelling at him. Instead he was making strange noises and pointing to his throat.

My God, he's choking on the fruitcake, Sean thought as he heard the downstairs door open. A chorus of "Dads" and "Seans" floated up from Libby, Bernie, Rob, and Marvin. Sean reflected that it looked as if the cavalry had arrived just in time to save Estes from choking to death on Libby's fruitcake.

Bernie burst through the door. "Hey, Dad," she said, waving what looked like a camera at him. "Look what we got. Evidence that Estes killed Hortense." Then she stopped short and looked down.

"Oh," she said. "What's with Estes?"

By now Estes was turning blue.

"He's choking."

It took a minute but Rob finally managed to dislodge the piece of fruitcake from Estes' throat. Sean explained what had happened as he told Rob and Marvin to tie Estes up; not that he was going anywhere, Sean reflected. The man looked in terrible shape. He doubted he could get anywhere right now. He was just leaning up against the wall, wheezing.

Sean borrowed Libby's cell phone and called the Longely Police Department.

"See," Sean heard Bernie say to Libby as he waited to speak to Lucy, "I told you that fruitcake was way too dry."

Chapter 36

Libby carefully smoothed down a wrinkle in the pale pink linen tablecloth. It was in surprisingly good shape, considering that her mother had gotten it on her honeymoon in Ireland. She used to say it was the only thing her father had let her buy.

Usually they didn't use the dining room to eat, hadn't even when her mom was alive and her dad was well, but tonight was Christmas Eve and Christmas Eve was special. Especially this one, Libby reflected as she checked the glasses and the silverware for last-minute spots. Thank heavens her father was as resourceful as he was. Otherwise . . . well . . . she wasn't going to even think about otherwise.

Libby's gaze rested on her mother's good bone china. She picked up a plate and turned it over. The pattern was called Prince Albert. She didn't know why she always forgot that. Because she loved it. She loved the gold rim and the delicate red and pink roses on it. *I should really use them more often*, she thought as she picked up a piece of her mother's crystal stemware and held it up to the light. Little prisms of light danced in front of her eyes. She should use these more often too.

Libby smiled as she glanced out the window. A light

snow was falling. The streets were quiet. Everyone was home celebrating. She and Bernie had closed the store an hour and a half ago, and they were staying closed till Monday. Libby was looking forward to that. They had a blessed weekend with nothing to do. Tomorrow, Rob, his mother, and Marvin and his father were coming over for Christmas dinner, but tonight it was just her, Bernie, and her dad. Given what had happened, that was fine with her. No. It was more than fine. It was perfect.

Libby turned as Bernie carefully set the white tureen full of pumpkin bisque on the table. Originally she'd debated serving the soup in a pumpkin but decided she liked the contrast of the pale orange and white better.

"The table looks nice," her dad observed as he came through the door.

The look of anticipation on his face made Libby smile.

He added, "I'm glad we're having an old-fashioned Christmas dinner."

Bernie laughed. "What? You don't want smothered cardoons and lobster stuffing?"

Sean shuddered. "No, thank you."

"I bet you've never tried cardoons."

"And I don't intend to."

"Don't knock them," Bernie continued. "Cardoons are from the thistle family. They're extremely nutritious, and they're really not that bad tasting."

Libby lit the candles. "They're not that great either, or as Mom would have said, 'Damning with faint praise.' "

They all sat down. Libby ladled the soup into everyone's bowl. It was simple but delicious, mostly just pumpkin sautéed with onion, seasoned with freshly ground salt and pepper and a couple of scrapings of fresh nutmeg; then she had pureed the vegetables, carefully combined them with some chicken stock and half and half, and heated the mixture through. Sometimes simple things are the best.

"Delicious," her father pronounced as he took a taste.

Libby reached over and took one of the Parker House rolls she'd just made out of the silver bread basket and broke it in half. She inhaled the smell of fresh yeast as she buttered it and took a bite. Nothing was better than rolls still warm from the oven. After this they'd have a capon stuffed with apples and apricots and corn bread, Brussels sprouts with chestnuts, green beans with toasted pine nuts, and potatoes lyonnaise.

They'd finish the dinner off with a buche de noel, assorted cookies, and two flavors of homemade ice cream—coconut and peppermint patty—served with a bittersweet chocolate sauce on the side. It was the meal they'd been having for as long as Libby could remember, and even though every year she and Bernie talked about changing it, they never did. After all, why mess around with perfection?

"I hear Eric Royal is taking a job somewhere in the Virgin Islands, working for a hotel," Bernie said as she dipped her spoon into her bowl of soup.

"Really?" her dad said.

Bernie nodded. "He said he wanted to get out of the business after this. Doesn't have the stomach for it anymore."

"I can't understand why," Libby observed.

Her dad took a bite of his roll. "Guess he doesn't like blood sports."

"Guess not," Bernie said. "Of course, he's going to have to come back to testify in Estes' trial if Estes' lawyer wants him to."

Sean dabbed the sides of his mouth with his napkin. "I don't think there's going to be a trial."

Libby put her spoon down. "Why do you say that, Dad?"

"Because Clyde told me they're going to try to get Estes off on an insanity plea."

Bernie snorted. "Good luck."

"I don't know," Libby said as she finished the last of her soup. "Anyone who kills someone just to increase the ratings of his television show is insane in my book."

"Maybe in your book, but not in the industry people I know out in L.A. They would think that what he did was perfectly justified. Maybe even admirable."

"You're exaggerating," Libby told her.

"Maybe by a little," Bernie admitted. "But not by much."

Libby put her spoon down. "I don't get it. If that was the case, why not kill Hortense on the show? Wouldn't that have been more effective?"

"Maybe too effective," Bernie reflected. "Maybe he was afraid that if he did that, he'd lose his sponsors or get the FCC down on him for too much violence."

Libby watched her dad shake his head. "Ironic, isn't it. Here he's working so hard to get the murders publicized and here's Bree trying so hard to hush them up. And all he wanted to do was get a buzz going for the show."

Libby took a bite of her roll. "So that's why he kept on saying the show was cursed, but the only thing doing the cursing was him." She shook her head, remembering what Estes had said about wanting to hire an exorcist.

"Exactly," Bernie said. She put her spoon down. "It always amazes me that people like to watch bad things happen."

"It wouldn't amaze you if you were on the force. Ever try directing traffic around an accident? Unfortunately for Estes," Sean observed, "he didn't realize the extent of Bree's influence, and he sure as hell didn't realize that his plans and her plans were at cross purposes and that in a situation like that—"

Libby finished the sentence for him. "Bree always wins."

Her dad nodded. "He never dreamed that she had the

ability to get the chief of police to hush up Hortense's death. So he decided to try again with Pearl."

"Well, Bree's performance was pretty impressive in that regard," Bernie said.

Libby grunted. The less she thought about Bree Nottingham, the happier she felt. She changed the subject.

"Poor Pearl," she said. "Why pick her?"

Her dad pushed his plate away and sat back. "Probably because she was the easiest one to get to. Estes knew that she had OCD. Everyone did. He knew that if he rearranged the lights slightly, Pearl would have to go over and fix them. And she did. She had to. She had no choice."

"But why did he come after you, Dad?"

"Yes, Dad," her sister repeated.

Sean rubbed his forehead with his fingers. "Because he thought I knew something, which I obviously didn't. By that time he was crazy. Here he was trying to create this situation and he kept on being stymied, and that made him do more and more coke, which was making him more and more paranoid; and on top of that, here you two were sniffing around, asking questions, and getting everyone all riled up. Then, in a final blow, I came along and asked Eric Royal that question about how the show was doing, and he freaked. Somehow Estes got it into his head that I was on to him, which wasn't true, but by that time he was too far in his own world to come on back to the real one. I tell you one thing . . ."

"What, Dad?"

"I will never look at another spray can of that white Christmas snow in the same way ever again."

"And I will never go on another TV show as long as I live," Libby said.

"But we won," Bernie pointed out.

"And it so wasn't worth it," Libby said.

"Maybe you're right," Bernie agreed.

Libby put her hand over her heart. "You're agreeing with me about something. I think I'm going to faint."

Bernie leaned over and hugged her. "You know I love you."

"I love you too," Libby said. Then she went over and hugged her dad.

"You just have to promise me one thing," her dad said.

"What's that?" Libby asked.

"No more fruitcake."

The following are some favorite holiday recipes from some of the best cooks I know. Enjoy!

Recipes from Deb Hutchison

Aunt May's Rum Balls

3 boxes Nabisco Vanilla Wafers
1 cup sifted powdered sugar
2 T cocoa
2 T white corn syrup
1 cup finely chopped pecans
5–6 T dark rum

Roll wafers very fine (or use a processor). Sift sugar and cocoa together. Mix dry ingredients together. Add rum and corn syrup and work a little at a time till it makes a firm ball. Roll into little balls (1 inch), then roll in powdered sugar. Ripen 3–4 days to 1 week.

The kids love them!

Date Pin Wheels

1 cup granulated sugar
1 cup brown sugar
1 cup shortening (butter or margarine)
3 eggs
4 cups sifted flour
1 tsp baking soda
½ tsp salt
1 tsp vanilla
½ cup water
½ cup sugar
1 box dates (pitted, cut fine)

Cream sugars and shortening. Add eggs, beat well. Add flour, soda, salt that have been sifted together. Add vanilla. Set aside. Chill. Can stay in frig overnight if wrapped tightly in wax paper.

Cook to a paste the ½ cup water, ½ cup sugar, and the cut dates. Cool.

Cut dough in half. Refrigerate unused portion. Roll remaining dough into rectangle. Spread date mixture on dough and roll up. Slice about ¼ inch thick. Bake on greased sheet for 10 minutes at 350 degrees. Repeat with second section.

Cajun Seafood Stew

16 oz shrimp

¼ cup flour, ¼ cup oil = roux

1 thinly sliced green pepper
1 thinly sliced medium onion
2 stalks chopped celery
2 cloves diced garlic
1½ cups water
1 can of tomatoes (1 lb)
¾ tsp salt
½ tsp red pepper
¼ tsp black pepper
1–2 tbs file powder

Make roux with flour and oil. Cook over medium heat, stirring constantly for 10 minutes or until golden brown. Add veggies. Cook 3–5 minutes. Stir in water, tomatoes, salt, and red and black pepper. Bring to boil. Add shrimp. Return to boil, reduce heat, and cook shrimp until pink (3 minutes). Stir in file powder right before serving. Serves six.

Bob Hutchison's Barbecued Ribs

This recipe comes from the *Costello Family Cookbook*.

Dry Rub Memphis Style

12 parts paprika
4 parts seasoned salt
4 parts black pepper
4 parts garlic powder
2 parts cayenne pepper
2 parts oregano
2 parts dry mustard
1 part chili powder

Stir this up and then store in glass jar. We use 1 tbs to equal 1 part. Rub this into your pork ribs and grill.

How to cook ribs:

Use baby back pork ribs (don't pull membrane).
Coat ribs with dry rub, amount by preference.
Cook in covered barbecue kettle with indirect heat (325 degrees or 50 coals) over drip pan for one hour.
Enjoy!

Susan Hawks' Christmas Desserts

Buche de Noel

Cake:

6 egg yolks
½ cup powdered sugar, sifted
1 tsp vanilla
6 tbs cocoa sifted
⅛ tsp salt
6 egg whites

Filling:

1 pint whipping cream
superfine sugar to taste
Rum, Grand Marnier, or other flavored liqueur to taste

Preheat oven to 325 degrees.

Line jelly-roll pan with parchment, extending several inches over ends. Oil well. Beat yolks until light. Add sugar gradually and beat until very creamy. Blend in vanilla, then cocoa and salt. Beat egg whites until stiff but not dry. Fold into cocoa mixture. Spread in prepared pan and bake until toothpick inserted in center comes out clean, about 25 minutes.

Immediately turn onto damp towel lined with parchment. Peel paper from cake. Roll cake lengthwise and let cool at room temperature.

Whip cream with sugar and liqueur to taste until quite stiff. Unroll cooled cake carefully. Spread with whipped cream. Using towel, roll lengthwise, ending with seam on bottom.

Carefully transfer to a serving plate. Before serving, dust cake with powdered sugar to look like snow. Decorate with meringue marzipan mushrooms, chocolate leaves, or marzipan holly and berries.

Ginger Snaps

Mix together:

¾ c. soft shortening
1 c. sugar

Add:

¼ c. dark molasses
1 egg

Sift together:

2 tsp baking soda
2 c. flour
½ tsp cloves
½ tsp ground ginger
½ tsp salt

Add dry ingredients to shortening mixture. Mix until just blended. Chill. Form 1-inch balls and roll in white sugar. Place on baking sheet with 2 inches between each. Bake at 375 degrees for about 8 minutes. Do not overbake—they're best when they're soft.

Recipes from Linda Kleinman

Holiday Potato Pancakes

For Six:

Use 6 peeled Idaho potatoes (one for each person). Grate potatoes. Press liquid out. Combine with 1 medium grated onion. Add between ⅓ and ½ cup Matzoh meal, 1 T salt, pepper to taste.

In a large cast-iron or enamel skillet, add 4 T of canola oil, and heat until extremely hot (almost smoking). Drop by slotted spoonfuls into pan. They should sizzle. Flip when brown.

Serve immediately with applesauce and sour cream. If you're doing these in advance, put on a rack and put in warm oven.

Variation: Make them smaller and serve with caviar and sour cream as an appetizer.

Holiday Pumpkin Bread

Sift together:

3⅓ cups flour
1½ tsp salt
2 tsp baking soda

Add:

3 cups sugar
½ tsp ginger
1 tbs cinnamon
1 tbs nutmeg

Mix well

Blend:

1 cup canola oil
⅔ cup water
4 whole eggs
2 cups unseasoned pumpkin puree

Optional: nuts, raisins, cranberries

Add above to flour mixture

Pour in either three greased 8" by 4" loaf pans with greased wax paper on the bottom or two 9" by 5" loaf pans.

Bake in 350 degree oven for 1 hour or until done. Cool. Wrap in foil. Let age overnight. Can age for 10 days. Freezes well.

Sorbets

Pineapple-Banana Sorbet

1 ripe pineapple
2 ripe bananas
¼ cup apple juice

Peel and core pineapple. Cut into chunks over a bowl to catch any juice. Put pineapple, pineapple juice, and bananas in a food processor. Process until pureed. Add apple juice, and process again until the mixture is very smooth. Turn into electric ice cream maker and freeze according to the manufacturer's directions.

Apricot Sorbet

1 16 oz. can apricots, drained and pitted
¼ cup lemon juice
1 cup water, 1 cup sugar, 2 egg whites

Puree apricots and lemon juice in processor. Place in bowl. Combine ¾ cup sugar and 1 cup water. Boil 5 minutes, add to puree, and chill. Beat egg whites until they form soft peaks, gradually add ¼ cup sugar, continue beating until whites form stiff peaks, and fold into puree. Freeze in two ice cube trays. As soon as edges are hard, put into a bowl and beat until smooth. Freeze again. Continue process two or three times. Serve in chocolate shells.

Strawberry-Rhubarb Sorbet

Combine 1 cup sugar and 1½ cups water in deep sauce pan. Bring to a boil. Add ⅛ tsp powdered ginger, continue boiling for 7 minutes. Add ½ lb rhubarb, trimmed, peeled, and cut into 1-inch pieces. Cover pot and boil for 10 minutes. Add a 12 oz. box of frozen strawberries with sugar syrup that has been defrosted. Remove pot from heat and cool. Put in ice cream maker and follow manufacturer's directions. Serve plain or with vanilla ice cream.

Murphy's Special Sauce

For use on or with chicken wings. This recipe was stolen from the vaults of the Murphy family castle. First, the ingredients are fairly simple if you use the generic variety. Cayenne pepper–based hot sauce made from hand-picked peppers by our Southern relations (so you know you're getting the very best). This is carefully simmered for 14 days on a 100-year-old iron wood-burning stove, using only 5-year-old aged cherry wood from North American cherry farms. Then it's time to add the honey mustard ingredients before properly storing for further use. The honey also comes from further Southern relations who use only killer-bee honey after interviewing each bee to see if he's up to the task. This, as you know, is quite time-consuming and adds to the cost of production, even in Mexico. The mustard seeds used for the production of the special sauce always came from the same plantation on an uncharted island in the South Pacific that has just been washed away in the wake of the recent tsunami, so everybody will be using a generic substitute before long. Serve warm over hot wings. Sides of blue cheese are acceptable.